THE MEDAL

B.P.SMY

B.P.SMYTHE.

B.P.Smythe studied engineering at Carshalton College and eventually became a member of the Institute of Quality Assurance.

For his published crime writing short stories and novels. B.P. Smythe was inducted into the Crime Writers Association for his achievements.

BOOKS BY B.P.SMYTHE

Sow And You Shall Reap - https://www.amazon.co.uk/dp/145677171X

From a Poison Pen - https://www.amazon.co.uk/Poison-Pen-collection-macabre-stories-ebook/dp/B01BKWT4EE.

From a Poison Pen VOL II - https://www.amazon.co.uk/Poison-Pen-ii-B-P-Smythe-ebook/dp/B01LFM1032

The Expired - http://www.amazon.co.uk/Expired-Barry-Smythe/dp/1911412728

Then There Were None - https://www.amazon.co.uk/Then-There-Were-None-Smythe/dp/1911412612

Short Tales With Long Memories - https://en.gravatar.com/barrysmythe

B.P.SMYTHE Amazon author page: www.amazon.co.uk/-/e/B006MCGVNU

For information on obtaining free complimentary PDF,
Kindle or paperback copies, contact B.P.Smythe at
barrysmythe@hotmail.com - Mob: 07814780856

To Victoria

Best Wishes

B. P. Smythe

III

TO BE RELEASED IN 2019

B.P.SMYTHE

GERTRUDE STICK   MAVIS BONE

MAVIS BONE PRIVATE INVESTIGATOR AND THE PERFECT MURDERS by B.P.Smythe

PLEASE BE AWARE, READERS MUST NOT DISCLOSE THE ENDING OF THIS BOOK. THIS ALLOWS OTHERS TO ENJOY THE BOOK TO ITS ENTIRETY. AT THE TIME OF PURCHASE, CUSTOMERS MUST SIGN A PLEDGE TO UPHOLD THIS. PEEKING OR THUMBING THROUGH PAGES OF COPIES ON BOOK SHELVES IS STRICTLY FORBIDDEN.
Author B.P.Smythe

barrysmythe@hotmail.com

Free paperback and kindle copies to Amazon and Goodreads reviewers: Contact barrysmythe@hotmail.com

THE
MEDAL
OF
PURITY

B.P.SMYTHE.

ISBNs:
Print: 978-1-911412-88-5
iBooks: 978-1-911412-89-2
Kindle: 978-1-911412-90-8

Published by BookPublishingWorld,
an imprint of Dolman Scott Ltd
www.dolmanscott.co.uk

CONTENTS

THE MEDAL OF PURITY

B.P.SMYTHE.

"The Medal of Purity" - an award given by Hitler's propaganda minister, Dr. Joseph Goebbels, to true Aryan bred Germans...

A STORY OF DISINTEGRATING FAMILY LIFE UNDER THE NAZI SYSTEM...

INTRODUCTION OF MAIN CHARACTERS:

"The Medal of Purity" - an award given by Hitler's propaganda minister, Dr. Joseph Goebbels, to true Aryan bred Germans...

This is the story of the **Borch** family, living in Berlin under the Nazi system... The father, **Dr. Karl Borch**, is promoted to SS-Sturmbannführer, becoming commandant of Pullhausen concentration-camp; his brief is to pioneer genetic pure-bred Aryan Germans, whilst the Waffen-SS are trying to recruit racially acceptable foreigners into the SS legions. His wife, **Frieda**, has Jewish friends, and is against the Nazi system, whilst their son and daughter, **Martin** and **Magda**, are staunch Hitler Youth party members, intoxicated with the banner-waving, drum-beating, searchlight grandiose of Nazi party rallies, held at Nuremberg - both are finding it hard to escape Hitler's toxic embrace. However, everything is good, just as the Führer has promised: everybody is now employed; no more hardship. The son and daughter have learnt at school that it was the filthy Jews who were to blame for Germany's economic problems, and for having lost the First World War. The filthy Jews are to blame for everything. That's why their shops have been smashed up and why they are banned from public life and public places. Everybody turns a blind eye to the Jew round-ups, to the stories filtering through about ghetto life and concentration-camp conditions. These are considered Jew-based troublemaking rumours, intended to undermine the party. Life is good for the Borch family with Jew servants and cocktail parties at weekends for important high-ranking SS party members and their families.

The Medal of Purity shows how decent German families can slip into a way of life that feels good - a life of privilege, earnt off the backs of slave labour. It also shows how ordinary people can be so easily caught up in the whipped-up frenzy of National Socialism, no matter the cost, as the Borch family find out.

CHAPTER ONE

It had all come to a head yesterday evening for the Binz family at their rundown apartment block in depression hit Dresden situated in the German state of Saxony. The ugly communal building they lived in, didn't do the city justice compared to the baroque and rococo architecture made famous in paintings by Canaletto.

Greta Binz was a blossoming seventeen-year-old pretty schoolgirl with long blonde hair from her mother's side. They had said prayers this New Year's Eve and were in the middle of supper. While the aroma of boiled cabbage still lingered, silence was the norm around the kitchen table even for this last day of 1930.

Heinrich, her stepfather, a tall fifty-two year old staunch Evangelical Lutheran preacher with a hooked nose and thinning greyish hair, sat in his vest and braces and sucked the bones of his oxtail stew while concentrating on the rough draft of his new sermon, already stained with gravy.

He'd recently been laid off along with most of the workforce at the tractor parts factory where he had been a machinist for eight years. Heinrich was bitter and blamed the corrupt politicians of the Weimar Republic for being out-of-touch with the masses, especially the lower classes. He now concentrated his preaching full time, finding God and persuading others to do so.

Ursula, Greta's short, stout, forty-eight year old mother with a prematurely lined face, sat stiff backed nibbling her supper wearing a housecoat. With her blonde hair in curlers, she was ready for another hell-fire evening service down at the Evangelical hall. Ursula's first husband was killed in the Great War, just after being awarded for bravery.

Greta picked over the fatty meat on her plate and considered. She raised herself, swallowed hard, and finally said, 'I've joined the BDM, The League of German Girls. All my friends have. They meet twice a week after school. This Adolf Hitler who runs it, is going to be our new leader, he will save the country. Everybody says so. He's going to save our Fatherland.' Greta stiffened and gave the Nazi salute. 'Heil Hitler,' she shouted. She had a wild look in her eyes. 'We all love him, we would die for him. Look! You get a medal for joining.'

From inside her blouse, Greta pulled out the silver iron cross medallion which dangled from her neck. The fine chain being hidden by the collar of her cardigan. 'It's called the Hünenkreuz Medal of Purity, and given to girls in the league as they are considered true Germans.' Greta showed them. 'He wants all German girls to remain pure. Not to have sexual relations with Jews or marry them—' She broke off as if the words had been splintered in her mouth.

Heinrich and Ursula stopped eating. They both looked at her.

Ursula's nostrils suddenly flared like those of a horse that had heard the dry rattle of a snake. 'No, you can't go,' she said immediately. 'I don't want you hanging around with other girls of an evening, for this Adolf Hitler. I've seen his posters. He's evil looking. I've heard him running down the Jews. Remember, Jesus Christ was a Jew. No wonder he doesn't like religion, I bet there's not one bit of God in him. And anyway, you've got your studies to attend do.'

'But, Mama, I'm nearly eighteen now. Most of the girls at school belong to the League of German Girls.'

'I said no, Greta, you've got examinations coming up. You've got to study. Things are hard as it is. We've no money coming in, and good jobs for women are hard to get, even at the best of times.'

She answered back indignantly, 'But I study every night, Mama.'

Ursula snapped. 'Shut up and finish your stew or you'll get the back of my hand.'

Greta raised her voice. 'Our beloved leader, Adolf Hitler, says the Jews are to blame for Germany's hardship. They're cunning and scheming and hold all the best jobs. Anyway, Adolf Hitler says women shouldn't work. They should marry pure German men and keep house and have lots of babies for the Fatherland.'

'Is your beloved Adolf Hitler going to pay next months' rent on this place?' Heinrich her stepfather interrupted. 'Your mother told you no. You have your studies to think of.'

Greta snapped. *'Who are you telling me what to do? You're not my real father.'* Greta threw her fork into the dinner in temper. The gravy spattered the table. *'All you ever wanted to do was come in my room and —'* She stopped herself.

A numbing silence followed. Heinrich slowly rose from his seat. Without taking his eyes off Greta, he slid the belt out from his trousers. 'I'm going to teach you, Girl, to wash your mouth out. I'm going to strap you all the way to that closet, my Girl.'

Greta stood defiant. 'You put me in that closet again, you Arsehole, and I'll go to the police.'

'You've had this coming, Girl, for a long time. Shouting at your mother and me with your profanities.' Heinrich lunged at Greta across the table and she screamed as the strap came down hard across her raised elbows. Then he was on her, moving quickly, knocking her back into the chair as she tried to pull away.

'Get off me, you Bastard,' she shrieked as Heinrich hauled her up by the collar.

Greta was screaming, trying to bite his arm as he frogmarched her to the closet. Heinrich, his face in a pleasing grin, strapped Greta's backside repeatedly while she yelled with each blow. She kicked and screamed, and then came a scuffle at the entrance. He yanked the medallion from her neck. 'You won't be needing this evil thing anymore. The swastika on it, is the sign of the devil, the sign of Lucifer.'

She tried to grab it back in the struggle. Greta shouted through her tears, *'I'll kill you both, you Jew loving Bastards!'* Then the closet door slammed shut and the bolt shot through. But the kicking and screaming continued for another ten minutes.

When Heinrich returned to the kitchen, he opened the wood burning stove and threw the medallion into it. 'That'll teach the bitch some manners, her Adolf Hitler purity medal,' he scoffed.

'Best place for it,' Ursula agreed. 'We don't need any Adolf Hitler telling us to hate Jews or how to run the country.'

*

After a while, Greta sat on the floor in the dark. She continued to whimper and plead. She was hardly coherent. She could feel the tears burning the back of her eyeballs like weak acid. Her eyes had become red and bleary.

The dull pink glow of the crucifix wall lamp looked down on her. Christ's downturned mouth seemed to emphasise her fate.

On the shelf below it, sat two candle holders for Mama's little altar, as well as a black bound bible with a gold leaf crucifix on the cover. The bible stared back at her, waiting to be opened. Wanting her to cleanse herself, to confess her sins, to find the true light. Greta picked it up and threw it against the wall. It hit the floor in a puff of dust. 'Bibles, I've had enough of bibles,' she muttered.

Greta pulled her knees up to her chin as she sat in the corner. She guessed it was going to be a long wait. They'd probably let her out after they got back from the New Year Eve sermon.

She looked over to the shelf, and her eyes fell on the drawer beneath it. Greta nonchalantly reached over and pulled it open. It contained one used candle and a box of matches. She opened the matches. There was just two remaining. Greta hesitated, and then struck one. The sizzle and flare illuminated her prison. Just for a second the shadow of the Jesus lamp swelled large over the ceiling, then reduced as the match set to a small yellow flame.

She blew it out and pondered. Greta held the smoking match for a while. She looked at the face of Christ on the crucifix lamp. The moulded features set in a contortion of agony, stared back at her. Greta held its gaze. Then her eyes widened as if awakened, as if Jesus had touched her. She wanted forgiveness, she wanted salvation. Greta threw her head back and cried out, 'Oh Lord, show me the way, for I have sinned.'

From her pocket she took out a miniature bottle of lavender water she'd stolen from her mother's vanity unit. She sprinkled it on the floor.

*

Heinrich and Ursula had just arrived back. It was 12:25 a.m. As the front door opened they looked at each other in bewilderment. Religious chanting was coming from the closet.

Greta sat cross-legged with the bible open at Revelations. She was shouting the passages like an Evangelical preacher, similar to Heinrich whipping up the crowd at one of his sermons. *'The ungodly are cast into a lake of fire and brimstone as an eternal punishment. And the beast was taken, and then with him the false prophet that wrought miracles before him, with which he deceived them, that had received the mark of the beast, and them that worshipped his image.'*

Heinrich and Ursula moved closer to the closet door and listened.

Greta continued yelling at the top of her voice. *'And the devil that had deceived them was cast into the lake of fire and brimstone, where the beast and the false prophet are, and shall be tormented day and night, forever and ever. But the fearful, and unbelieving, and the abominable, and murderers, and whoremongers, and sorcerers, and idolaters, and all liars, shall have their part in the lake which burneth with fire and brimstone, which is the second death...'*

Ursula hesitated, and then interrupted knocking sharply. 'You praying in there, Greta?' She gave Heinrich a puzzled look.

Greta yelled back, 'Oh, Mama, I've found the way. Jesus came to me, Mama, while I was in here. He showed me my wicked ways. How I've been sinning and how disrespectful I've been to you and father. I want to be saved, Mama. Open the door so we can pray together.'

Ursula slid the bolt back.

Greta was kneeling. Her face was red, and hair stuck to her cheeks from sweat and tears. A candle glowed in one of the holders on the shelf. 'Oh, Mama, I've been so bad, both of you pray for me. Please Mama. Help me find the way.'

Ursula looked astonished, and then was about to say something when Greta continued. 'Let's all pray together, Mama, right here and now in front of this crucifix lamp. He gave me the sign, Mama. I saw tears run from his face. Mama, look on the floor.'

Underneath the crucifix lamp a small pool of water had collected.

Ursula crossed herself.

Heinrich stood perplexed. He looked at Greta and Ursula and then said, 'I've seen this once before in a chapel in Rome. It's a sign from Jesus Christ himself.' Heinrich looked up to the ceiling. 'Halleluiah, praise the Lord. That cupboard...closet, is a shrine. It's a holy place now.'

'Let's all pray together then,' Greta urged them with excitement. 'We can all get in here and kneel.' Greta's face twisted with pain. 'Mama, I have to come out first. I need to use the bathroom badly.'

'Okay, but you hurry, Girl. The Lord don't take kindly to young sinners. Oh, and bring some cushions with you, and two candles with a box of matches from the kitchen dresser. We can light them in the closet for this new holy place'

'Yes, Mama.'

They waited until she arrived back, then Heinrich and Ursula stooped their way first into the closet. With the cushions placed, they all knelt down.

'Did you get the candles?' Ursula asked.

Greta rolled her eyes back. 'Sorry, Mama, I forgot.'

'You stupid, Girl,' Ursula said giving her a scalding look. 'Go get them now and hurry.'

Heinrich joined in with a little dig. 'Thy lord is waiting, Girl.'

Greta raised herself in the cramped space and manoeuvred her way out of the closet. In an instant, she slammed the door shut and shot the bolt home.

'What are you doing, Greta?' Ursula shouted and knocked on the inside. 'Greta, are you playing games?' She shouted again, *'Open the door!'*

Heinrich looked at Ursula. 'She's teasing us, the Bitch.' He leant over and thumped with his fist. *'Open this door, Girl, or you'll get my belt again. That's a promise.'*

They heard something being dragged. It rattled against the door.

Greta had wedged the doorknob with one of the wicker chairs from the kitchen.

Heinrich pounded with his clenched fist again. *'Open this door, Girl. The joke is over. Your mother and me are getting angry.'*

Ursula shouted, *'Open the door this instant, Greta. Do you hear?'*

Greta lit two candles and placed them in saucers either side of the closet door. For a while she stared; it looked like the entrance to a holy place. The noise from within very quickly collected her thoughts, and made her realise what she *should* be doing.

Greta smiled at their cursing as she busied herself. From her school bag she took out her gloves and put them on. She took out the signed photograph of Adolf Hitler she'd been given at her BDM meeting and kissed it. She said, 'I'm doing this for you, my Fuhrer, so we can be together, perhaps not in body but in mind.'

Then, she went into the small lounge and set about creating a drunken New Year's Eve party. Carefully upsetting bits of furniture; a chair here, a table lamp there, some framed photos upturned, scattered about the sideboard. The contents of the fridge were next; some Bratwurst sausages and Sauerkraut with Stollen cake, all broken up to look half eaten and laid out on a few plates. Greta threw some bits onto the carpet and trod them in. She filled up two dishes with biscuits and crushed some of them into the carpet.

She went to Heinrich's secret stash, his favourite Schnapps. He kept it hidden in his writing bureau along with all the sermon paraphernalia. The key was on a piece of string which hung down the back. Of course Ursula knew, however, she let him have his petty concessions.

Greta had seen him fortify himself before a sermon on a number of occasions. Again, it was another one of their little shared secrets. Visiting her bedroom as a little child was another of his shared secrets. As she hugged her Teddy with tears streaming down her face, he would look at her with his finger pressed to his lips and whisper, 'Don't tell your mother or the Bogey man will come for you.'

Greta half-filled some glasses with Schnapps and knocked one over onto the coffee table. Holding the bottle, she spilt some onto the sofa and the adjoining faded rug. Then, Greta remembered Ursula's sedatives. Kept on her dressing table, she'd been taking them for almost a year.

Coming back to the lounge, she tipped a handful of the pink capsules onto the coffee table amongst the dregs of Schnapps and onto the carpet.

Greta stood for a moment and looked at the result. She was pleased. A New Year's Eve drunken party and then praying for forgiveness in their confession box afterwards. A tragic accident from a lighted candle.

Greta made her way back to the closet with two bottles of Schnapps.

Heinrich had swapped places with Ursula to be nearest the door. He was now using his shoulder and weight as a battering ram. With each heavy thump he cursed her. *'Open this door, you Bitch. Enough is enough. Do you hear me, Girl?'*

Ursula shrieked abuse at Greta. It was as if her mouth was a scalding furnace. *'Why was I cursed with, Satan's child...a devil's child...a devil witch?'*

Heinrich banged on the door again. *'Open this door, Girl, at once. I'm telling you. I'll strap you from here to Vienna when I get hold of you.'*

However, the closet door wasn't going to budge. The chair was a good wedge fit; she couldn't have wished for a better barricade.

Greta was ready for what she had to do. There was no turning back. She raised one of the bottles. Then her hand began to shake. She grasped it tightly with her other hand.

She was having second thoughts. She was going to chicken out. She couldn't go through with it.

Greta closed her eyes amongst the banging and the cursing. She muttered to herself, 'Relax...just relax.'

She released her hand and the bottle stayed steady.

When Greta's parents had started using the closet for her punishment as a confession box, Heinrich had fitted an air vent at the top of the door. It was a small austere wire mesh grill, nothing fancy, in keeping with their little makeshift prison for sinners. The mesh so fine, you couldn't see through it. However, it had its uses. Such as providing an escape for unwanted smells if one was locked in there long enough, as Greta could verify.

And when she'd been sitting trapped inside scheming her plan, the significance of the vent began to grow; akin to a prisoner yearning for freedom while looking at the sun streaking through the bars of a cell window high above out of reach.

Without further hesitation, she poured the bottle of spirit through the grill vent.

Heinrich erupted. '*What you doing, Girl?*' The schnapps was splashing all over him.

Ursula screamed out, '*What she doing? What's that smell, Heinrich?*'

'Smells like liquor or something.' Heinrich pummelled the door again. '*What you doing, Greta? You're making me and your mama upset now. Open this door!*'

Greta hoisted the second bottle of Schnapps, and it glugged its way through the vent amidst more banging, more cursing and more profanities.

The closet floor by now was drenched. Greta looked down to see the liquor seeping out. Now was the time. She tipped over one of the candles into the emerging stream. There was a *Whumph!* A pale blue chasing flame shot under the door and up the outside where some spillage had occurred. Greta dropped the bottle in shock. It smashed on the floor as she backed away.

Heinrich yelled, *'What the hell! We're on fire...Ursula, Christ sake, help me.'*

Ursula shouted, *'We're on fire, help us somebody. Greta, there's a fire!'*

Heinrich started screaming in a terrible high pitch that Greta had never heard before. Not even when he'd had them all fired up in one of his frenzied sermons, all a slobbering and a gibbering. Then came more high pitch screams from both of them with terrible thudding and pounding. The bolt was beginning to shear off – the retaining screws being far too inadequate for such punishment. However, the chair still held solid as a rock, right to the end.

Greta had to get out quickly. The place was filling up with smoke. The closet door was completely on fire and she shielded her face as she listened to the pounding and their agonising pleas. She waited until the noise had turned to helpless whimpers mingled amongst the crackle of wood and sizzling. Then eventually, only slight movement and moaning, and then, silence.

Greta put a cuff to her nose. The strange sweet sickly smell of burning flesh became nauseating, overpowering.

With one hand up to protect her face from the inferno, Greta used Ursula's cardigan as a mitten to pull away the chair and then slide back the bolt. She stamped out the flaming cardigan as sparks singed her legs. As the closet door swung open, flames belched out and Greta flinched back from the searing heat. She threw some extra candles and the other bottle of schnapps into the closet and then backed away.

Next, with a lighted rolled up newspaper, Greta went to the lounge and torched the curtains. They instantly began to flare up as she quickly retreated. Then she changed into her white nightdress and removed her shoes and socks. She had to hurry before her only exit was cut off.

Moving quick to the front door, Greta felt her neck and suddenly realised. Her Hünenkreuz Medal of Purity was missing. She remembered her father was holding it and grinning. She raced back to the kitchen and checked the table and dresser, then all the drawers. Nothing.

Greta dashed back to the smoke and burning in the hallway. Shielding her face, she made for the front door again and then realised she needed money. Any sum just to tide her over for small purchases. She spotted Ursula's handbag. She looked inside the purse and found nearly ten Reichsmarks. Greta remembered her stepfather saying to spend money fast. Every day it was buying less because of the Wall Street crash.

She stuffed the cash down her panties.

Another thought occurred to her. With Ursula's charred cardigan she blackened her face and white nightdress. It had to look good. Just escaped with her life while sleeping in the bedroom.

Greta opened the front door and peeked out onto the dilapidated walkway. Smoke immediately billowed past her. The evening was quiet. She stepped out and started yelling, *'Fire! – Fire! Help me someone, fire!'* She ran to the next apartment and started banging on the door. *'Fire! – Fire! Help me, my parents are in there.'*

In those few seconds while she waited for help, Greta felt elated. It was the first time in her short miserable life, she was actually free of those two Jew lovers. No more going home with that gnawing pit in her stomach.

CHAPTER TWO

It was late October 1938 for the Borch family, who lived in a large six bedroomed residence in central Berlin along a smart tree lined road just off Wilhelmstrasse. With its oak panelled walls and sweeping staircase, the stained glass windows helped to finish off a grand house that was built in the 1920's.

Thirty-four year old Dr Karl Borch was a SS-Totenkopf eugenics research physician and had been married to Frieda for the last fourteen years. Slim with a tall frame and light brown hair, his blue eyes and Germanic features make him look a near perfect Aryan. Although childhood sweethearts, he'd married Frieda when she became pregnant at nineteen years old with Magda. Frieda Borch on the other hand had a full figure and liked her Swiss chocolate. At five feet, four inches, she wore typical German flaxen hair braids, wrap around style, above a heavy featured face with a pasty complexion.

Both Magda and her eleven year old brother Martin were conscripts in the Hitler Youth. With National Socialism taking over all aspects of German daily life, even their school lessons were based on Nazi ideology. School textbooks had been rewritten and include Nazi versions of German history. Mathematical problems now involved calculations about bombing and killing invalids. They were taught Nazi beliefs every day in subjects such as Ideology and Eugenics.

All schools were single sex, and girls and boys were educated quite differently. Girls did not study foreign languages, and their maths and science lessons were linked to cooking and childcare. This was all part of a deliberate plan to prevent women having careers. A woman could work until she became married, and then she was expected to give it up and become a housewife and bear children for the Fatherland.

Martin, Karl's eleven year old son, had a Hitler Jungvolk meeting to go to. Although short for his age from his mother's side, he'd inherited his father's good looks and light brown hair, that he combed over to look like the Fuhrer.

In his bedroom, he put on his Hitler Youth uniform with its brown shirt and black shorts. He expertly donned a thin black tie. Then he tightened his belt, taking a moment to run his finger over the embossed image on the rectangular buckle, showing an eagle with a swastika gripped firmly in its claws. Above the eagle were engraved the words *Blood and Honour*.

His final touch was the party armband, shiny and black, emblazoned with a striking swastika. Martin gazed into the mirror and admired himself. *Not bad*, he thought, grinning at his wiry image.

*

His fourteen-year old sister Magda was a member of the BDM - The League of German Girls. Tall for her age and also with her father's striking looks, she'd inherited her mother's flaxen hair which she wore in plats down her back.

Standing to attention at her BDM meetings, wearing a uniform that comprised of a narrow, dark blue calf-length skirt, white ankle socks, black flat-heeled shoes and a white blouse with a dark tie, she would raise her hand in a Nazi salute as the party flag was hoisted.

Magda was so committed she would die for the Fuhrer. Her bedroom wall was full of Adolf Hitler posters.

Unbeknown to her family, Magda was sometimes bullied at school and at her BDM meetings because of her glass eye. She'd lost her eye because of an infection when she was a baby. The leader of the bullying is a fifteen year old tall blonde pretty girl called Helga. Helga is the group leader in the BDM and automatically a school class leader when the teacher isn't present. Helga does her best to get all the other girls to gang up on Magda.

Magda hadn't told her parents. She'd been taught it would be weak to go to her family for support, as her first family are now the Fuhrer and her BDM comrades.

That evening, Magda showed her parents a school letter. It informed them, that all the BDM members at her school would be going to visit the Fuhrer. They would be travelling to his residence, the Berghof at Berchtesgaden on the Obersalzberg in the Bavarian Alps. The four day visit would be to give the Fuhrer Christmas presents.

Out of politeness, Magda asked her parents for permission; although her parents knew it was a foregone conclusion, as children answer first to their Hitler Youth leaders and are classed as property of the state. However, Magda with her long yellow hair braids hanging down her back, still looked longingly at them for their approval.

*

For homework, Magda and the rest of her class had to draw their own family tree with birth certificate proof. This was a compulsory national socialist eugenics exercise all schools had to carry out to ensure families had true third generation Aryan traceability. Today was important as the charts were being collected and would be sent to the Reich Information Centre for Genetic and Racial Hygiene.

Magda's class had been told, any pupil that didn't submit a chart would have their parents accountable and therefore wouldn't be able to go on the school visit to see the Fuhrer. Only proven true Aryans would be able to greet the Fuhrer. Magda wanted to see him more than anything. She would give her life for Adolf Hitler.

That morning on her way to school it was raining. The tram platform was slippery as Magda found out. While she was getting off, she skidded and fell onto the kerb outside her stop, badly cutting her knee. The tram conductor with some passengers, helped her back onto her feet. Someone else picked up her satchel and schoolbooks.

Magda cried with the pain. Holding a handkerchief against the wound, she held onto the tram conductor. The driver in his cab looked around, concerned, trying to see what the delay was about.

'Will you be okay, Young Lady?' The conductor offered his concerns. 'That's a nasty cut.'

Magda gritted her teeth and stiffened, ready to take the weight on her knee. Choking back the tears with some sniffs and wiping her eyes, she concentrated on the matter at hand; trying to walk to her school.

All at once, Magda's face brightened. She saw Ingrid walking briskly towards her with a worried look.

Ingrid was her best friend at school, although she did look Jewish from her father's side. With her dark hair and prominent nose, there had been rumours. However her features and eye colour had measured up to the required tests and parameters they'd all undertaken for Aryan traceability. Ingrid's parents reinstated their bloodstock, being German born and second generation shopkeepers selling leather goods.

Never-the-less, Ingrid suffered because of her looks, similar to Magda with her one eye, from Helga's incessant bullying and sarcasm. The suffering they sometimes endured was probably the common bond for their friendship.

They also shared a secret. Ingrid had shown Magda her grandmother's brooch she kept hidden behind the lapel of her blouse. It was beautiful and dangerous. A Star of David Jewish heirloom. She had been forbidden to take it out of the house. The shared secret made them feel special. They knew something the other girls didn't.

In the strict national socialist world they found themselves in, with marching songs, Heil Hitler greetings, saluting the swastika flag, going to camp with all the basic amenities that boys loved, and studying cooking and childcare to be a good Aryan housewife; the brooch somehow rebelled against the system. It was the same as listening to banned radio broadcasts of American jazz music, which they frequently did together in Ingrid's bedroom under the pretence of doing their homework, while putting on her mother's makeup. It was there they tried out the Jitterbug – an American dance craze which they'd seen on BDM films warning against decadent Negro music.

As Ingrid approached she asked, 'Magda, what's up?' The formal greeting of Heil Hitler was forgotten.

'I just slipped getting off.'

'Oh, you poor thing,' Ingrid crouched down to take a look.

'Better get her to school and let someone in first aid have a look at it,' the conductor said as he eventually mounted the platform, to all the passenger's relief and rang the bell.

With her arm around Ingrid's shoulder, Magda limped the short distance to school.

'Nurse should be in soon. Her bicycle's not there at the moment,' Ingrid said, glancing at the cycle rack. 'Let's get you to the classroom. You can rest up then.'

'Thanks, Ingrid.' Magda winced as she adjusted the red stained handkerchief, the blood still oozed down her shin onto her sock.

No one else had arrived when they reached the classroom. Ingrid unpacked as usual and put her satchel and books into one of the numbered lockers. The keys to them all had been lost years ago, so she just shut the door.

From the windows, the cycle rack wasn't visible so Ingrid suggested, 'I'll check out if nurse has arrived. If not I'll wait for her, let her know about you. Will you be okay while I'm gone?'

Magda nodded and forced a smile.

Ingrid disappeared through the door. Magda heard her humming the strains of the *Horst Vessel* national anthem as she made her way to the nurse's office. She'd be a time; it was on the other side of the school next to the canteen.

The next one in was Helga, looking gorgeous as ever with her school books under her arm. She sneered and saluted, 'Heil Hitler,' and then looked mildly concerned with a partial sympathetic smile as Magda told her about the accident.

Helga winced and put her hand to her mouth when Magda pulled away the handkerchief and showed her the wound. Helga asked her, 'That does look nasty. Can you walk on it?'

'I guess so,' Magda said glumly.

'Look, don't move yet. I'll check out if nurse is in,' Helga said, turning to the door.

'Ingrid's gone for her,' Magda cautiously replied.

Helga spun round, *'Ingrid! What she doing poking her Jew nose in?'* Helga had turned ugly.

'Listen, one-eye, it's *my* job as Mädel Führerin to sort out first aid, not her.'

Magda tried to make light of the cruel remark. 'She helped me to school, she was only thinking of...'

Helga ignored her. She unpacked and then slammed her locker door shut.

Magda flinched and then heard her mutter, 'Trust that Jew to look good in front of me.'

Helga made for the door. She said with a mocking sneer, 'If anybody wants me, tell them I've gone to first aid.' Under her breath she mumbled, 'I'd better see if the nurse is in. Get myself involved before that Jew sticks her long nose in.'

With that remark, she slammed her way out of the classroom.

Magda heard Helga's distant sarcastic laugh fade away. Then there was silence.

It was still early. Her class members hadn't arrived yet. Magda looked at her knee. The blood had congealed at last. She dabbed the wound and flinched as it smarted. As other classes began to arrive, she heard the clacking of shoes on the stone passageways. Then the opening and shutting of doors. The excited exchanges amidst squeals of girlish delights, all peppered with running footsteps.

Magda felt alone. She looked at the classroom door. Then she looked out of the window. Rivulets of rain made their way down the glass in ever changing patterns. She looked at the wound on her knee. Finally, she looked at the locker doors, and she continued looking. She looked at them so hard, her eye lids could have been nailed there.

*

Magda spent most of the morning in first aid with Frau Huber, a grumpy middle-aged, overweight nurse with facial hair. It was suggested she should go to hospital, however, by lunchtime Magda could walk on it without limping. So, with a generous bandage around her knee, she made her way back to the classroom. As Magda entered, she was confronted by the stern looking Headmistress, Frau Fuchs. A tearful Helga was at her side while Frau Koch the resident teacher was at her other side. The rest of the class stood to attention with grim expressions.

'Ah! Just in time, Magda.' Frau Fuchs said. 'I'm afraid you have to be included in this.' The headmistress put her arm around Helga's shoulder and then continued. 'We have a thief amongst us. Someone has stolen Helga's family tree chart from her locker. If it's not returned she won't be allowed to travel and meet the Fuhrer on the coming school trip.' She looked hard at the girls and then added, 'I understand this chart with her family's birth certificates was discreetly hidden, not on show as there are no keys for the locker doors.'

Frau Fuchs paused and looked at their faces individually for any hint of guilt but they all stared back at her with blank expressions. She continued, 'It's highly unlikely other girls have been in here, this room is not shared with any other class.' The headmistress again, looked accusingly at the girls and then said, 'The thief knew where to look.'

No one moved, it was deathly quiet.

Frau Fuchs added, 'I understand, if this is a practical joke between some of you, then no more will be said if it is handed in now.' After another deathly silence she wasted no time. 'Right, everybody, I want you all to empty out your lockers and then your pockets.' Frau Fuchs was in a no nonsense mood. 'I don't want to call the police, but I will if I have to as this is an important state document.'

After a few minutes, everything was out on the large teacher's table in their individual piles. Frau Fuchs walked around their belongings and sifted through the usual items of gym clothing, books, magazines, hair brushes, combs, mirrors, keys and of course the family tree charts that had to be handed in today.

Some of the girls muttered under their breath, *'She can't do this... I'll tell my parents... don't like being accused... my dad will sort her out...'*

Frau Fuchs caught a few whispered threats, 'Now listen, you can moan all you like,' she said, countermining the remarks. 'Better this way than in front of the police?'

Then she nodded to Helga to double check the items.

Helga slowly moved along the table sifting through belongings, picking up clothing. Suddenly she stopped. Slowly she pulled out from underneath a pile of clothing her family tree chart. She held it up with a look of disbelief. Helga looked at the owner.

Ingrid shuffled uncomfortably and said, 'What's up?'

'You know what's up, that's my chart, you thieving Jew?' Helga held it out for her to see.

'I didn't put it there,' Ingrid snapped, 'and I'm not a thieving Jew.'

'Alright you're a lying Jew,' Helga said with a dark sweet smile. 'Look, my name is on the chart.' Her finger pointed to the spot.

'Now, Helga,' Frau Fuchs interrupted. 'There's no need for those remarks.'

Helga wasn't listening, she'd seen something sparkle under the lapel of Ingrid's folded gym blouse. She lifted the item and showed Frau Fuchs.

Frau Fuchs gasped, 'Dear God, it's a Jew brooch.'

Pinned to Ingrid's blouse hidden on the underside of the lapel was a beautiful `Star of David` gold brooch with a menorah set in the middle depicted in small diamonds. All eyes looked at Ingrid.

Helga started up. 'I was right all along. You are a thieving Jew, and you stole my chart.'

'Now that's enough, Helga,' Frau Fuchs replied. 'We can't have –'

'*That's a lie!*' Ingrid exploded. '*Somebody put it there.*' She looked in desperation at the Headmistress. 'It's a sick joke. I'm not a thief!'

'Oh yea! So what's with the Jew brooch?' Helga said with a sneering grin.

Ingrid looked down at the floor ashamed. 'It was my grandmother's. She gave it to me before she died.'

Frau Fuchs put a hand to her mouth in shock. 'Your grandmother was a Jew.' The headmistress quickly sorted Ingrid's family tree chart from the pile. She studied it for a moment and then said, 'There's nothing here to say she was?'

The other girls looked at Ingrid stupefied.

Helga sneered. 'I knew she was a thieving Jew.'

Ingrid exploded. *'You could have planted that chart in my locker. You've never liked me.'*

'Because, you're a thieving Jew.' Helga spat out the anti-Semitism. 'My dad says all Jews–'

Before she could finish, Ingrid lunged at Helga knocking her to the floor – kicking, clawing and screaming she shouted, *'You fucking, bitch, you set me up?'* Helga rolled with her fending off punches and blows.

'Girls, stop it!' The Headmistress rounded on both of them. 'Ingrid, *that's enough!'* Stocky Frau Fuchs managed to break up the fight and hold them apart.

Ingrid screamed, *'I didn't steal your fucking chart!'* The tears started to flow. *'Some ones playing jokes! Setting me up.'* She looked in desperation at the headmistress. With tears streaming down her face she said, 'Honest, Frau Fuchs, I haven't stolen anything.'

The Headmistress held up her hands to quash any further arguments. 'I would be willing to forget the chart as a practical joke, Ingrid. However, I consider it my duty to inform the security services about your grandmother's brooch. It is unforgivable, your family never mentioning your Jewish ancestry. Collect your things, Ingrid, and come with me.' She smiled at Frau Koch to take charge of the class again.

Twenty minutes later, Ingrid was escorted by two Gestapo officers into a car. One of them turned to Frau Fuchs. 'You have done well, Headmistress, finding the Jew's brooch. Reich

Security will make a note of your awareness and dedication. It will not go unnoticed.'

Frau Fuchs beamed. 'I was only doing my duty as a loyal party member.' She finished with a Hitler salute.

The officer clicked his heels and responded with the same salute. Then he leaned into the headmistress and whispered. 'You have no idea how cunning Jewish girls can be hiding things. We've come across it in the work camps. The parents even get them to hide family jewels, diamonds and the like.' He leaned in closer still. 'You know in women's places.'

Frau Fuchs put a hand to her mouth in shock.

*

The plan had backfired as far as Helga's chart was concerned. Magda had meant to get rid of it so she wouldn't have been able to go on the school trip to see the Fuhrer. There wouldn't have been time for her family to get copies of all those documents and birth certificates again. That would have meant a nice visit to Berchtesgaden free of Helga. Trouble was, just as she was taking the chart from Helga's locker to hide behind a wall radiator, someone approached. Magda had to hide it quickly underneath a pile of gym clothes in the nearest locker available. Not realising, the locker belonged to Ingrid.

Magda considered. She did feel guilty about Ingrid. Her actions had led to the Jewish brooch being discovered. Then again it was her fault bringing it to school. Her parents had warned her. On the other hand, it did reveal her Jewish ancestry. Magda convinced herself, she belonged to the Fuhrer now. He wouldn't tolerate sympathy for a Jew. She had to be strong.

Within a couple of days, Magda's guilt had been replaced by renewed National Socialist zeal. This included extra swastika pendants pinned to her wardrobe and a new portrait of the Fuhrer on her bedroom wall.

*

When Magda had come home from school and told her family what happened to Ingrid, leaving out her involvement of course, Frieda became worried. Through the girls' friendship, Frieda was good friends with Ingrid's mother, Hildegard Bauer.

To make matters worse, the Gestapo had checked parish records and discovered Ingrid's deceased grandmother, from her father's side, had a Jewish maiden name of Yehuda Adler. This meant Ingrid's parents had lied on their family tree chart. Her father, Ulrich, was immediately arrested and held at Gestapo headquarters in Berlin.

Ingrid's parents worked a small shop selling shoes, handbags, umbrellas and gloves at Spandauer Strasse just off the big shopping centre of Alexanderplatz. The large two bedroom apartment above, came with the shop and was where the Bauer family lived. They were not exactly well off, however, the shop brought in a substantial income to keep their heads above water - With a steady flow of customers, especially at weekends, who required shoe repairs and purchases in the lower price range compared to the bigger showy stores on Alexanderplatz.

Frieda liked going to the Bauer's shop. She liked the personal service and would take tea and cake with Hildegard while having the odd chinwag.

However, that all changed after Ulrich's arrest. Frieda went to their shop and couldn't believe what she saw. The anti-Semitic graffiti daubed on the window made her put a hand to her mouth in shock. The premises was deserted with a notice pasted on the large window stating: NO ENTRY - PROPERTY OF THE REICH. SUSPECTED JEWISH OWNERS. TRESPASSERS WILL BE SEVERELY PROSCECUTED.

Keeping a watchful eye, Frieda made her way to the rear of the shop and saw the fire escape staircase. She knew she had to be careful. Not only for herself. She could also jeopardise her husbands' important position.

Frieda made her way up the metal steps and wrapped on the back door. She noticed a curtain twitch and then heard a key being turned and a bolt slid back.

When the door opened, Frieda couldn't believe her eyes. Hildegard and Ingrid were dressed in thick jumpers and gloves looking pale and cold. They were both wearing Star of David armbands. The only kitchen light was from four candles placed on a table and a dresser.

Frieda hugged them both. 'Dear God. This place is freezing,' she said.

Thirty-five year old Hildegard broke down in tears while Ingrid explained, 'They've turned off our water, gas and electricity. It's all my fault for wearing the brooch and punishment for not telling the authorities my father had a Jewish grandmother on the family tree chart.'

A slim Hildegard with pointed features and dark hair in a bun, put her arm around Ingrid. In-between sobs she said, 'No Ingrid, it's our fault. Sooner or later they would have checked anyway. Your father and I should have come clean and told them at the outset. They told us this is our punishment because we lied to them, not because of the Jewish ancestry.'

Frieda looked worried. 'You poor things. What are you going to do?'

'I don't know.' Hildegard wrung her hands with worry. 'They've frozen our bank account and the little money we had in the apartment went on food. We haven't eaten for three days.'

Frieda gasped and said, 'I can't believe they'd do that. It's too horrible for words. What about Ulrich? Are they going to release him?'

'They could send him to a concentration camp. They won't tell us anything.' Hildegard looked anxious. 'The Gestapo forced us to wear these armbands. They said we'd be shot if we were caught without them. It's like a death sentence, we can't even get served in shops wearing them.' She asked in desperation. 'Could your husband help us, Frieda? He must have connections?'

Frieda gave them both a reassuring hug. 'I'll do what I can, but meanwhile I'll get you some food.' She took out a handful of Reichsmarks from her handbag and handed it to Hildegard. 'Keep this safe. You may need money at some time. Even the Gestapo can be bribed,' she said with a smirk.

Hildegard and Ingrid grabbed her arm and thanked her.

'Now, you two, make me a list of what you want and dig out some large shopping bags I can use.'

With the list, Frieda went to the downtown shops where she wouldn't be recognised. Stocking up with tinned food, fruit, bottled water, candles and some toiletries, she made her way back to their apartment. The early November afternoon was cold and a light snow had started to fall.

At some distance away she froze. An SS Stormtrooper was now standing on guard in the shop doorway. She had to get past him to get to the rear of the premises.

Frieda hovered until his attention was diverted by a window cleaner who'd come to the shop to carry out his regular two-week wipe over. While arms were raised in protest - it looked like the cleaner was owed money from previous work - Frieda managed to duck down the side entrance as the Stormtrooper laughed and pointed to the defaced window.

Safely inside, as the shopping contents spilled out onto the kitchen table, Hildegard and Ingrid as hunger gripped them, immediately broke into the water and cans of tinned food and began drinking and eating without glasses or plates. Frieda looked on in shock.

Halfway through their gorging and burping they stopped. They looked at Frieda embarrassed. Hildegard felt awkward. 'You must think we're animals?'

'No – no, of course not. I'd be the same if I hadn't eaten in days. Carry on, you poor things.'

Ingrid fetched some plates and glasses from the dresser and served out the remaining food that had been opened. The two of them sat at the table, more civilised this time.

Frieda broke the tension and pointed to the cardboard box. 'I got you both Black Forest Cake for desert. I hope you like it?'

Hildegard smiled and thanked her. 'We owe you a great deal, Frieda. You risked your life for us. Anybody helping Jews, even half Jew families like us could be executed.'

'Listen, You Two. I'll do my best. It's monstrous how you've been treated. I'll speak to my husband tonight. See if he can do anything to get you out this mess.'

With hugs and kisses, it was dark as Frieda left their apartment and cautiously made her way down the fire escape. The Stormtrooper had gone, however, a replacement could be along anytime. With this in mind, she walked briskly until the apartment was out of sight and then took a tram home.

*

'I'm sorry, Frieda, there's nothing I can do.' That evening Karl was working from home. In a small converted upstairs bedroom that doubled as his office, he was explaining to her. 'My hands are tied. The Gestapo are a law unto themselves. The Bauer family should have come clean to begin with. They've only got themselves to blame.'

The doctor still in uniform sitting at his desk, paused from his work and looked up at her with a sympathetic smile. 'Look, Frieda, I know they were your friends but you have to distance yourself now. That husband of hers, Ulrich whatever. He's probably on a train to a concentration camp right now. And with the other two, it's only a matter of time.' Still with a sympathetic expression he explained, 'With my new position, Frieda, I can't afford any scandal. If you help these people you'll only get us both into trouble.'

'Scandal, is that all that concerns you?' She said mockingly. 'These people are starving, Karl, and you're worried about a scandal. No food, no heating. It's disgusting how they're being treated.' Frieda was angry with him. 'All you have to do is have a word with the Gestapo. Tell them who you are. Use your connections. Get their water and heating turned back on, that's all I ask.'

Karl sighed with submission. He raised himself and came round to her. He put his arm around Frieda's shoulder. 'Okay – okay. I'll see what I can do. I can't promise anything, Frieda, but as they were your friends I'll make an exception and try and get their situation improved.'

She beamed and kissed him. 'Thank you darling, thank you so much.' With a spring in her step she turned to him at the door. 'I'm getting cook to prepare your favourite for supper. White bean soup followed by Bratwurst sausage and potato dumplings and then apple pancakes and cream.'

Karl smiled back. 'Sounds good to me.'

When Frieda had gone he picked up the telephone and dialled the number.

'Gestapo headquarters.'

'SS- Sturmbannführer Dr Karl Borch speaking.' Karl wanted to use his newly promoted title to impress. 'I would like to speak to SS-Gruppenführer Heinrich Muller.'

'One moment please.'

Karl waited and then.

'Good evening, Doctor, what can we do for you?'

'Ah, Heinrich. It's about the Jew scum living above that locked up shoe shop on 15 Spandauerstrasse. A Jewess and her daughter. My contacts tell me their hiding other Jews there. You know, under the floor boards, behind wall panels, that sort of thing. They've seen Jews coming and going of a night time.' Karl paused and then said hesitantly, 'It's a personal matter, Heinrich. You see, they were friends of my wife before it was discovered they had Jew ancestry. To save us both any further embarrassment, I would be very grateful if you could immediately investigate and delouse the apartment. You know. Make sure it's empty by tonight.'

'I'll make a note. 15 Spandauerstrasse you say. Leave it with me, Doctor. I'll take care of it and get it fumigated.'

'Oh, and if you could report a Jew found in hiding, it would help to appease my wife. Make her see there was nothing that could be done.'

Heinrich Muller laughed. 'Sounds like she's really been bending your ear, Doctor.'

Karl laughed with him. 'You could say that. Oh and by the way, give my kind regards to your wife. We expect to see you both at our New Year's Eve party.'

Karl gave a slight sigh of relief as he put the receiver down. Then he turned his attention back to his office work.

*

The next day, while her husband was attending to business at his medical centre in Berlin, Frieda made her way by tram to the Bauer's apartment. It was another cold November morning as Frieda flitted in and out of a few local shops stocking up with some more provisions for the mother and daughter.

Expecting a guard on duty forbidding entry to shoppers as with other Jewish shops, she was surprised to see the shop window and door entrance boarded up. Keeping a watchful eye, Frieda made her way down the side entrance and climbed the rear fire escape. When she reached the top it was the same. Boards had been nailed over the fire escape entrance and windows with a few swastika stencils stating PROPERTY OF THE REICH. NO ADMITTANCE.

She listened out and then wrapped on the window board. Taking a risk again, Frieda wrapped harder this time hurting her knuckle. Still no sound or movement from inside. With one last look, hesitating on the top step, she descended the stairs thinking the worst.

*

Over supper that evening with her husband, she nonchalantly enquired about the Bauer's welfare. Had he managed to improve some of their living conditions?

Karl had rehearsed his reply. With a sympathetic expression he explained to her. 'I telephoned Chief Muller this morning to see what he could do for them. He told me they'd been arrested. The Gestapo had received a tip off last night concerning the Bauer's harbouring Jews. They went in during the night and true enough, found a young Jewish male hiding under the bed. They also found a stash of anti-party leaflets with him and a small printing press under the floor boards. All three of them were arrested and taken away.'

Frieda gasped with astonishment. 'I can't believe...'

'I'm sorry, Darling, under those circumstance they'd committed high treason. There was nothing I could do for them.'

Frieda shook her head in bewilderment. 'The Bauer's didn't...didn't seem the type. Just ordinary shop people.'

'You have to remember, Frieda, Jewish blood runs deep. Having Jewish ancestry they would of course be sympathisers. It would only be natural. And let's face it, the Bauer daughter looked more Jewish than some girls living in Palestine.'

Frieda with a lost look murmured, 'I know, but...'

Karl interrupted. 'And as Doctor Goebbels highlighted, the Jews are very cunning. Especially some of the European ones without the Zionist features. They are still amongst us all with their deceiving ways. Taking us into their confidence. Trying to build false relationships. One can easily be fooled

Frieda, as yourself for instance, even me.' Karl affectionately reached for her hand across the table and gave it a little squeeze with a strained smile.

CHAPTER THREE

At supper, while a portrait of Adolf Hitler looked over the Borch family, their elderly maid Gertrude served dinner and poured the wine and then stood behind waiting on them. Sharon, their half-Jewish younger maid was on her hands and knees polishing the floor in the other room.

During their meal, the radio in the background preached the daily mix of Goebbels propaganda: "... *for 1938, unemployment in Germany is the lowest it has been in years, thanks to our good Fuhrer. The creation of the autobahn promises more jobs for more men, and we await the day when, as our great Fuhrer has promised, there is an automobile for every family...*"

Although some time ago, Magda and Martin still chatted excitedly about the Hitler Youth Rally they'd been to last year at the Berlin Olympic Stadium where the previous Olympic Games of 1936 had been held. That Saturday there had been over eighty-thousand Hitler Youth. In their separate legions amongst the drumming and waving of flags, Magda and her brother had marched in step as the band played Horst-Wessel-Liedamongst. Then her brother had performed military-style manoeuvres which his local *Hitlerjugend* had practiced for an entire year; ending with a night time grand finale which included spelling out the name 'ADOLF HITLER' with flaming torches.

Young Martin Borch and his boys group had been lucky. With his light brown hair combed over, Führer style, and wearing the summer uniform of black lederhosen with brown short sleeves and party armband, he'd sorted himself an ideal place to view near the concrete podium with its giant swastika. Looking up he waited, shaking with excitement like thousands of others. Then the buzzing started. Gradual at first, but becoming more and more audible until Baldur von Schirachthe the Reichsjugendführer - Leader of the Hitler Youth, introduced the Fuhrer to them.

The tumultuous welcome as their saviour stepped up to the microphone was unbelievable. Martin told Magda afterwards, the Führer had looked at him and smiled.

She was jealous and said he'd looked at her as well.

Hitler had given a speech in which he spoke candidly about his own youth and painful adolescence, and then ended by telling them: 'You, My Youth, are our nation's most precious guarantee for a great future, and you are destined to be the leaders of a glorious new order under the supremacy of National Socialism. Never forget that one day you will rule the world!'

When he'd finished, Magda and Martin in a whipped-up frenzy, shrieked, 'Sieg Heil,' many times with thousands of others until they were nearly hoarse.

For this evening meal, Frieda had told cook to prepare one of their favourites as a celebration for her husband's promotion. White bean soup followed by Bratwurst sausage and potato dumplings and then apple pancakes and cream.

While everyone tucked in, Magda told her parents about her school friend Gretel and what she had witnessed that afternoon while queuing in a shop. A Jew had been hit over the head by the shopkeeper for standing in line and then everybody cheered as he ran out of the shop bleeding from the wound.

They all laughed apart from Frieda who forced herself to grin. She knew, even with their daughter, they had to be careful. A number of parents had been reported by their children for dissent, for not towing the National Socialist line.

Karl told his children he had a surprise for them. With a nod to Frieda, who already knew, he told them he'd been promoted, and in the new-year they would be moving to a bigger house in the country.

Dr Karl Borch initially trained as a pilot in the Luftwaffe, however, his problems with airsickness combined with his colour blindness forced him to take his second chosen career in medicine. Karl qualified and worked for the SS-Totenkopf as a eugenics research physician at the Reich's Office of Medicine in Berlin. He'd worked hard over the years and knew this promotion was long coming. His new post would be as SS-

Sturmbannführer, Commandant of Pullhausen Concentration Camp.

Pullhausen was a small sub-camp of Dachau Concentration Camp near Munich which was around three-hundred miles south of Berlin in Upper Bavaria. With its quiet location, it was ideal for the Reich's secret eugenics programme he'd be working on. Being near the larger camp of Dachau, it would provide Pullhausen with an endless supply of available prisoners for experiments.

Magda and Martin frowned. Magda asked, 'What about school? What about my friends? My BDM group?'

Karl tried to quash their worries and make pleasant excuses. 'Don't worry, you two. There'll be a school and Hitler Youth groups at the camp and you can still see your friends. They can come and stay whenever you want.'

Magda and Martin continued to grumble. 'It's not fair. Why do we have to move? Can't we stay here while you go to your new work,' they said in unison.

Karl tried to make light of it. 'Look, we're going to have a grand farewell party on New Year's Eve and you can invite all your friends with their parents. And my new boss, the very important SS-Oberstgruppenführer Dr Klaus Müller and his wife will be there. He's the Reich Protectorate of Upper Bavaria.'

The prospects of a party with their friends seemed to soften the mood. Magda asked again. 'And you say we can visit our friends or they can visit us at any time?'

'Yes of course, you two. There's nothing to worry about. And just think, it'll be an exciting new adventure. A new house. New garden. Make new friends at the camp in your Hitler Youth groups.' Karl could see he was winning them over. 'Now after dinner you can both make a list of friends who you want at the party.'

*

Over the next week, Frieda and her maid went shopping for their forthcoming New Years' Eve farewell celebration. Although a bit early, Frieda wanted to make sure to get in quick with her food orders and furniture hire before the Christmas rush started. She spent two days picking out an evening dress for the occasion and, because of her short plump size, would have to visit again to confirm the alterations were correct. Then there were the caterers, choosing the right menu and of course the celebration cake. The flowers and the iced carvings were next. An iced bust of the Fuhrer, centre piece on the table would be fitting she thought, and bunting everywhere with the swastika depicted in each little triangular flag.

The family chauffeur drove them in their black and cream Mercedes Benz with the soft top. This time of year the hood was up with the car heater blasting away.

While shopping, they saw Berlin filled with giant flags and banners. There seemed to be an ever increasing abundance of military personnel on the streets.

While pavement café life relaxed in the winter sun, people ignored the daily round up of Jews being herded into trucks or looked away and pretend it wasn't happening. A few shop windows had *JEWS FORBIDDEN* daubed on them including the same message displayed on trams and buses.

That evening on the ninth of November while having dinner, the family heard shouts and screams outside. They moved upstairs to the bedroom windows for a better view into the street below and saw rioting taking place. The sound of breaking glass mingled with flames and cries from burning shops.

Karl looked through his binoculars and with the aid of the street lights he could see looters running from one shop to another. There was no sign of any police but storm troopers were everywhere. They already had a group of people with their hands raised against a wall. Other rioters were armed with sledgehammers and axes and were shouting *'Smash the Jews.'*

Karl told his family not to follow him and went outside. Some Jewish shops across Wilhelmstrasse had their windows smashed and one was on fire. There was broken glass everywhere. Sharp slivers sparkled on the ground from the light of the street lamps.

The crowd scattered as a group of soldiers moved in. Some ran into the road while others looked for a safe place to watch the show. A cacophony of voices shouted, *'Stop! Please, stop!'* He recognized the protesting shop owners. They had Jewish beards and were wearing Kippahs. As the soldiers threw their merchandise into the street including clothes, shoes, jewellery and food items, mayhem broke loose. People screamed and cursed, *'Jewish Pigs!'* Others seized the opportunity and gathered up what they could carry and headed for home.

Karl was stunned, he witnessed people he'd known a long time, just blatantly scoop up articles that didn't belong to them and scurry away.

Those Jews that dared to challenge the looters were pushed to the ground by the soldiers and were kicked and beaten with coshes. Then an army truck pulled up and they were bodily thrown into the rear compartment.

He'd seen enough. This was madness. Reckless and stupid. A waste of goods and property that could have been put to good use by non-Jew shop owners. Now the premises were rendered unusable.

As far as he'd been told in closed door meetings and conferences, the Jews were to be quietly eliminated from society. To what extent would depend on the resources available. Euthanasia for the feeble minded had been suggested. Others to labour camps and factories in the East to boost Germany's manufacturing economy. The remainder for medical research, in the most humane way of course. However, these mindless clashes would only stir up resentment. And Karl felt sure, the one thing the party needed to solve its Jewish problem was a willing Jew not a resentful one; certainly where his new work was concerned. The last thing he needed at Pullhausen was a camp full of bitter fired up Jews.

Karl decided he wouldn't put anything in writing, but have a quiet word with his new boss Oberstgruppenführer Dr Klaus Müller at the New Year's Eve party.

*

Magda's love for the Fuhrer was so intense that she was willing to put up with four days of expected bullying from Helga while on holiday to see the Fuhrer at the Berghof. She was infatuated with him and prayed to him every night. Under her blankets with a torch, Magda would read *Der Mädelschaft*, the Nazi magazine for girls. Then when it became late she would lie back and shut her eyes and recite the Jungvolk prayer she'd learnt. 'Führer, my Führer, give me by God. Protect and preserve my life for long. You saved Germany in time of need. I thank you for my daily bread. Be with me for a long time, do not leave me, Führer, my Führer, my faith, my light, Hail to my Führer!' Then she would fall asleep clutching the magazine, dreaming of that November rally in the Berlin Olympic Stadium.

*

One morning, a few days later after the register had been called, Magda was asked to come to the front of the class. Her teacher Frau Koch, patted her shoulder with pride and presented her with a small gift box. It was for the family tree chart she had submitted. The Reich Information Bureau had marked her as the purist Aryan in the class.

While all the pupils stood, Magda opened the box and gave a sharp intake of breath. It was the Hünenkreuz Medal of Purity. Awarded by the party to the racially pure, the silver medallion with the German shaped iron cross and diagonal swords sat on a red velvet cushion.

Magda lifted it out. It was beautiful. On the back was inscribed her rare blood group - AB Negative. The Reich Information Bureau knew her blood type from the chart. This in itself was a privilege. She knew each of the elite SS wore a blood group tag around their neck as well as being tattooed under the arm. Frau Koch urged her to put it on. Magda slipped the chain over her head. The class applauded her apart from Helga Meyer. She just stood and sneered.

CHAPTER FOUR

Two weeks before Christmas, the Borch family were assembled on the platform at Berlins' Anhalter Bahnhof Station.

The station was adorned with swastika flags, and stirring party music blasted from the loud speakers. The smell of coal and steam along with whistles and shouts, filled the senses as Magda spotted many girls from Berlins' other BDM troops. Spaced out along the platform there had to be over forty of them clinging together with parents and luggage. No doubt, presents for the Fuhrer were safely stored away in suitcases.

She could see girls from her own group. Some of their mothers hugged them and became tearful. She saw two of her friends and waved to them. They responded, looking carefully first in case Helga was watching, then they gave a big smile and an excited wave.

Just then, Helga Meyer appeared with her family. She gave Magda a cold stare and then turned her back to talk with girls who had gathered. It is obvious Helga was the ringleader.

Without her around, Magda mixed well with most of the girls. The problem was the others were afraid of Helga. She was clever and witty and had perfect Aryan good looks. As well as being head girl at school, she had also been promoted to Mädelscharführerin – girl supervisor of Magda's BDM group.

Helga's father, Hans Meyer, was a small arms manufacturer and in business with the husband of the wife who was the Gebiets Mädel Führerin - the Berlin regional leader of the BDM. Helga's family were well known and successful with her father's company being awarded National Socialist honours by the Reich Armaments Ministry for reaching production quotas. This meant Helga was the teacher's favourite at school as well as amongst her BDM superiors. Helga couldn't do a thing wrong and made it clear from early on, Magda with her false eye was going to be the classroom butt for her jokes.

The Reichsbahn's Class 52 steam engine with the five pale green coaches softly hissed expectantly on platform three ready for the ten hour, five-hundred kilometre overnight journey to Berchtesgaden, with stops at Nuremberg and Munich. Within thirty minutes the girls were all aboard and waving goodbye to tearful mothers as the train chugged slowly out of the station amongst the roars and smoke of the engine.

Later after visiting the dining car for tea, the girls were climbing onto each other's bunks, chatting and squealing incessantly in their overnight sleeping carriage. The smell of lavender and new bed linen permeated the air.

No one came near Magda. Lying on her bunk with the curtains pulled, she heard Helga's taunts including all the old eye jokes, with bursts of laughter including the hurtful collective singing that Helga had managed to start up. Especially her version of *Lili Marlene*. '*Underneath the eyelid in the empty slot, Magda wants an eyeball to match the one she's got. A glass one for Christmas might come her way, so who can tell, who can say. Oh Magda with one eyeball, Oh Magda can only pray.*'

Magda punched her pillow as the tears welled up.

By eight o'clock that evening the cruel singing had subsided. After traveling two-hundred kilometres it was dark outside with a temperature of minus five degrees. A blizzard was raging. Then all of a sudden the train slowed to a stop. The girls' attentions were diverted. They were all looking out of the window because of the holdup.

Magda heard voices along the carriage and then a rail steward called out for everyone not to be alarmed. The stop was due to a partial snowfall on the line.

Magda raised her blind and looked out. She couldn't see anything. No lights only total blackness with swirling snow beating against the window. She thought to herself they were in the middle of nowhere.

Poking her head out of the curtain, Magda could see twenty-eight year old Frau Schulz, her tall BDM adult supervisor with her arm around Helga's shoulders. It looked like Helga wasn't feeling well. 'Come with me, Dear, and we'll get you some fresh air,' she said, and walked with her up the carriage.

Once Helga had gone, the other girls settled down and Magda knew it was safe to approach. They seemed a bit embarrassed at first without Helga being there. It was obvious she led them on. Magda asked the girls what the problem was with Helga. They told her she was suffering from travel sickness.

All of a sudden an inward warmth of relaxation flooded through Magda. Secretly she hoped the bitch would drop dead, but that was wishful thinking.

At that moment, Magda needed to use the toilet. The supervisors had provided an endless supply of biscuits with orange and black-current drinks for the overnight journey and Magda had made full use of the freebies. The problem was, the toilet was at the end of the carriage where Helga and Frau Schulz had gone.

Magda excused herself from the other girls and made her way up the carriage. The temperature inside the train was warm with the heaters working flat out. As she opened the door into the lobby compartment she suddenly shivered with the cold blast that hit her.

The carriage door window was down while Frau Schulz, still with her arm around Helga's shoulder, looked up and said, 'Magda, can you keep Helga company for a moment, while I go and check on the other girls?'

'Can I pay a visit first, Miss?'

'Yes of course you can.'

When Magda came out of the toilet, Frau Schulz had gone.

Because Helga couldn't get into the toilet, she'd reached through the window and opened the carriage door to be sick. At that moment she was leaning out, bent over and heaving onto the railway track. Hair stuck to her face from the icy wind and snow.

Magda, knowing she'd been told to stay with Helga, put her hand sympathetically on her shoulder and asked, 'You gonna be okay?'

Helga spun round and swallowed hard. Then she said to her coldly, 'What do you care, One Eye? Why don't you piss off!'

Magda took her hand away in shock at the offensive remark. She stepped back while Helga was sick again.

She was thinking, this was going to be a long painful holiday even though she hoped to meet the Fuhrer. And this was only the first night. But if...?

Magda looked at Helga's back convulsing with the moans of travel sickness. There was nothing to lose. Even if it meant the holiday would be abandoned. Even if it meant not seeing the Fuhrer. The plan was to knock her out of the carriage onto the track and lock the door. At least she'd have her own satisfaction.

Magda checked either way through both carriage windows that looked into where they were standing. She felt like a prisoner preparing to make a break for freedom. It was quiet. This was it. It was now or never.

She braced herself. Stepping back to give herself room for a good run-up, she took a flying leap at Helga. At that moment Helga heard something and turned. The pair of them collided and they began to wrestle with each other by the door entrance. Then with one almighty push, Magda knocked Helga out of the carriage.

Her scream was carried away by the noise of the blizzard as she plunged headlong down a steep embankment.

Magda immediately slammed the carriage door shut and pulled up the window. She took deep breaths. *What the fuck have I done?* She thought. She had to act quickly. *The toilet, get yourself into the toilet.*

Just in time, as she slid the lock to engaged, the carriage door opened and Frau Schulz called out, 'Helga!'

Magda answered, as near to Helga's voice as she hoped. With a long drawn out horsy moan she replied, 'I'll be okay, Miss. Its travel sickness, just let me rest up in here for a while.'

'Alright, Helga. By the way, where's Magda?'

Magda replied in a sickly whine 'She left, Miss, went back to the others. I told her I'd be OK.'

'Selfish little brat,' Frau Schulz mumbled.

Magda smiled at the remark.

'You sure you'll be okay, Helga?'

'Yes, Miss. I'll probably go to bed early. Sleep it off.'

'Best thing, Helga. I'll come and look in on you later.'

'Thanks, Miss.' Magda heard the lobby door close and breathed a sigh of relief. Then she slid the toilet bolt back and peeked out.

At that moment, the train lurched and rolled about ten feet and then stopped. Suddenly a steward opened the lobby door and called out. 'Please be aware the line has been cleared and we will be moving shortly.'

Magda held the toilet door shut until the steward had gone. Then she quietly slipped out of the entrance and stood by the carriage window taking stock. All she had to do now was get back to the others quickly and be seen.

It was then she heard something. A rustling scratching sound. She looked out of the window and, *'Arghhh!'* Magda screamed as a hand slapped against the glass. She recoiled back and put a fist to her mouth in terror.

Magda looked to see if she'd been heard. It all seemed quiet. She took a step forward and peered out.

A snowy cap appeared at the bottom of the window followed by the terrible white apparition of Helga. Her lips and nose were frozen blue and there was ice on her eyebrows and fringe. Helga had managed to haul herself up the steep embankment. Her hand slapped the glass, the fingers frozen and useless.

The pleading eyes of Helga looked at Magda. One hand tried the handle, but the fingers had no grip. Helga was saying something - shouting something in her cold silent world.

Magda leant forward and smiled. She put a hand mockingly to her ear and mouthed the words, 'Speak up.'

In that instant, Helga knew she'd been trapped.

As the whistle blew, Magda symbolically put a hand over her false eye and did the Hitler salute with the other one.

Then the train lurched a bit, then lurched a bit more. Helga's blue lips were pulled back showing her teeth in a muted scream. And then she was gone.

The train lurched again and stopped. As Magda made her way down the carriage she passed some girls chatting excitedly as they would be on the move soon. Now she had to consider her options.

Passing through into the sleeping car, she saw the bedding cupboard. Magda couldn't believe her luck. It was plum next to Helga's bottom bunk. Helga had chosen the one in the best location of course; nearest the amenities and with the biggest picture window view. The other girls didn't argue. No one dared. They didn't want to be singled out like Magda. Be at the mercy of Helga's cruel sarcasm with the others ganging up.

With a rolled up blanket and two pillows she moved quickly onto the bunk and pulled the curtain. The rest of the girls were still in the dining car. Probably having a late snack because of the delay. Magda stuffed the pillows and blanket under Helga's sheets. The mound looked realistic enough. Could she get away with it until morning? If they found Helga alive, Magda knew she'd be finished. She might even be executed, knowing Helga's father and his connections. Hanged or guillotined like so many anti-Nazis.

Magda nervously fondled her neck. She thought, the more distance the train could get between that little brat the better.

Suddenly she froze. The medallion. The Hünenkreuz Medal of Purity around her neck! It was missing. She had it in the toilet. 'Shit!' She whispered. Magda tried to think. Her mind was racing. *Shit! – Shit! – Shit!* She thought, *where the hell did I lose that?*

Magda nonchalantly retraced her footsteps up the carriage scouring the floor. She looked into the lobby and then the toilet. Nothing. She'd grappled with Helga. It must have fallen off. Perhaps the bitch had torn it off. *'Shit! – Shit!*

Dear God! Even if Helga didn't survive, if they find it with her then they'll know she was mixed up with it.

Magda felt her neck again. The thought of being laid out staring into a bucket and hearing the guillotine blade swish down above her head, jerked her into reality. She had to go and find Helga, and find her quick before the train moved off.

She peered through the window. It was blowing a blizzard outside and she couldn't see anything. Grabbing the handle, Magda opened the carriage door. The icy blast of wind smacked at her face. It took her breath away as fine snow blocked her good eye, nose and mouth. Wiping her face she looked both ways to make sure she hadn't been seen and then jumped down.

Magda hit the frozen ground and screamed as she rolled halfway down the embankment. She was covered in snow and it was freezing. Being dark as well she could hardly see ten feet in front of herself. Her fingers were getting numb, she had to be quick. With a hand shading her eyes she scoured the ground and saw something moving. Magda trudged down the embankment towards it.

Helga was crawling slowly on her stomach completely covered in snow trying to get up the slope and then slipping down again. Her pitiful attempt made Magda stare for a second. Then she noticed something in her hand.

With the snow up to her calves, Magda turned her face against the biting wind and moved nearer. She grabbed Helga's arm. The hand was blue with cold and the stiff frozen fingers had locked themselves around the Hünenkreuz medallion.

Magda tried to prize them off, however her own fingers were numbing up. Then to her horror, Helga's other hand grabbed at her ankle and Magda stumbled and fell. She cried out while Helga rolled on top of her whining and moaning. Magda thrashed around and tried to push her off. Helga's face was so close in her face, she could see an expression of relief thinking help had come. Magda with all her remaining energy punched her square on the nose and blood spattered the both of them. She punched Helga again and managed to pull herself free.

Just then above her in the swirling blizzard she heard the train horn sound. Jesus it was going to go without her. Magda looked up and could just make out the long dark shadow of the carriages. It was still there but for how long?

This time, holding Helga's arm and with a foot placed firmly on her whimpering head to give her leverage, Magda forced the fingers open and took the medallion. She breathed with relief at the sight of it.

Leaving Helga moaning with flaying arms clutching at nothing, Magda made her way with difficulty up the embankment. As she reached the top, she collapsed onto one knee with exhaustion. The horn sounded again and now it was life or death. The train began to move slowly, inch by inch.

Magda raised herself and cried out in pain. She began to stumble desperately in the direction of the open carriage door. Now it was moving faster. She had to break into a run to save herself. With one last desperate attempt, Magda flung her body into the entrance and clutched at the doorway. Her legs were swinging widely outside, while she tried to haul herself onto the moving carriage. As the train picked up speed she managed to drag herself inside further. Knowing time wasn't on her side, Magda tried to stand up and collapsed. She tried again and this time she used the hand rail to heave herself up.

Now she had to reach out and close the swinging carriage door. Holding onto the rail, she watched it sway backwards and forwards until she saw her chance and grabbed at the handle. With an almighty pull, Magda slammed it shut.

She winced at the sound and held her breath and then looked into the carriages either side through the lobby windows. A few people were sitting and reading but no one had heard her. She was alone. 'The toilet, get to the toilet,' she muttered to herself.

With the bolt slid to engaged, Magda tried to smarten herself up in the mirror. Using yards of toilet roll she washed the blood off her face and dabbed snow off her hair and clothes. Her fingers were tingling, she was getting some feeling back. Now all she had to do was get back to her bunk and change clothes without being seen.

One hour later, Magda was playing cards with the girls.

Frau Schulz had taken her time over supper with the other BDM leaders and spoilt herself with a Brandy. And why not, she had thought. First night of the holiday, a chance to relax, all paid for by the Hitler Youth and parents.

Having eaten her favourite - braised lamb shank followed by a delicious crème brulee, Frau Schulz slowly ambled down the lounge car feeling warm from the brandy. As she approached Magda she asked, 'Have you seen Helga?'

Magda looked up nonchalantly from her cards, calm and relaxed. She also held a winning hand. 'Yes, Miss. I popped back to see her but she was in the toilet. She told me she was feeling a bit better and was going to bed.'

Frau Schulz relaxed a bit further, hearing the good news. The last thing she wanted was to be up all night with some schoolgirl vomiting all over the place. 'I'll pop in to see how she is. Thank you, Magda.' She smiled and made her way to the sleeping car.

Magda knew her deception was probably going to be short lived. She braced herself ready for the alarm call, when Frau Schulz would realise the rolled up blanket with two pillows was some kind of joke being played.

However, nothing happened. All seemed well. Frau Schulz had popped her head in, seen Helga all covered up and relaxed even further. Now it was decision time. Should she have an early night or return to the dining car with the BDM troop leaders for another brandy? Also the thought of those dark chocolate truffles that someone had brought along to share, did help make up her mind.

*

Magda did get to see the Fuhrer and hand him her present. It was a Christmas hamper her parents had made up with a card inside showing their address in Berlin. Her parents reasoned, if one was going to give a present to the Fuhrer, one had to make sure he knew who it was from.

Magda, proudly wearing her Hünenkreuz Medal of Purity medallion, queued with the other girls in the large reception hall at the Berghof. When he appeared, they all gasped in awe. It was like God had walked into the room. The Fuhrer with his entourage looking on, started down the line smiling and chatting to the girls until he came to Magda. He looked at her medallion and gave Magda an affectionate pat on the cheek.

It was if she'd been electrocuted when the Fuhrer touched her. She vowed she would never wash her cheek again.

*

After Helga's friends had reported her missing, a thorough search was carried out. Trains following behind had been warned to keep a look out.

It was two days later that a maintenance worker had discovered the body of Helga at the side of the track. It appeared she had managed to climb up the steep incline. A passing train must have cut her in two. Of course the driver couldn't have seen her in the dense blizzard weather.

The newspapers and radio didn't go into specific details. They just said she died outside on the line from her injuries while playing some sort of prank with friends. Never stood a chance in the severe cold weather, it had dropped to minus ten-degrees.

There had to be over three-hundred people at Helga's funeral. All her friends and class including BDM girls were there. It was a freezing day and some of them were stamping their feet to keep warm. As the coffin was lowered, draped with a giant swastika flag, they each dropped a white rose onto the casket. Magda didn't, she took hers home as a memento.

CHAPTER FIVE

On the evening of the New Year's Eve farewell party, as Dr Klaus Müller the SS-Oberstgruppenführer Reich Protectorate of Upper Bavaria and his wife made their grand entrance, the whole gathering saluted him and shouted, 'Heil Hitler.' At that moment the hired dance band started up playing the Horst-Wessel-Lied National Anthem, and over sixty guests stood to attention and patriotically sung the words.

Frieda had excelled herself. A long table had been laid out with a help yourself buffet while extra staff handed out champagne and canapes. Guests queued as the large overweight chef served them slices of roast suckling pig, and then with their overladen plates, they made their way to the hired gold painted tables and chairs situated under the white satin sheeted canopy.

While waiters circumnavigated tables topping up glasses, the guests chatted and dined amidst the strains of a Viennese waltz from the band.

Magda and Martin, wearing their Hitler Youth uniforms, were presented to the Oberstgruppenführer. Dr Klaus Müller the Reich Protectorate of Upper Bavaria, wearing a light brown uniform and matching Jack boots, was a short middle aged fat man with a large stomach and chubby fingers; most notable when clutching his champagne glass. They listened enthralled as he informed them how vital their father's work was for the country and the Fuhrer. He told them the youth of Germany were the nation's most precious guarantee and that one day they will rule the world as the Fuhrer had said. He also commented on Magda's medal. She made sure her Hünenkreuz medal for racial purity was on display around her neck. Magda puffed out her chest when the Oberstgruppenführer told her she must be proud to wear such an award.

Sometime later, the Oberstgruppenführer and Karl were alone together in the drawing room relaxing with brandy and cigars. 'A wonderful evening to end the year for 1938, Karl. Yourself and dear wife have done a splendid job of entertaining.'

'Thank you, Oberstgruppenführer.' Karl beamed that he was pleased. 'We wanted to put on something special as a farewell to our friends and for my promotion.'

As he drew on his cigar the Oberstgruppenführer became serious. 'You know, Karl, your new commandant's position at the camp is going to be a hard and difficult one which requires complete commitment regardless of the difficulties that may arise. Remember, you are sworn to secrecy regarding the work that is being carried out.'

'Of course, Oberstgruppenführer, I understand perfectly.'

The Oberstgruppenführer swigged his brandy and reminded him. 'Remember, Karl, the Jews are the eternal enemies of the German people and must be eliminated. If we do not succeed in destroying the biological foundation of Jewry, then one day the Jews will destroy us the German people, if we let them. Our work, your work in fact, is part of the Lebensborn programme, not just to destroy the Jews but to eradicate through forced sterilization those who are mentally ill - the feebleminded, the epileptic, the schizophrenic, the crippled including the deaf and blind.' The Oberstgruppenführer stared into space with his thoughts. 'The Aryan race must be Nordic looking, tall long legged and slim. He will have a narrow-face with a narrow high-built nose and a prominent lower jaw and chin. The skin will be white and only tanned by the sun. Not the inferior African black man's skin or like the American degenerate Nigger skin. The hair will be smooth, straight or wavy - possibly curly in childhood. The colour will be blonde. This will be done in your camp through a breeding plan of male and female pure Germans to make babies for the Fatherland, for the Fuhrer.'

The Oberstgruppenführer swigged his brandy again and then continued. 'With your team of doctors, Karl, we are counting on you to understand the science, so as to be able to change facial features, eye, hair and skin colour through transplants and grafting experiments. Make just acceptable peoples, perfectly acceptable to swell our nation as a master race.'

Karl smiled inwardly. The desired features of an Aryan certainly didn't match the physical build of the Oberstgruppenführer.

The Oberstgruppenführer relaxed. The brandy was now talking. 'Never forget, Karl, the eternal Jew is always scheming and crafty by nature.' He sat back and reminisced. 'I remember back in 1933 when I'd brought my first Jew to book. It was just after I'd joined the party. At the time, the Jew was landlord to my father's farm. I helped my father run the farm. I remember the day my father died. I was at the horse market. The Jew landlord had visited the farm to collect his rent and found my father dead in the barn from a heart attack. Knowing money was tight and my father still owed rent, the Jew landlord stole a horse from my father's stable. Sometime later I confronted him. The Jew swore blind he hadn't taken it. Then a couple of months later I saw it up for sale at the local horse market.

'That evening we had a party meeting at the beer hall. We all got liquored up and afterwards a crowd of us went out to the Jews farm. We called the Jew out and then beat him up. His Jew bitch wife was screaming so we knocked her unconscious. Then we dragged them back into the farmhouse and set it alight.' The Oberstgruppenführer raised himself and stubbed out his cigar thoughtfully. 'Still...Although it was some gratification, I never did see the horse again.' He looked at Karl and smiled. 'Enough of my rambling. Shall we get back to the party?'

As they made a move for the door, Karl stopped him. 'Oberstgruppenführer. I saw the riots in the street recently.

The Jews being taken away. Shouting, screaming all whipped up with hate and terror. I was thinking of a more passive approach. To calm them at the camp where their cooperation would be beneficial. Especially before their fate. To be gassed or sterilised or used as a specimen.'

'What did you have in mind?' the Oberstgruppenführer said interested.

'A band made up of Jewish musicians. Playing as the prisoners arrived, got out the trucks. Also at rollcall when selections would be made.'

The Oberstgruppenführer replied, 'Wasn't it Shakespeare? If music be the food of love, play on.' He laughed and Karl joined in pretending to get the Joke. 'Yes, a good idea, Karl. Let me know what you need in the way of instruments. I'm sure our budget can run to it. Now let's join the others and get a refill of your wonderful brandy.'

With the rest of the evening a success, it wasn't until the third hour of the New Year that the last guest had departed. Karl and Frieda finally slumped into bed exhausted and were quickly sound asleep.

Until the first Wednesday of January 1939 had arrived, which was moving day, the following few days were busy with last minute packing and arrangements. This included leasing the house to a high up Gestapo official and his family.

After a tearful farewell to their house, with Frieda and Magda sniffling into their handkerchiefs while hugging neighbours and young friends' goodbye, they were finally driven to Berlin station. The three-hundred and sixty mile train journey to Pullhausen concentration camp would take about ten hours.

*

At the end of the car journey from Pullhausen station, they saw a big house approaching with SS guards on sentry duty flanking its wrought iron gates. As the black 1938 Horch Limousine staff car with swastika pendants attached to the headlamps swept through the entrance, the guards saluted.

Within half an hour of exploring, Karl stood in his huge office and admired his highly polished leather topped desk. He felt he'd arrived at last and the party were beginning to recognise his achievements. He looked through a window into the rear garden and saw two Jews in their striped uniforms digging and weeding some of the flower beds.

For a moment he wondered what it would be like to be a Jew. At the bottom of society. Forevermore to be a slave with no hope of freedom. Akin to those that worked for the Roman Empire which lasted five-hundred years. Generation after generation of families serving their masters. This was how the Fuhrer had said it was going to be. The only exception being, the German Empire was going to last a thousand years. Himmler had said ten thousand years. Even so, the Fuhrer had predicted after the war was won that every German family would have a Jew or a foreign servant. It would be a new Utopia so every day would be a holiday. No more work. No more money worries. The conquered world would serve

Germania, as Hitler had promised to call it, economically and financially.

Karl was glad to be a German in this exciting time of history.

While Karl busied himself in his new role as commandant, Magda helped her mother sort items and furniture around the new house. As it was extra-large, Dalia, a young Jewish woman had been seconded from the camp to help as a maid with the daily chores along with the existing staff of Gertrude and Sharon. Dalia knew how lucky she was to be out of the striped smock and not to have her head shaved, even though she was forbidden to talk unless spoken to. Although cook gave her leftovers and scraps from meals, she knew it was a hundred times better than the rations in the camp.

A few days later, Karl's boss the Oberstgruppenführer, arrived by a chauffeur driven Mercedes-Benz flanked by two military motorcyclists. Carrying a new propaganda film issued by Joseph Goebbels, he summoned Karl and his senior SS staff to watch the twenty minute reel showing how well the Jews were being treated at Pullhausen Concentration Camp.

Ensconced in Karl's new office with the curtains drawn, and the flickering leader tape from the projector counting down on the wall mounted white screen; the selected few watched clean and well-dressed prisoners relaxing outside their huts. Some played cards while others smiled and watched children play. The film with its friendly narration switched to people tending their patch of garden or just sunbathing. Inside the freshly painted canteen an abundance of food was on display. As men, women and children queued, the narrator complemented the hearty meals available. The film portrayed a holiday atmosphere, ending with children eating ice-cream and sweets.

With the curtains pulled open, the audience applauded with some offering praise for the skilful deception. The Oberstgruppenführer raised his hand to quieten them and addressed the gathering. 'Gentlemen, this film must be shown to all Red Cross Inspectors that visit Pullhausen Concentration Camp. On no account must they see this camp's medical block and its equipment. Always use the excuse there is a Typhus outbreak in the camp and the area is under quarantine. Remember you are sworn to the utmost secrecy. This is by order of Heinrich Himmler personally.'

An hour later, as the short bulky frame of the Oberstgruppenführer squeezed into his staff car he saluted and said, 'I have every faith in you, Karl, to carry out Himmler's orders to pioneer a master race. If that cannot be achieved.' He gave an ironic laugh, 'then all our necks are on the line.'

CHAPTER SIX

By 1942, fifteen year old Martin Borch had risen to a Hitlerjugend Streifendienst - an elite Hitler Youth group that helped SS Garrisons in concentration camps. He was now stationed in the main camp at Dachau three miles away. His sister Magda on the other hand wasn't content living a cosseted existence because of her father's connections in her new home next to the camp at Pullhausen. With little social life among people of her own age and wanting to do something positive for the fatherland and the National Socialist cause, she became a BDM section leader working in the ethnic German resettlement programme called Osteinsatz.

Magda had volunteered for *land service in the east* where BDM girls could volunteer for work in the areas of Poland annexed to the Reich. This consisted of amongst things - teaching German to farming families and handing out clothes and food stamps including various rations to help the repatriation of ethnic Germans.

Magda had struck up a friendship with a young Polish maid in a resettlement camp near the city of Lodz. They both had been detailed to serve a couple of Red Cross officials who were there for a week carrying out inspections. They were there, courtesy of Heinrich Himmler, to show the world press including neutral countries how well resettled Germans and deported undesirables were living under National Socialism. This they hoped would quash rumours that had been spreading, concerning the welfare of refugees that were being transported to the east.

The camp was given an extra special clean, prior to the Red Cross party arrival. With freshly painted huts, new curtains, rugs and bedding, Magda just assumed this spring clean was the norm.

At 18 years old, Magda was tall for her age. She still wore the regimental white socks with her long flaxen braided hair, pinned up Gretchen-style. This was in keeping with the young women in Dr Joseph Goebbels propaganda films. Some of the other girls envied Magda because it was the 'in style' and you needed long hair to make the Gretchen braids look good wrapped around your head.

Like most of the BDM girls working at the resettlement camps, Magda was very innocent in the ways a regime which she chose to follow, could be so brutal. However, it came as a shock when she was personally confronted with the results of the Fuhrer's racial laws and policies.

Magda had heard rumours about terrible things that were going on in the ghetto at nearby Lodz. She'd only seen posters and propaganda films with laughing families, all eating together, tending lovely gardens, children playing in their best Sunday clothes; everybody without a care in the world. Sometimes the films would make her homesick. However, the stories filtering through telling otherwise, seemed to increase. Magda decided to find out for herself what the real truth was.

On the pretence of doing some shopping, she aquired a lift into Lodz and boarded the tram that ran through the ghetto. The tram windows were painted on the inside so no one could see through, and the doors were ominously locked. The German authorities had cut off the ghetto from the rest of the town and made it strictly out of bounds.

The journey through the ghetto picked up no passengers. It was purely to get people from one side of Lodz to the other.

Magda sat at the back on her own. She noticed little peepholes had been scratched on the painted windows, so she scratched some more. What she saw made her put her hand to her mouth in horror. Jewish children wearing the Star of David stood in rags, half-starved against the barbed wire fence. As the tram passed, one child, a small girl, had her arms outstretched as if pleading to the driver. A boy lay motionless, spread out at her feet with painfully thin matchstick arms and legs. Further away on the pavement she saw bodies, some naked – just skin and bone. As the tram rumbled on, she saw through her peephole two Jewish men pushing a cart, picking up bodies along the road as they went.

For many years Magda had been taught the Jews were the enemy. They were not Aryan but subhuman; the reason Germany had lost the First World War. They were to blame for the following depression and high inflation. The Fuhrer had said the Jews were to be punished. They were be sent east into exile to labour camps similar to the type her father was in charge of, well away from German civilisation. However, she had never seen suffering on such a scale. This must be wrong. The Fuhrer couldn't know how these people were being treated. He would put a stop to it. It was inhumane. You wouldn't treat animals that way. The Jews were to be punished, yes. Have their homes, businesses and land confiscated. Be made to work and earn an honest living, but not this. Being shut off from the outside world with women and children being starved to death. The treatment she had seen had to be reported.

When she arrived back at the resettlement camp and told her BDM friends, they were horrified. Some didn't believe her. Magda confronted Anna, the Polish maid. She was too afraid to talk about it.

Magda immediately went to see her camp Gebietsführer. She had written a report and handed it to him.

In silence, while she stood to attention in his office wearing her BDM uniform with its blue skirt and white blouse bearing a small swastika on the sleeve and her cap with its party badge sitting on her Gretchen braids. The Gebietsführer sat and read her account of what she'd seen.

He smiled at her and folded the report. 'You must keep this to yourself, Magda,' the Gebietsführer told her.

'But why?' She asked him in astonishment. 'All my group know and my friends, It's terrible how these people are being treated.'

The good-looking blonde Gebietsführer, in his mid-twenties and wearing a black uniform with highly polished Jack-boots, came around from behind his desk and told Magda firmly, 'You would be wise to tear the report up and say no more.'

Magda said defiantly, 'I want my report sent to Berlin, to Reichsjugendführer, Artur Axmann, himself.'

'Don't be silly, Magda, this can do you a great deal of harm,' the Gebietsführer said, trying to reason with her; but she wasn't going to be intimidated.

At 18-years-old, Magda was 5-foot-10-inches tall, taller than the Gebietsführer himself, and very single minded. She snatched the report from his hand, 'Then I'll send it myself,' she said with a defiant sneer.

'Don't be stupid, Magda. The report should be sent through the proper channels, as you very well know.'

She snapped back at him, 'So they can be censored like all the other letters?' At that, she turned on her heels and stormed out of his office.

As the door slammed, he was already picking up the phone.

Two days later, Magda saw her chance while the Red Cross officials were on their own in a camp hut comparing notes. She handed them the report and told them what she had witnessed firsthand.

As she expected, she heard no more about her report and assumed it probably had been shown to higher officials and excused as a young girl's imagination running away with her.

However, Magda's report, which she had signed with her Hitler Youth membership number, had eventually reached the desk of Heinrich Himmler, via the Red Cross.

In view of the eyewitness account and other stories that had been circulating around the Lodz ghetto, the Red Cross wanted to come and see for themselves. They planned to send a three-man delegation in one month's time.

Himmler had exploded with rage. He wanted to know who had leaked the information. It didn't take long. Magda's camp Gebietsführer had telephoned and sent a warning letter at the time to the Staff Leader, head of Magda's district. But the letter had been ignored and pigeon-holed. The silly ramblings of a girl, the Staff Leader had thought to his misfortune.

Himmler had shouted down the telephone. 'I want a full investigation and anything that can be dug-up about this Borch girl. I want her reclassified as feeble minded and put away somewhere. And inform her family as good German's they are to disown her, never to see her again. Do you understand me?' he screamed.

Three weeks later, Magda was summoned to the Gebietsführer's office. Two plain clothed Gestapo men in leather coats and a SS doctor from the Race and Settlement Department stood with the Gebietsführer. The doctor held a document and read from it. 'Are you Magda Borch?'

She nodded, 'Yes, why, what's this about?' Magda flashed a worried look at her Gebietsführer and then at the three officials.

SS Dr Joachim Eisele, with his pointed features and a faint duelling scar on his left cheek, ignored her. 'Magda Borch, by order of the Fuhrer and of the Third Reich you are arrested for treason against the National Socialist Party for distributing subversive literature for reasons of dissent and to incite the enemies of the state. You will be escorted to collect your things and then come with us for questioning. Is that clear?'

'Treason, what do you mean treason? Because of my letter about the treatment of the Jews?' Magda was flabbergasted. 'You wait till my father hears about this. He's an SS- Sturmbannführer and Commandant of Pullhausen Concentration Camp. He'll have *you* arrested before the days through.'

The doctor came over and without hesitation, before she could move, hit Magda across her mouth with the back of his hand. Her head snapped back and blood poured from her lip. As she fell, the other two Gestapo men pinned her arms back and snapped on a pair of handcuffs. The doctor leant down and was about to hit her again, when he noticed the silver medallion around her neck. 'Ah, the Hünenkreuz, the Medal of Purity.' He yanked it off and looked at it thoughtfully. 'She won't be needing this where she's going,' he said to the others. 'The Bitch probably stole it anyway.' The doctor laughed and put it in his pocket.

Magda was placed in a holding cell at Gestapo headquarters in Lodz while charges and a statement were officially written up. Then she was sent under guard to the Westerberg Reformatory Detention centre for Girls, north of Berlin.

Karl Borch was notified and informed of his daughter's fate by Heinrich Müller - Chief of the Gestapo. Over the telephone her father was told she was being held for treason against the state. The Gestapo Chief made it clear to him that she was fortunate to have a father who had a high position in concentration camp security. Otherwise she would have faced the guillotine along with other dissidents who'd been sentenced before her. Her father was told his family was to have no contact with her until her views and thinking had been corrected and she had been truly rehabilitated into the National Socialist way of thinking. The Gestapo Chief made it clear to Karl that he should invent a story about his daughter being quarantined for typhus, and if the truth ever leaked out she would be executed immediately.

That evening at dinner, Karl broke the news to his wife and son. Frieda collapsed in tears while Martin sat stone faced. How could his sister have become such a traitor? To go against the Fuhrer. Karl told them they must not mention it to anyone. This sat well with Martin. The last thing he needed was his small Hitler Youth group, made up from the sons of senior camp guards and officials, to find out about his sister. Martin could imagine the shame and humiliation he would suffer. He decided he would kill himself with his SS dagger if the truth was ever discovered.

*

Over the next few months, Magda's life at the reformatory consisted of soul-destroying hard labour, semi-starvation and unpredictable punishment. All designed to break her spirit and lead her to renounce her Jewish sympathy and find true National Socialism.

Greta Binz was one of those designed to break her spirit.

At 30 years old, she was an Oberrottenfuhrer, a section leader in the BDM and in charge of Magda's reformatory block. Greta Binz had the looks of the true perfect Aryan female. Some of the staff remarked she looked like the German film star Lilian Harvey. Tall with a perfect figure and blonde hair braids that framed a regal looking face, her china doll complexion was every bit a likeness to the actress who starred in many of the Fuhrer's favourite musicals. That was where the similarity ended. Magda had heard from the others in the reformatory that Greta Binze was one to watch out for. She had a vile temper and took sadistic pleasure in using her riding whip on any of the girls for the slightest misdemeanour.

Greta was an ardent National Socialist who craved for advancement. Already a member in the National Labour Service as Reichsarbeitsdienst, which secured her the position as section leader in the reformatory, she was ready for the next step up to be a Lagerführerin - a women's camp assistant leader at Ravensbrück or Dachau.

She'd applied for promotion three months ago and sent the application form to regional head office, but had heard nothing since. Greta had been to see Gisela Hoffmann, the Stabsführer of the reformatory. The Stabsführer - staff leader, a stern slim woman with high cheekbones in her late forties, with greying wavy hair and a side parting, had other things on her mind.

Dr. Jutta Ruediger, the Hitler Youth National Leader of the BDM was coming for an inspection visit in two weeks. Besides dismissing Greta's promotion question with a wave of her hand, she made it quite clear, just as she had told the other section leaders; her block, consisting of sleeping quarters, toilets and workshops had to be spotless, in time for the inspection. If any deficiencies were highlighted, the BDM leader of that block would be dismissed, with a covering letter to national office giving the reasons for expulsion.

That afternoon, Greta, now in a bad mood with no promotion in sight and with more pressure and work heaped upon her because of this inspection visit, had all the girls including Magda lined up in the sewing workshop.

With their heads bowed, Greta holding her riding whip strutted up and down the line screaming abuse at them and reiterating the words of her boss. Magda put her hand up defiantly, while the others were too afraid to move an inch. Greta stopped in front of Magda and raised her whip. 'Yes, what is it you filthy Jew sympathiser, and you better have a good excuse for interrupting.'

'Please, Miss, we've had no hot water for bathing for three days. If you want us to wash the floors as well, can we have some coal for the boiler?'

The others shifted uncomfortably. Greta Binz couldn't believe what she'd just heard. With a red face pulsating with anger and spittle oozing from the side of her mouth, she shouted with a sarcastic sneer, *'You, filthy Jew lover. Do you think I give a rat's arse what you wash in?'* The whip came down repeatedly across Magda's face as she raised her arms to defend herself. *'We have no coal because the Jew allied bombers have destroyed the coal yards.'* The others scattered as Magda backed away, then she tripped and went sprawling. Greta Binz stood over her. *Thwack - thwack - thwack -* with her riding whip, thrashing away with a fixed grin of delight while Magda pleaded for her to stop. *'What coal there is goes to good German families, not Jew lovers like you,'* she screamed.

Eventually, physically exhausted by the flogging, Greta Binz stopped herself. She took out a handkerchief and wiped her forehead. 'This goes for the rest of you if the cleaning isn't up to scratch, do you hear me?' They all nodded and continued to look down. 'Now clear up this mess.'

Magda was moaning in pain on the concrete floor. Two girls grabbed an arm each and dragged her back to the sleeping quarters. They filled an old tin kettle and put it on a wood burning stove. With Magda laid out on her bottom bunk, one of the girls supported her head as she tried to drink some tea. Another girl dabbed her wounds with warm water.

'Best not to put your hand up again,' one of the girls joked.

Magda forced a smile. 'Fuck her,' she said.

*

On the morning of the reformatory inspections, Dr. Ruediger, Reichs Deputy of the BDM, wearing an immaculate blue blazer and party armband with a matching blue skirt and white blouse, all finished off with a military cap and chinstrap, arrived in a gleaming black Mercedes with two other high-ranking officials from the German welfare department. A red carpet was laid up the steps to reception.

Gisela Hoffmann, in full Stabsführer regalia, lined herself up with her section leaders to greet the Reichsreferentin. After a Nazi salute they shook hands and then one of the reformatory girls, washed and dressed in spotless work clothes, curtsied and presented the doctor with a bunch of flowers.

The delegation toured the vegetable gardens and then walked through a variety of workshops filled with busy girls at sewing machines; some of them making uniforms or darning socks, others producing coarse flannel underwear - all for the glorious Wehrmacht fighting at the front.

The inspections had gone well and by lunchtime a meal had been prepared in the large communal dining hall. For the occasion, the guest silverware and candelabra were polished and set out with swastika-embroidered napkins made in the sewing workshop. The raised staff table on a stage at the front with its gleaming salvers and spotless white dining-cloth overlooked six other much longer tables.

Each reformatory block had its own table of fifty girls. Just this once, they would be wearing laundered and pressed work-clothes and have a specially prepared nutritious meal. It had to look the norm. There were to be no hiccups.

The reformatory had never been state audited or had to submit an expenditure account. The yearly budget they received was more than ample, even after Gisela Hoffmann had taken five-thousand Reich marks from it, and hid the money in a biscuit tin under the floorboards in her bedroom.

Gisela Hoffmann, with her six section leaders and Dr. Ruediger by her side, watched as 299 girls filed into the dining hall and stood stiffly to attention at their tables with heads bowed. The one empty place belonged to Magda Borch. Greta Binz had her on punishment detail scrubbing the toilet block floor. As they were about to sit, Dr. Ruediger asked if she could wash her hands.

'Of course, Doctor Ruediger,' the Stabsführer replied. She glanced at her section leaders. 'Greta, show the good doctor where she can freshen-up.'

Greta beamed at the opportunity to help the Reichsreferentin.

The doctor followed Greta Binz down a flight of steps to a washroom. Magda, on her knees with a bucket beside her, looked up.

'Borch, get out of here,' Greta Binz shouted, proudly showing her authority. 'You can come back after we've finished.'

Magda quickly stood up and bowed, 'Yes, Oberrottenfuhrer.' Then with her bucket and mop, she moved swiftly out of their sight.

'She's on punishment detail,' Greta Binz relayed to the doctor as she offered a towel to dry her hands.

'Ah,' the doctor said with a smile, 'discipline above all, my dear, is the key to the future of our Fatherland. We must treat all those, who's hereditary is in doubt or have wandered from the path of our National Socialist faith, as we treat a stray dog that we give a home too. We feed it to make it trusting, and we beat it if it is unruly, to instill fear and respect for its master.'

Greta Binz beamed at the Reichsreferentin, 'You're so right, Doctor Ruediger.'

The doctor smiled at her and said, 'Thank you, My Dear,' as she finished drying her hands. 'Now, let's go and eat.'

With the doctor leading and her attention diverted, Greta Binz quickly reached across the sink basin and put something in her pocket and then continued up the stairs behind her.

After a brief walk they made their way back into the dining hall.

Everyone waited for Dr. Ruediger. When she sat down they all followed. The reformatory girls as always were forbidden to speak.

For the next forty minutes, during a meal of cold ham, potatoes and cabbage, followed by cream cakes and coffee, the Stabsführer chatted with the doctor. The section leaders looked on in admiration and listened intently to the doctor. From time to time Dr. Ruediger asked them in turn about their racial awareness. How it was so important that BDM girls remain pure in body and spirit, to avoid racial defilement.

The doctor finished off by saying, 'Only choose a spouse of similar or related blood. Be aware of worthy and unworthy races, about breeding of hereditary diseases. The task of the Girls BDM League is to raise our girls as torchbearers of the national-socialist world. We need girls who are at harmony between their bodies, souls, and spirits. And we need girls who, through healthy bodies and balanced minds, embody the beauty of divine creation. We want to raise girls who believe in Germany and our leader and who will pass these beliefs on to their future children. We want girls who believe absolutely in Germany and in the Führer and who will also pass on this faith to the hearts of their children. Then National Socialism and through it Germany, will endure forever.'

Overcome by the speech they all stood up and applauded the doctor. Then they raised their glasses and shouted, 'To the Führer.'

Dr. Ruediger raised her glass and then realized in shock, the Reichsieger ring was missing from her index finger. It was the one presented to her by the Fuhrer himself. She slapped her forehead. 'Goot Gott in Himmel!' She remembered now; she'd taken it off to wash her hands. She leant across to the Stabsführer, 'I have left my ring in your washroom,' the doctor said looking worried. 'Can you please get the girl to fetch it for me?'

The Stabsführer clicked her fingers for Greta to go immediately and get the ring.

Greta moved swiftly down the steps and felt for the ring in her pocket. She peered around the washroom door and saw the Jew lover, Borch, on her knees scrubbing. Hopefully, this was going to get her into the Stabsführer and Dr. Ruediger's good books, with a possible well deserved promotion.

The short walk to the sleeping quarters took less than a minute. Greta took out the ring and hid it under Magda's mattress. Her bunk wasn't hard to pick out. Some dried blood from the beating remained on the pillow.

Greta made her way back and set a worried look on her face as she climbed the stairs. 'I'm sorry, Doctor Ruediger, I couldn't find it.' With a sympathetic look she continued, 'I looked in the washroom, even asked the girl Borch on punishment duty.'

'But I know I left it there when I washed my hands,' the doctor confirmed with a worried look at the Stabsführer.

Greta leant over and whispered in the Stabsführer's ear.

'Yes, you're right, Greta, we should check her out,' the Stabsführer agreed. She stood up and said, 'Doctor, would you excuse us for a moment. Greta and I will soon clear this matter up.'

'I insist I come with you,' the doctor said. 'I'd like to check for myself.'

The three of them descended the stairs and took the short walk to the washroom.

Magda still on her knees scrubbing, raised her head to them.

'Borch, get up,' Greta said.

Magda got up immediately and stood still with her head bowed.

'Now listen, Borch.' Greta meant business. Holding her riding whip, she slapped it into the palm of her other hand, menacingly. 'A ring has gone missing, Borch. A very precious ring belonging to the Reichsreferentin here. It was left on the wash basin this morning while you were working. Have you seen it or do you know anything about it?'

'No, Oberrottenfuhrer, I have seen no ring.'

'Don't speak to the floor, Borch, look at me.' Greta jerked Magda's head up with the riding whip under her chin. 'I'll ask you again, Borch, where is the ring?'

'I have seen no ring, Oberrottenfuhrer, honestly,' Magda pleaded.

'Turn out your pockets, now, quickly,' Greta barked.

Magda fumbled nervously and produced a small bar of caustic soap and a broken pumice stone.

'Search her quarters,' the Stabsführer said, 'no one else has been down here. They're all in the dining hall.'

Magda protested, 'But I'm telling the truth, honestly.'

'Shut up, Borch, and come with us,' Greta said.

With Greta clutching Magda's collar, they quickly frog-marched her to the block sleeping quarters.

At the entrance, they were met by the smell of stale sweat. 'Show us your locker?' Greta shouted.

Magda pointed over to the wall.

There were two books and some toiletries in the cubbyhole. Greta with a sweep of her hand, scattered some old toothbrushes, used bars of soap and combs onto the floor. She flicked through the books and tossed them idly away. 'Nothing here,' she said to the Stabsfühere and the doctor. Then she barked at Magda, 'Show us your bunk, Borch?'

While the doctor looked on, Greta and the Stabsführer searched through Magda's rough cotton blankets and then under the blood speckled pillows.

'Nothing,' said the Stabsführer. She turned to the doctor with a look of dismay, 'I'm sorry, Doctor Ruediger, there's nothing here.'

'I told you I didn't have it,' Magda protested to them again.

'But it must be here somewhere,' Dr. Ruediger said, very near to tears. 'It's most precious. The Führer himself presented the ring to me.' She knew weeping was a sign of weakness and as supreme leader of the BDM she couldn't afford to display any vulnerability at the loss of a personal item when so many soldiers were sacrificing themselves at the Russian front.

Greta could sense this was her moment. 'Let's just check the mattress.' She lifted the threadbare item and felt underneath. At that moment something dropped onto the floor. All of them stared down at the beautiful gold party ring emblazoned with its swastika on silver oak leaves.

Greta stooped to pick it up. 'Is this what you're looking for, Doctor Ruediger?'

Magda interrupted, 'I didn't know that was there, someone must have put–'

'Shut up, you thieving Jew lover,' Greta shouted.

'But honestly, I had nothing to do…'

'I told you to–' Greta lunged forward with her riding whip.

'*Stop–stop,*' the doctor said, pulling Greta back by the shoulder. 'We'll have to deal with this through the proper channels.'

'Borch, go to my office and wait there,' the Stabsführer said sternly.

'But I'm innocent, I honestly didn't–'

The Stabsführer interrupted. 'I told you, Borch, go to my office now or else.' She looked over at Greta who was itching to use her riding whip.

Magda took the hint and quickly walked out with her head down.

The doctor couldn't contain herself. She put the ring on and admired it. Then, to the Stabsführer's amazement, she flung her arms around Greta and hugged her. 'Thank you - thank you, my dear. You are a clever girl for finding it.'

'Yes, well done, Greta.' The Stabsführer said smiling, so relieved the ring had been found. The last thing she wanted on this state inspection visit was any complications.

'My dear,' the doctor said, still with her arm around Greta's shoulder, 'if there is anything I can do for you within my capacity as Reichsreferentin, please let me know.'

Greta glanced sheepishly at the Stabsführer, then said hesitantly, 'Well, there is something actually, Doctor Ruediger. It concerns my promotion...'

*

Still protesting her innocence, Magda was sent to the reformatory infirmary. She didn't mind so much, she was excused duties and the beds were cleaner. She was even allowed a hot shower and a clean smock. They kept her isolated and set a date for her examination.

A week later, Magda was visited at her bedside by a psychiatrist and a doctor from the regional eugenics court. During a one-hour examination using a tape measure and callipers, they inspected Magda's head to non-Aryan charts including the colour of her eyes and hair. Also taking into consideration that she had been classified as a dissident Jew sympathiser and stolen from a senior party official; it was inevitable they finally classified Magda as schizophrenic with feeble-minded tendencies.

In accordance with the 1935 Nuremberg race laws - The Protection of German Blood and Honour - Dr. Walter Schreiber had no hesitation in stamping Magda's medical card, *For Sterilization*.

Magda was taken to the Wessenberg Maternity hospital where sterilizations were carried out. They told her, *examinations had shown she had a slightly inflamed appendix and it should be removed.* Misleading patients whose mental health was still rational and capable of reasoning was standard procedure. Through experience, it was better for everyone if patients were rendered, cool and calm, unaware of their fate.

That afternoon, a nurse came in and shaved off her pubic hair. Then they wheeled her into the operating theatre.

*

Three weeks later after convalescing, Magda returned to the reformatory. Soon afterwards, she was called into the Stabsführer office. Sitting by the side of her was an SS doctor; he held a syringe under the table, just in case.

The Stabsführer coldly informed her, 'Magda Borch, I have to inform you that on the 12th December 1942, you were sterilized in accordance with the 1935 Nuremberg race laws - The Protection of German Blood and Honour - because of being classified as a schizophrenic with feeble-minded tendencies. I also have to inform you, it is forbidden for you to marry a man who is not sterilized himself.'

Magda burst out crying, then the rage took her. She started screaming at them, *'You Bastards! What have you done to me? I hate you and your disgusting National Socialism. I hate Adolf Hitler.'* All of a sudden, she was out her chair leaning over their desk lashing out at them. She picked up the lamp and telephone and threw it at them.

'*Now, Borch, control yourself,*' the Stabsführer shouted back. '*You'll only make matters worse.*'

93

As scalding abuse erupted from Magda's mouth, the doctor and the Stabsführer leant back fending of her blows. Eventually they managed to get to their feet and tried to restrain her, shouting at her to stop. *'Enough, Borch, enough, you Stupid Girl.'* Wrestling her to the floor, the doctor managed to inject Magda with his syringe, and she collapsed within twenty-seconds.

The SS doctor wasted no time. He informed the Stabsführer he had no other choice. The doctor reached for the telephone and asked for the Reich Führer's office. After a brief discussion with his secretary, he was put through to Heinrich Himmler himself. They spoke for a couple of minutes with a lot of head-nodding by the doctor. Finally, he put the receiver down. Without saying a word, the doctor took out Magda's medical records from his briefcase. His gold pen hovered over the section box, headed, State Recommendations. Then the SS doctor slowly wrote - *For Extermination.*

CHAPTER SEVEN

Over the next year, part of Pullhausen Concentration Camp was transformed into a pioneering medical research centre with an endless supply of prisoners for experimental purposes. However by January 1943, Karl's relationship with his wife Frieda had become strained because of Magda their daughter. Frieda thought her husband could have done more to protect Magda. She had wanted to visit Magda at the reformatory but wasn't allowed to. There were also the rumours, although strictly secret, she'd heard about her husband's work.

Never being an ardent National Socialist, Frieda couldn't come to terms with the knowledge she'd gained, including seeing over the years, thousands of prisoners passing the house in trucks one way, but never leaving to make room for others. The camp capacity and the figures didn't add up. And then there was the smell, the smoking chimney and the falling ash. Frieda had worked it out for herself. Because of this, most evenings had ended in rows between them. So

Frieda decided to leave Karl and return to Berlin to live with her mother.

*

A week after moving back in, Frieda was shopping for her elderly mother along Dorotheenstrass. As they lived local, her sister's family had taken care of her mother the last few years, however, now she was here, Frieda knew it was her duty to share some of the chores.

The first thing that had surprised her was the extensive bomb damage. She'd last been in Berlin six months ago and the change to the city was significant. Where complete rows of shops once stood, there were now intermittent broken spaces of brick and rubble which had been partially cleared up as best as possible for party moral and the newsreel cameras. She also felt there was a wariness amongst everyone that hadn't been there before. Although the shops and restaurants were full, people didn't seem to engage or smile. Frieda envisaged the bombing had some share in that. Huddled together in shelters and underground U-Bahn stations for hours on end must have drained nervous conversation for every ounce. Then there was the new state restrictions she'd read about. People couldn't miss them pinned to lampposts and public buildings. These listed amongst others, forbidden conversation regarding foreign news, verbal dissent concerning the situation on the eastern front, defamatory jokes about National Socialist Policy, refusing to address each other with Heil Hitler on meeting someone and departing their presence. And much more.

The food rationing didn't help. While doing her shopping, Frieda could clearly see allowances had been cut yet again and food stamps reduced. The lack of traffic and private cars confirmed petrol was now a luxury and road usage was confined to essential journeys only.

Looking on the bright side, it did allow her to cross the road more easily. And on this gloomy January lunchtime, Frieda did just that making her way to the Café Wintergarten for a coffee and a slice of Stollen cake.

Pushing through the revolving door, the warmth hit her as she perused the diners and then eyed the waitress in a smart black uniform with a white apron and matching cap.

'Just the one?'

Frieda nodded.

Passing faces looked up at her as she followed the waitress to a single vacant wall booth.

Leaving her with the menu, Frieda slid her shopping under the table and slipped off her thick coat.

A few minutes later the waitress was back and flipped her pad.

'A coffee and some Stollen cake please.'

The waitress made her notes, nodded indifferently with a, 'Thank you, Frau,' and then disappeared through the kitchen swing doors.

Frieda sat back and took in the café aroma. Coffee and almond smells seemed to be fighting for domination as she surveyed the customers, which were mostly made up of women and the elderly, as expected. The eligible men folk of course being away at the front fighting the Russians or the Allies.

Although the restaurant was nearly full, the service was surprisingly quick as the waitress came back and set down the coffee and cake. Then with a polite thank you, she disappeared through the swing doors again.

Frieda sipped her coffee and nibbled the Stollen cake. It was a bit dry but she couldn't complain. Cheap cake and coffee could be luxuries in six months' time. God knows what they'd be eating then if the war swung the other way.

She took a newspaper from her bag. A large front page photo of Dr Joseph Goebbels stared back at her with a caption stating he was appearing at the Sportpalast on the 18th February to give a speech on Total War. Frieda had learned from the newspapers that Germany was slowly winning the war and was certain for all out victory. Dr Joseph Goebbels had announced on the radio it was going to be a long slog with sacrifices, however, he told the people, we must have faith in the Fuhrer who will deliver the final blow to the Bolshevik hordes and the Jew ridden Allies and rid the world of International Jewish Conspiracy.

Frieda couldn't help wonder, if Germany was winning the war how come it was being bombed every night. She glanced at her watch. It was still time to get some browsing in along the fashionable shops on Kurfurstendamm.

'Everything to your satisfaction, Frau?'

Suddenly the waitress had appeared from behind and startled Frieda. As she jumped to the voice, she spilt the coffee she was holding. 'Oh! Dam! I'm sorry....' She raised herself and quickly dabbed at the dregs on the table that were spilling on to her dress.

'I'm sorry, my fault,' the waitress said, as she helped her dab here and there with another table serviette.

'That's okay...I'll be alright thank you. No damage....'

A few other tables were looking over at the commotion and then lowered their heads as Frieda glanced around. She felt embarrassed being so clumsy.

'I will get you another coffee, Frau, and a clean tablecloth, again I'm sorry...'

Frieda assured her, 'No...No. My fault...I'll just pop along to the washroom to freshen up.'

The waitress sped off through the swing doors.

As Frieda stood up, she pushed her bags under the table and nonchalantly made her way to the women's sign on the fancy decorated white and pink washroom door.

There was only one other person that looked up as she entered. A smartly dressed mature lady who then carried on titivating in the mirror.

Frieda moved to an elaborate wash hand basin with fancy brass taps and started dabbing at the coffee stain on her dress. While she ran the water she took in the fancy pink tiles and the tulip shaped mirrors. It was a better styled toilet than the one she was sharing with her mother. Still, she had to be thankful for small mercies. There were many now who shared the public toilets because of the bombing.

On the vanity unit there was a selection of cheap perfumes with compliments. Using one of them, Frieda delicately puffed the scent behind each ear. Then after a bit more fussing, she finally moistened her lips and applied a thin red gloss lipstick. She used this as she thought it counteracted her heavy features and white complexion. Then she raised herself slightly in the mirror. At 5ft 3ins with her German style flaxen hair braids, she felt conscious about her short height and full figure. She would have preferred another couple of inches and be a stone lighter, in line with the Aryan concept of the perfect National Socialist wife.

With one last look, Frieda straightened her dress, closed her handbag and moved to the door. Before leaving, she put two-Reichspfennigs into the tipping saucer as she passed the lady concierge sitting idly on a stall reading a magazine.

When Frieda arrived back at her table there was a fresh cup of coffee sitting on a new tablecloth. She took a sip and then a bite of the Stollen cake, delicately dabbing the crumbs around her mouth with a napkin. And then she froze.

Frieda slowly unfolded the white napkin. There was a message written in ink.

Her eyes swam over the blue scribble before they focused. It read, Frieda, meet me at the Pergamon Museum tomorrow on the steps of the altar at twelve mid-day. She read it again to take it all in.

Frieda slowly folded the napkin, looking around furtively as she placed it in her handbag. All seemed normal. Everybody carrying on with their business. Nothing out of the ordinary.

The waitress came up behind her again, however this time she recognised the voice.

'Is everything to your satisfaction, Frau?'

Frieda half turned and looked at her. It wasn't anybody she recognised although she had the opportunity. The waitress wouldn't have looked out of place fussing around her table.

'Yes, it was very nice. Did...did you see anybody at my table while I was away?'

The waitress shook her head and looked puzzled. 'No, Frau, is there a problem?'

'No – no, it's okay.' She searched her face once more and then said, 'I'll just have the bill please?'

'Thank you, Frau.' She politely nodded and then was gone.

Three minutes later, she came back and left the bill in a saucer on the table. The waitress discretely left while Rita checked the amount. They hadn't charged for the coffee.

*

Frieda arrived at the Pergamon Museum twenty minutes early. Knowing that last night's air-raid could be disruptive to her journey, she'd decided to take the tram and walk the rest of the way.

With few visitors around, she clearly had a view of the alter steps from her partially concealed position at an adjoining lobby entrance. While she waited, two elderly couples sat on the steps to have their sandwich lunch. The museum was a popular place for the aged. With the heating on, they could switch theirs off at home and spend the day perusing and chatting in the cafeteria. It also had its own air-raid shelter.

At just gone twelve, a woman approached. She looked around nervously and then set herself down on the steps hugging the extreme side wall. Frieda saw her look at her watch. It was obvious she was waiting for someone.

Frieda edged closer to the lobby door for a better view. The woman was well wrapped up for the outside cold. A scarf covered most of her face.

She began to move towards the steps and then hesitated. Now, with this person only thirty feet away she was confronted with the dilemma. Was she going to harm her? She may have a knife concealed, even a gun. Frieda tried to reason with herself. She couldn't think of any enemies she'd made. Christ, she'd only been back in Berlin a week. Then again was it someone her husband had crossed? A former camp inmate or their relation wanting to get revenge? However, this person knew her name was Frieda. Camp inmates or their relations wouldn't have known that.

There was only one way to find out. Frieda walked directly up to her and spoke. 'Was it you who left the message on the napkin?'

The woman looked carefully around and then lowered her scarf. 'Frieda it's me, Hildegard.'

It took a few seconds and then recognition kicked in. 'Jesus, Hildegard. I thought...I thought...you were...'

'In a camp? Even dead? No such luck, Frieda. I'd heard through a resistance contact your husband set us up.' Hildegard nervously lifted her bag and pointed a partially concealed Luger pistol at her.

Frieda looked at the gun and then at a much thinner Hildegard she'd seen from five years ago and swallowed hard. 'I...I was told...my husband told me you were arrested for hiding Jews.'

'That was a lie and you know it?'

Frieda protested. 'No, honestly, Hildegard, that's what he told me. I even went to your place and found it boarded up.'

'Keep your voice down. Don't draw attention to yourself.' She waved the pistol from under her bag. 'Sit next to me for Christ sake and pretend we're friends having a chat.'

Frieda did as she was told and said, 'So what do you want? Are you going to kill me?'

Hildegard ignored her question. 'After you left our apartment a friend of my husband came to see us. He was in the resistance and had a contact working the switchboard at Gestapo headquarters. The contact overheard your husband telling that Gestapo pig Muller to round us up because we were hiding Jews. Myself and Ingrid managed to get out just in time. We've been staying at resistance safe houses ever since. My husband wasn't so lucky. They shipped him off to Sachsenhausen Concentration Camp where he was shot as a political prisoner.'

Frieda put a hand to her mouth in horror. 'Oh my God, Hildegard. I didn't know, honestly. Karl lied to me. He said you'd been caught for hiding Jews. He told me you and Ingrid had been rounded up and taken away.' Frieda pleaded with her. 'What else was I supposed to think?'

'Ok – ok, I believe you had no choice. But you didn't exactly worry about us after that, did you? To busy planning your husbands' farewell party for his high up Nazi friends than concern yourself with the Bauer's anymore. Just like all the others. Turned their heads the other way when they saw Jews beaten up and then put in trucks and driven off.'

Frieda looked down ashamed. 'You're right. I should have done more. I didn't know at the time. I suppose...I didn't really want to know...to tell the truth. My husband's work included.' She looked up. 'I've only been back in Berlin a week. I've left my husband for good. I found out what they were doing to prisoners in his camp.' Frieda buried her head in her hands. 'It's too awful for words.'

Hildegard replied sarcastically, 'I know what they're doing to them, Frieda. In the resistance we get first-hand knowledge from inside the camps and from the front. You have no idea of the slaughter that's going on. The newspapers lie. They tell Germans the Jews are deported to work camps to help the war effort. In reality, thousands of Jews are being gassed every day and then cremated in ovens. All the Jewish families I used to know have been wiped out. The position at the front is not good either. Thousands of German soldiers have died in vain at Stalingrad. The Sixth Army there is on the verge of defeat.' Hildegard pressed the luger into Frieda's ribs. 'Now listen carefully. The resistance know who you are. You've been followed the last few days. Because of your husbands contacts you could be useful to us. I was chosen to sound you out. The only reason I'm not going to kill you is because you gave us food and money that time. Risked your own neck.' Hildegard looked around and then lowered her voice. 'Now here is the deal. Our sources tell us your daughter Magda is at Dachau Concentration Camp.'

Frieda cried out. 'Magda, you've heard from Magda? Is she still alive?'

Hildegard pressed the concealed Luger into Frieda's ribs again. 'Shut up and listen.' She looked around. One or two people glanced over at the outburst and then carried on with what they were doing. 'We know for sure her name is on an extermination list. Provided you help us, we can get her name removed. Our contact at Gestapo headquarters is open to bribery.'

Frieda was desperate. 'Tell me what you want? I'll do anything to help her.'

'Give me your newspaper.'

Frieda took it from her bag and handed it over.

Hildegard showed Frieda the front page picture of Dr Joseph Goebbels. 'Dear Uncle Joseph will be appearing at the Berlin Sportpalast on the eighteenth of February. No doubt to stir up the mob by telling them the Fuhrer wants Total War. Even if it means throwing themselves onto the National Socialist bonfire before surrendering. This propaganda monster will drag every man, woman and child into the abyss. He has to be stopped before millions more die and we become slaves to the Russians and the Allies. With Goebbels dead it would be a sign from the people. A protest. Upon Goebbels death we have generals close to Hitler who would assassinate him and then negotiate for peace. This is our only chance. However, we have to have someone who can get close enough to pull the trigger, or as in this case, plant the bomb.'

Frieda protested, 'How would I do that?'

Hildegard explained, 'Someone like yourself, an important Commandants wife would be doing her National Socialist duty by joining the Frauenschaft women volunteer group to organise the meeting at the Sportpalast. You know. Wash and clean floors. Set out chairs. Hang up decorations and flags. Make coffee and tea for the helpers. Distribute propaganda leaflets on seats. That sort of thing. There calling for volunteers at this moment. Then when you get the chance, plant the time bomb under the rostrum where Goebbels is speaking.'

Frieda swallowed hard. 'You want me to kill Joseph Goebbels?'

*

The four of them were gathered in a partly bombed safe house on Tiergarten Strass across the road from the park. Ingrid, now a thin striking nineteen year old with her mother Hildegard and a worried looking Frieda, watched as Max, the young agent working for the underground resistance group Red Orchestra, showed Frieda how to prime the bomb. On an old wooden table in the kitchen lay two pounds of Nobel 808 green coloured plastic explosive with a dummy copper time pencil protruding from it. 'Make sure you have a small pair of pliers with you. The last thing you do is to crush the end of the copper time pencil like so.' He demonstrated to her. 'The crushed glass vial inside, releases an acid of cupric chloride that begins to corrode a thin wire holding back a sprung loaded striker which in turn hits a percussion cap. This sets off the attached detonator which is inserted inside the plastic explosive. 'You will want to be far away, Frieda when that happens, believe me.'

Frieda put a hand to mouth with shock and then said, 'How long have I got?'

'The white labelled time pencil you will be using is good for two hours give or take ten minutes. However, the long delay ones are not fool proof. They've been known not to explode. The longer the time delay, the less amount of cupric chloride acid inside. Sometimes it's not enough to corrode the trigger wire. I suggest if Goebbels begins his speech at around five-thirty in the evening, you will want to prime it at four o'clock to allow for delays of any kind.'

With an anxious expression she asked him, 'But how do I hide all that until the time?'

'The plastic you can shape to any size. It's like plasticine.' Max picked up the slab of explosive and manipulated it in his hands. 'I suggest on the day, you keep it in your handbag. Then at the desired time you slink off to the ladies washroom. Lock yourself in a cubicle to do the priming.'

'So it can't go off before hand?' she said worried.

'No only when it's primed, believe me,' he told her with a reassuring grin.

'And if I do this for you, my Magda will be safe?' She asked him in desperation.

'I can't promise anything. I can't vouch for her safety but she'll be removed from the extermination list.'

'Frieda buried her head in her hands and then looked up. 'OK, I'll do it.'

*

The Sportpalast, just off Potsdamer Strass, was busy on this 18th February. The building was sealed with guards at every entrance. Frieda that afternoon, with an army of volunteers consisting mostly of middle-aged and elderly women, had been inducted into the Frauenschaft Women's League. After taking the oath of allegiance to the Fuhrer, they began to distribute Nazi propaganda material on the fourteen thousand seats in the auditorium. Frieda, in her small group, wearing a smart brown suit and a canvas shoulder bag containing leaflets, had fortunately been allocated an area nearest the front.

She had discretely eyed the huge rostrum with the giant swastika flag hanging beneath it. Stormtroopers with Alsatian dogs had already searched there as well as under seats and in the gallery areas. Security were not taking any chances. Gestapo spies and contacts had expressed a certain wave of unease amongst the population and the party faithful, because of how the war was progressing. The situation at Stalingrad didn't help. Security knew of the Red Orchestra resistance and its leader Leopold Trepper. There was a reward on his head, alive or dead.

Frieda checked her watch. She'd left it as late as possible. It was ten minutes to four o'clock. Her black leather handbag was in the ladies cloakroom along with all the other coats and bags. Manned by an elderly official, Frieda had been given a numbered reclaim ticket.

Using Max's advice she had double wrapped the plastic explosive. He'd told her it smelt of almonds and if not securely covered it was sure to be sniffed out by some guard dog straining at the end of a Stormtroopers leash.

With a casual glance at the others, Frieda made her way to the cloakroom and, mumbling to the attendant about needing a few minutes to freshen up, handed over the numbered ticket.

The elderly woman attendant smiled as she took it and then, partially squinting at the number, disappeared behind the many racks. Thirty seconds later she came back with the same smile and handed over the wrong handbag.

'That's not mine I'm afraid. This is grey.' Frieda smiled back. 'I have a black one with a gold clasp.'

The attendant frowned and looked at the ticket again. 'Well it was the same one on the bag. Are you sure?'

Frieda could feel her impatience rising but told herself to keep calm and not to draw attention to herself. 'Yes I'm perfectly sure. Perhaps it's the next one to it if you'd kindly look.'

She took the bag and disappeared behind the racks again. Then she reappeared and said, 'Did you say a black one, Frau?'

'Yes with a gold clasp,' Frieda replied calmly.

A moment later, back she came with a black handbag with a gold type clasp.

Frieda began to feel a rising panic in her stomach. 'Err no. This is still the wrong one.'

'Oh dear.' The attendant thought for a second and then said, 'I'm sorry about the mix-up. Would you like to come behind and see if you can find it yourself?'

In that instant, a horrible thought flashed through Frieda's mind. Perhaps they'd rumbled her. Found what was inside. Wanted her to actually pick it out. Then she realised that wouldn't make sense. They could just have handed her the correct bag in the first place.

'Thank you.' Frieda followed the attendant behind the counter and was immediately surrounded by shelves displaying coats, bags, umbrellas, boots, hats and even balaclavas.

The attendant took her to the bag section, to the number location of her ticket.

Frieda spotted the bag straight away on the rack above. 'That's mine.' She took it down with a sigh of relief. 'It's got the wrong ticket on it.'

'One moment.' The attendant took the bag from her. 'Dear God, it's heavy. Whatever have you got in here?'

Frieda laughed nervously. 'Oh it's just plasticine for my kindergarten class. I'm their teacher. There's my cigarettes and lighter as well.' Again panic flooded over her. She expected the Gestapo to jump out.

'You don't mind me checking. Just a precaution you understand. Some of these handbags are quite expensive.' The attendant moved away and fiddled with the clasp. Once opened, she felt inside and found the lighter with a packet of twenty Eckstein. Then she partially lifted the wrapped parcel. 'Plasticine you say?' She squeezed the slab and then gave a reassuring smile. 'That's fine, Frau. Sorry again about the mix-up.'

Frieda was relieved she hadn't found the detonators or the plyers wrapped with it. 'That's okay, easy mistake. A lot of handbags look the same.'

Making her way to the ladies washroom, she found an empty cubicle and locked herself in. Frieda removed the wrapped explosive from her bag. She put her cigarettes and lighter in her pocket. Frieda looked at her watch. It was five minutes past four. She had to get a move on. With the toilet seat down she spread out the contents. Frieda carefully picked up the copper time pencil and slid the No.8 detonator into its end. Then she pushed the assembly into the Nobel 808 green coloured plastic explosive. With the pliers, she held the copper tube ready to squeeze.

Frieda closed her eyes for a second. What if the delay was faulty? It might blow up in her face, not that she'd know much about it. What if it went off too early or too late, killing innocent people. Then other thoughts flashed. How could she be doing this? Was she mad?

This was high treason. If she was caught they'd show no mercy. She'd heard from her husband how the Gestapo had cut off the fingers of a woman in the Czech resistance, one by one, to get her to reveal the partisans who'd shot the Obergruppenführer, Reinhard Heydrich.

It might be the same for her. They'd want to know the names of the people who'd organised it. Set her up. They'd want information on the Red Orchestra. Something she knew nothing about. The thought of screaming in agony for answers she couldn't give the Gestapo, made her open her eyes.

Frieda breathed in. She swallowed hard. She remembered the precarious position of her daughter. Also, that evil lying bastard of a husband. And her son Martin whose mind had been warped and twisted by his father and the Nazi system.

She gripped the pliers and mumbled, 'This is it. No turning back.'

With a crunch, she crushed the end of the copper tube. Frieda held it for a second, mesmerised. Then adrenalin kicked in.

She put the plastic bomb in her leaflet bag and then shoved her black handbag with the plyers inside, behind the toilet cistern. Hopefully it would be awhile before it was discovered. She cleared any remaining mess and washed her hands in the sink. They smelt of almonds, Max was right. Then she checked herself in the wall mirror. With one last look around, she pulled the toilet chain for effect and slid the bolt of the cubicle door.

The washroom was empty as she peered out. She checked the other four cubicles, they were vacant as well. Steadying her leaflet shoulder bag, Frieda made her way out into the corridor and back to the main hall. The others in her detail were still placing leaflets. She hadn't been missed.

Frieda eyed the rostrum. There were too many people about to make an attempt to deliver her parcel. The minutes were ticking buy, so was the time bomb in her bag. She had to think of something quick.

Frieda looked around in desperation. Both sides of the hall had decorative streamers draped over the first and second floor balconies. She thought the second floor would be her best bet. The streamers there, were hanging near powerful spotlights. A good excuse for a distraction.

She made her way up the stairs to the first floor, placing leaflets on seats as she went and then up the stairs to the second floor. High up now, the area was deserted of personnel.

Frieda moved towards the balcony rail and looked over. The helpers below seemed to scurry around like ants. She checked the other surrounding balcony areas. Satisfied it was all clear, she reached for the streamer decoration and draped it over the hanging spotlight. Then she moved back quickly.

Although the spotlight casing was hot, Frieda knew she couldn't rely on the paper streamer catching fire straight away. That could take ages, if at all.

Frieda took out her lighter. She checked around again and then reached over. On the second flick, the flame remained and she lit the streamer in two places. It immediately began to flare up. Now she had to be quick. Choosing the farthest end of the balcony, she descended the stairs. As she reached the lower first floor flight, she heard the first warning shouts.

Officials and security were rushing towards the stairs, the nearest end. Frieda knew it was now or never. She walked briskly down the wall side of the hall to the front end. Helpers had crowded towards the opposite balcony side and were looking up to where the streamer was now being put out with a fire extinguisher. With their backs to her. she ducked under the giant swastika flag that provided a backdrop to the rostrum. Frieda knew she had only seconds.

In the dark, she took the bomb from her shoulder bag and hid it behind some wooden supporting struts. She was glad she had primed the bomb in the toilet. Under here she could hardly see a thing. Now was the tricky part. Getting out and not being seen.

The curtain flag twitched as Frieda eyed her chances. Everybody was still looking up at the smouldering streamer. With lightning speed, Frieda slipped out from under the flag, and not drawing attention to herself, she stood still and looked up with the others.

After a few minutes, with the fire under control, people began to move around and carry on with their jobs. Apart from some small water spillage and the odd bit of charred streamer still floating down from the ceiling, there was no damage, certainly not enough to stop Dr Joseph Goebbels meeting.

Frieda with a look of innocence asked her supervisor what had happened. She was told some idiot had draped a decoration around a hot spotlight and the decoration had caught fire. Frieda put a hand to her mouth in shock and replied, 'Lucky it hadn't happened at the meeting with all those people there.'

An hour later, nearing five o'clock, the Sportpalast doors opened and people began to pour in. With the main hall filling up, most of the volunteer groups had left after their detailed work had been completed. Frieda with her group of fifteen, had to work on a bit extra to get finished. Now they were assembled in the staff area and being thanked for their cooperation by a Nazi official.

Suddenly the doors opened to a buzz of outside cheers and glimpses of press photography.

Dr Joseph Goebbels, in a smart beige uniform wearing a large emblazoned swastika armband had arrived with his entourage. He smiled at Frieda's group and gave them a salute. They were in awe of him and returned a similar Heil Hitler salute.

Then Dr Joseph Goebbels addressed them. 'The party are very grateful for your help, Ladies. It is Frauenschaft women volunteers like yourselves, true German Aryans who are the backbone of our home front and party organising. Time and time again the Frauenschaft are called upon to do their duty in all weathers to lend a hand with such things as first aid in hospitals, collecting scrap metal and other materials for the war effort, providing refreshments at train stations, running cookery classes for brides and schoolgirls, collecting winter clothes for our troops at the front and much more. This is done by you without any thought of repayment or profit. With this in mind I have decided, as you have stayed late today doing your volunteer work, and as a fitting example to our party, to award you all with the Hünenkreuz Medal of Purity. This non-military version is awarded to the racially pure and conscientious members of the Frauenschaft.'

Frieda's group beamed at the Reich Minister of Propoganda.

He continued. 'Also included in your award will be front row seats tonight at the meeting, and during this you will all be invited on stage to be presented with your medals.'

On those words the group burst into appreciation. The women cheered and thanked him excitedly. They all knew, front seats at the meeting were reserved for the high ranking military officials. This was an unbelievable surprise to them all.

Frieda tried to look pleased wearing a fixed grin of pleasure. The minutes were ticking away. To make an excuse to leave would single her out as a possible perpetrator. And any excuse would certainly be checked out by the Gestapo afterwards. No doubt this would include her son Martin. He would be arrested as a suspect in the conspiracy.

Then there was Magda. She would do anything to help her daughter. If this is what it took for her daughter to survive, then she'd have to stay behind and die in the explosion.

Max had informed her the blast was powerful enough to take out Goebbels and the first three rows of top Nazi officials. Now there would be fifteen innocent people including herself sitting at the front or on stage. Then again, what are the lives of fifteen innocent people including herself compared to the millions that could possibly die if the war continued?

As her group made their way to the front seat chairs she could see the hall was filling up fast. Frieda selected a seat and sat down. She checked her watch. It was five-forty. The thing could go off at any moment.

Five minutes later, the far doors opened to a tumultuous roar as the speakers blasted out the Horst Wessel Anthem. On cue, Dr Joseph Goebbels and his entourage walked in a solemn stride down the central gangway while fourteen thousand people stood with an arm raised salute. At the front end of the hall, the doctor climbed the steps by the side of the rostrum and was greeted by Albert Speer, the Minister for Armaments. Against the curtained backdrop, the giant golden eagle with the swastika in its claws looked down on them.

With everyone seated, the doctor addressed the audience. 'Only three weeks ago I stood in this place to read the Führer's proclamation on the 10th anniversary of the seizure of power, and to speak to you and to the German people. The crisis we now face on the Eastern Front is at its height. In the midst of the hard misfortunes the nation now faces in the battle on the Volga, we are gathered together here at a mass meeting to display our unity, our unanimity and our strong will to overcome the difficulties we face in the fourth year of the war.'

Underneath her coat, Frieda clenched her fists. She was no hero. The prospect of being blown to pieces or maimed at any moment jarred all her nerves. Hoping no one would notice, she closed her eyes from time to time waiting for the inevitable.

Dr Goebbels looked down at his notes and then continued. 'I do not know how many millions of people are listening to me over the radio tonight, at home and at the front. I want to speak to all of you from the depths of my heart to the depths of yours. I believe that the entire German people has a passionate interest in what I have to say. I will therefore speak with holy seriousness and openness, as the hour demands. The German people, raised, educated and disciplined by National Socialism, can bear the whole truth. It knows the gravity of the situation, and its leadership can therefore demand the necessary hard measures, yes even the hardest measures. We Germans are armed against weakness and uncertainty. The blows and misfortunes of the war only give us additional strength, firm resolve, and a spiritual and fighting will to overcome all difficulties and obstacles with revolutionary zeal.'

The audience stood and shouted their approval including Frieda and her small group of women. She had to look as loyal as the others although she felt sick. The people were being brainwashed. They would jump out the window if he asked them.

It was at that point the doctor looked down at Frieda's group and motioned for them to come up on stage with him.

Frieda with the others climbed the steps and formed a line behind the doctor.

The doctor pointed to them as an example and said, 'Our enemies maintain that German women are not able to replace men in the war economy. That may be true for certain fields of heavy labour. But I am convinced that the German woman is determined to fill the spot left by the man leaving for the front, and to do so as soon as possible. For years, millions of the best German women have been working successfully in war production, and they wait impatiently to be joined and assisted by others. All those who join in the work are only giving the proper thanks to those at the front. Hundreds of thousands have already joined the Frauenschaft League of Women and I hope hundreds of thousands more will join.'

The doctor motioned to Frieda's group. 'Like these women behind me who have helped organise this meeting. Their volunteer work is invaluable. And for this reason I am awarding them a special party medal. The Hünenkreuz Medal of Purity. This is in honour of the Frauenschaft they represent.'

An official walked on with a box of medals and stood by the side of the doctor. Dr Joseph Goebbels went down the line of women and placed the Hünenkreuz Medal of Purity medallions with their red and gold striped ribbons, around each of the lowered heads. After he'd finished, the audience applauded.

With Frieda's group back in their seats, the doctor continued with his speech amongst the some fanatical cheering and applauding. Frieda's nerves were at breaking point. She had developed a nervous tick which she hoped nobody would notice.

Forty minutes later Dr Goebbels finished off the evening by saying, 'The nation is ready for anything. The Führer has commanded, and we will follow him. In this hour of national reflection and contemplation, we believe firmly and unshakably in victory. We see it before us, we need to only reach for it. We must resolve to subordinate everything to it. That is the duty of the hour.' The doctor raised his arms and shouted, *'Let the slogan be, now people rise up and let the storm break loose!'*

His words were lost in an unending stormy applause as the crowd rose to their feet screaming *Heil Hitler* over and over again. Frieda joined them knowing the bomb had failed to detonate and Magda could not be saved.

It was seven-forty-five that evening when she left the Sportpalast. It was cold with a fine drizzle as she made her way to the safe house on Tiergarten Strass. Turning the corner into the strass, two military trucks sped past her and pulled up at the safe house. With shouts and guard dogs barking, SS soldiers piled out and proceeded to hammer on the front door.

Standing the other side of the road with a gathered crowd, Frieda watched as the soldiers didn't wait for an answer. Two of them using their shoulders and rifle butts, smashed the door down and entered. A moment later the occupants, Max, Hildegard and Ingrid, all handcuffed, were being roughly manhandled at gunpoint into the rear of a truck. Other soldiers brought out armfuls of leaflets and another two carried what appeared to be a printing press.

After further shouts they climbed back into the trucks, then pulled up the tailgates and sped off into the dark.

Frieda realised, a few minutes earlier she would have been caught with them. It was her second close shave tonight. Nevertheless, Frieda felt devastated. She had accomplished nothing. Dr Joseph Goebbels was still free to squirt his propaganda poison, and her Magda was going to be gassed, hung or shot.

On the way home passing a bomb site, she tore the Hünenkreuz medallion from her neck and, muttering, 'You know what you can do with your Medal of Purity, Doctor Goebbels.' She tossed it in disgust amongst the rubble.

CHAPTER EIGHT

By 1944 Karl's son Martin was now seventeen years old and wearing the field-grey uniform of a Rottenführer. Still helping the SS garrison at Dachau Concentration Camp, and in charge of his Hitler Youth group of eleven boys, he was now having doubts like his mother about the true fate of the prisoners being held there. With most of the camp strictly out of bounds, his group were mainly confined to the supplies and accounts office. Numerous times they'd been told by the camp commandant, Gottfried Weiss, the crematorium with its chimney was for the disposal of clothes and rubbish and sometimes for terminally ill prisoners that had died. Never-the-less, they all had a dignified funeral with their ashes spread on a garden of remembrance. A similar excuse for the gas chambers. That was where the prisoners showered.

Martin had his reservations. He'd seen the condition of some prisoners coming and going from the local quarry as they passed near his compound and was horrified. They were like walking skeletons.

Since a young boy, he'd been indoctrinated to believe the Jews and the Communists were to blame for Germany's downfall. They were the reason for the loss of the First World War and the depression. Martin had been taught ever since he was five years old that the long nosed Jew, according to the party propaganda pictures, was the corrupt money lender. As a child he'd read kindergarten books showing the Jew as the Bogey Man who would ply children with sweets and then lead them into the woods to be killed and eaten. The Jews and the Communists deserved to be removed from society. Concentration camps were where they could be forced to do hard work for a change instead of scheming and profiteering amongst their own kind. However, Martin didn't know along with the thousands of others, that the Final Solution plans had been agreed by the top SS officials at the Wannsee conference. These plans in turn had been handed down to the commandants of concentration camps and their garrisons. Above all else, it was top secret. Each SS guard involved with the extermination process had to swear an oath to his commandant never to disclose what was being carried out.

This was the reason Martin's father had not mentioned his real work.

One cold November early morning, Martin had been ordered to the office of Greta Binz, the SS- Erstaufseherin at the female camp. He'd been detailed to escort the office cleaner, a young Jewish female prisoner, to her barracks. Prisoners crossing check points from one compound to another had to be escorted.

As Martin knocked and then entered the office, Nineteen year old prisoner number 201718, wearing a striped smock which showed the Star of David and a head scarf, stood to attention while Greta Binz inspected her cleaning.

As his eyes wandered around the office they settled on a lampshade. The skin coloured material stretched out around the lamp was patterned with a tattoo design. Martin was fascinated. He'd never seen a lamp like that before. The coffee table it sat on was also weird looking. The four legs looked like bones. Perhaps animal bones. Martin's attention was soon diverted to the matter at hand.

Wiping along the top of a cabinet and then at the back of a book shelf, Greta Binz instantly froze. A small amount of dust was visible on her finger. The SS- Erstaufseherin barked at the prisoner. 'You filthy, Jew.' She showed the prisoner her finger. 'You were supposed to have cleaned. Look at it. I could have you hanged for this.' She looked at Martin and instantly calmed. 'You like this girl? I can see you do, Herr Rottenführer. Perhaps while I'm at rollcall you'd like sex with her, yes?' Greta Binz turned to the prisoner and barked. 'Tell him your name, Jew?'

'Rachael Blinski, Mein Erstaufseherin.' She stared at the floor.

'Take off your clothes, Jew.'

Without hesitation, the prisoner removed her smock and stood their naked trembling.

Martin breathed inwardly. He was overcome by her beauty. With the head scarf removed, long dark hair cascaded down her white back. The prisoner couldn't have been more than twenty years old. She was obviously on special privileges to retain a figure like that. He'd heard the rumours about Binz and her appetite for young women.

Martin used his discretion. SS- Erstaufseherin, although a woman, still had connections above his rank. A wrong word in the right ear could prove a major hurdle when he applied for his next promotion. 'That is most kind of you, Erstaufseherin. However, as a true National Socialist I must abide by the Nuremberg Race Laws which refuse me to have sex with a Jew.' Martin smiled agreeably. 'Although I must add, a very shapely Jew.'

Greta Binz smiled. 'You Hitler Youth, are so ambitious. You never relax and have fun.' She turned to the prisoner and shouted. 'Get dressed, Jew.'

She quickly put her smock back on and stood to attention with her head bowed.

'Escort the Jew back to her hut, Rottenführer.'

Martin clicked his heels and did the Hitler salute. 'Thank you, Erstaufseherin.'

With the prisoner in front, Martin escorted her from the office to the compound checkpoint. With another salute and a click of heels to the SS guard on duty, he said, 'Rottenführer, Martin Borch reporting to escort prisoner to her hut on the SS Erstaufseherin's orders.'

The bored looking guard in his small covered post looked the prisoner up and down and then at Martin. With a nod he lifted the barrier so they could go through.

Thirty yards later they reached the prison compound. As Martin turned the corner of a hut he froze. In the middle of the compound for all to see was a woman hanging from a gallows. Her body, dressed in a prison striped smock displaying the Star of David, twisted in the breeze. The head hung to one side disjointed from the noose.

Martin swallowed hard. He'd never seen a woman hanged. His prisoner looked to the ground and stood very still. Then he nodded for her to lead on. At the next hut they climbed the steps and entered. Martin cupped his nose. The place smelt awful. It was quiet. He asked her, 'Where is everybody?'

'They're on work detail, Herr Rottenführer. At the quarry and the arms factory.'

It was a freezing day. Martin made his way to the central wood stove to warm his hands. It was then he heard a cough. He looked at the pile of striped smocks stacked up against the wall. Buried beneath them he heard wheezing. He looked at the prisoner. She was staring transfixed and trembling. Martin pulled at the clothes and jumped back. Lying there was a boy. Dressed in oversize adult clothes he looked no more than twelve or thirteen years old.

She fell to her knees and grabbed Martin's leg and pleaded. 'Please don't tell, Herr Rottenführer. He's my brother, Ezra. He's all I've got now. They'll send us to the gas chamber with everyone else from this hut if you do.'

Martin pulled back. 'Get off me.' He was shocked. 'Your brother.' Then he looked confused. 'What gas chamber? How did he come to be...?'

She quickly added, 'On arrival at selections, my elderly mother and brother were sent to be gassed immediately as they were considered nonessentials. You know, not fit enough to work. The Sondakommandos who pull out the bodies after gassing found him alive. They reckon he must have collapsed immediately and had his face near a floor drainage grill. They resuscitated him as best they could and then hid him from the guards. One of the Sonda had come from my village near Frankfurt. He knew I had a brother.'

At that moment an older female prisoner appeared and froze when she saw Martin.

Rachael shouted at her. 'Not now, Erika. We have enough coffee.'

In her hand she held a pouch. Erika instantly hid it behind her back.

Martin was too quick for her. He looked at the star on her smock. 'Show me what you have, Jew, or I'll report all of you.' He looked at the other two and pulled his Walther P38 pistol.

Erika, the mid-forty Hungarian Jewess stood stiffly to attention in her striped smock with her shaven head bowed. She slowly held out her trembling hand clutching a leather pouch.

Martin took it from her. It was heavy and laced up at the top. 'What is it?'

Erika blurted out, 'It's only a coffee ration, Herr Rottenführer.' She kept her head down and stared at the floor.

It was deathly quiet. Only punctuated by the wheezing of the boy.

Martin slowly untied the neck of the pouch. He instantly recognised the cordite powder. 'What is this for, Jew?'

Rachael, still sitting on the floor, grabbed his leg again in desperation. 'Please don't tell on us, Herr Rottenführer. They're murdering our people. We want to blow up the crematorium to stop it.'

'What!' Martin tried to pull away from her. He pointed his pistol at her.

'She clung on and pleaded, 'They're killing all the Jews, Herr Rottenführer. Men, women and children in the gas chamber.'

Martin said astonished, 'What gas chamber?'

She looked up at him. 'Where they're supposed to shower.'

He shrugged her off. 'You're lying, Jew.'

Erika interrupted. 'She's right, Herr Rottenführer. The trucks arrive everyday with Jews. Thousands are gassed and then burnt in the crematorium.'

Martin in his innocence said, 'But that's for clothes and rubbish.'

They both looked at him dumbfounded. 'Clothes and rubbish?'

He looked confused. 'Yes... we were told when we arrived here.'

'Erika shook her head. They lied to you.'

Martin looked at the staring faces. 'But I don't understand. Why would they kill people when they could use them for labour?'

Erika explained. 'Because the SS hate the Jews so much they want to kill them. They fear a world Jewish conspiracy if they're not eliminated. Their fear overrides any rational alternative to murder. That is why the men folk in the camp want to blow up the crematorium.'

Martin looked at the pouch. 'That's what this cordite is for?'

'Yes.' Erika explained. 'We've been collecting it from the arms factory. We don't want to kill anyone. Just plant a bomb to destroy the crematorium.'

Rachael was crouched holding the hand of her brother Ezra. She looked up at Martin and added in an emotional tone. 'Please don't report us. We just want to stop their murder.' She looked at Erika. 'Let's face it. We're all going to be killed anyway. So if we can stop them just for a while, a few weeks even until they repair or build a new one, it'll be worth it.'

Martin still looked confused. 'I can't understand why they would...'

Erika cut him short and shouted. 'Why would we risk our lives if we were lying?'

Rachael stood up. She said defiantly, 'I'm not worried about myself. Just save my brother.' She nodded in his direction. 'He's only thirteen. Could you steal a boy's Hitler uniform? Dress him up and conceal him amongst your group?

Tell the others he's a new recruit or something? Smuggle him out of here before the SS find out?'

Martin levelled his pistol at them and considered. If he killed all three now he'd be a hero. The cordite. Foiling a plan to blow up the crematorium as well as finding a Jew boy in hiding. Then he considered further. He'd never killed anyone before, especially a woman or a boy. Somehow the expected back slapping and plaudits seemed hollow, a sour taste in the mouth. Then what if they were telling the truth? The constant sweet smell and ash from the crematorium chimney? He'd often wondered. The constant trucks that had passed with people? And why strictly out of bounds if only burning rubbish?

Martin lowered his pistol. 'If it's true what you say, I'll help you. I'm going to find out for myself.' He levelled the pistol at them again. 'But if you're lying, they're not killing the Jews. Then I'll report you.'

Rachael grabbed Martin's hand and tried to kiss it. 'Thank you, Herr Rottenführer.' She was overcome with emotion.

*

Although the crematorium and the showers were strictly out of bounds, Martin knew the camp infirmary was his best bet. It lay in the SS compound. All he had to do was fake stomach cramps or some illness that didn't require too much of a doctor's close attention. That would hopefully get him a bed for the night. Then under cover of darkness he could check out what took place when the pact trucks delivered prisoners to the showers.

A day later, Martin went to see his commanding officer with stomach cramps and diarrhoea. Knowing the ever present risk of a typhus outbreak he was sent immediately to the infirmary.

Martin doubled up in pain as the doctor poked and prodded his stomach. Then he was given some fowl tasting medicine. Fortunately a spare bed was available so he flopped onto it groaning, while five other SS guards laid on their beds and ignored him.

By three o'clock that morning the snores of the others had helped to keep him awake. The sweeping search light from the guard tower and the headlights from the passing trucks, flashed through the infirmary windows and danced across the bunks and walls. With a night orderly busy reading a book under a lamp in the adjacent room, Martin saw his chance and crept out of the door into the small lobby. He crouched down as three trucks passed him and pulled up the other side of the courtyard at the sign marked SHOWER ROOM.

Instantly some SS guards appeared with dogs and let the tailgates down. They shouted 'Raus – Raus,' as the prisoners clambered down from the rear and were herded into line. Men and barking dogs panted steam from condensation in the earie floodlight glow of a cold night.

Around eighty male prisoners of mixed ages began to descend the concrete steps to the showers. As the guards followed them down, Martin waited and was about to do the same, when another two SS guards wearing gas masks, climbed the steel ladder to the roof. He recognised what was being carried by one of them – a canister of vermin repellent. A guard then lifted a roof hatch while the other one began to prize open the lid of the canister.

Martin knew the factories and workshops around the camp were alive with rats. They did considerable damage chewing through electrical wiring and food sacks.

One of his duties as a Hitler Youth leader was to check the store's supplies coming into the camp. His superiors had informed him, the canisters labelled ZYCLON B were to combat infestation. A factory would be evacuated and sealed off, and then the crystals inside the canister released through a hole that was quickly sealed afterwards. Once in contact with the air they would give off Prussic Acid and kill anything that moved.

Halfway down the stairs Martin paused. He could see the men stripping and hanging up their clothes. The guards constantly called out, 'Make sure to remember your peg number when you return to collect your clothes.'

As they entered the shower room indicated by the name plate above the doorway, every fourth man was handed a bar of soap and told to share it out. Then the steel door was slammed shut and the lever pulled down.

Martin edged nearer. So far as he could see, everything seemed normal. A minute later all hell broke loose. A massive cry rose up from those locked inside followed by banging and horrendous screams. The agonising noise lasted for about ten minutes. And then came silence.

One of the guards lifted a peephole flap, and after ten seconds gave the thumbs up. From a cupboard, two gasmasks appeared and the guards snapped them on. Martin thought they looked like monsters from another planet.

With a nod to confirm he was ready, the other guard pulled the lever up and opened the steel door.

Martin edged himself down the stairs. He had a clear view into the shower room. For a second his eyes disbelievingly scanned a scene that could have come from the depths of hell. The white naked bodies of prisoners had formed a pyramid to the top of a ceiling grill. As if the highest one was trying to draw his last breath from it. A strong pungent smell lingered and caught the back of Martin's throat. It made his eyes smart.

Suddenly voices behind him were getting nearer. Martin grabbed a gasmask and slipped it on, just as half a dozen prison workers, known as Sonderkommandos wearing striped clothes, filed down the stairs under an SS escort. Without thinking he quickly began to collect the clothes off the pegs and immediately saluted the SS-Oberscharführer. The officer responded with a nod and Martin carried on with his chore as if it was his job.

With the Sonderkommandos leading, the escort entered through the door marked SHOWER ROOM. Martin hovered near the entrance and saw the prisoners set to work pulling at the tangled heap of bodies.

One by one the white limp corpses were stacked onto carts and wheeled through the adjacent unlocked entrance. Some discarded shoes and undergarments lay on the shower floor. One of the guards shouted to Martin and pointed. Martin entered and quickly gathered up the items.

When all the bodies had been moved into the next room, the prisoners began to hose down the walls and floor to wash away vomit and excrement. They politely stepped aside as Martin pretended to check for other discarded items while edging nearer the entrance where the bodies had been taken.

At the doorway he stiffened and dropped the garments in shock, then he quickly regained his composure in case he was seen.

The bodies were now being lifted from the carts onto tables, where Sonderkammandos with pliers were removing gold teeth and carrying out intimate body searches. Martin assumed they were looking for contraband. Small valuables such as gold or diamonds. After processing, other prison workers lifted the bodies back onto carts and wheeled them out of another entrance towards the crematorium. The crematorium! Now it all made sense.

Martin had seen enough. Rachael and Erika were telling the truth. The Jews were being killed in their hundreds, possibly thousands.

He made his way back up the concrete stairs. Two SS guards with dogs glanced at him and then carried on chatting while having a smoke. Crossing the courtyard he saw in the distance the headlights of more vehicles approaching. Martin ducked down out of sight and discarded his gasmask.

As he watched, a new wave of prisoners were already clambering down from the rear of the trucks and being ordered into line.

Martin slipped through the first door of the infirmary. The night orderly on watch was still busy reading his book. Within a minute, he'd tiptoed behind him and made his way into the ward and then onto his bed. The snores from the other patients assured him he hadn't been spotted.

As he lay on his bunk amongst the smells of stale sweat and surgical spirit he felt a twinge of uncertainty. He'd always been led to believe the Jews and the communists were to be resettled in the east. Not murdered like this. His sister Magda had said something similar. She'd seen Jews being starved in the Lodz ghetto. Their emaciated bodies being collected up in carts. No one had believed her of course. The authorities had labelled Magda feeble minded and sent her away for correction so she may one day find the true path of National Socialism. Martin had considered Magda a blot on the family honour. A disgrace to her parents as well as to her Hitler Youth comrades. His father had advised him to forget about his sister.

He had until now.

Martin stared at the ceiling in the tiny glow of the orderly's reading lamp and tried to think of her. What she had reported about the ghetto must have been true. Even when they gave her the option of tearing up her report, and no more would be said. She still had the courage to reveal what she had seen, knowing the consequences.

And he'd done nothing to help her. Too young of course at the time.

He closed his eyes as other things clouded his memory. A lot had happened these past few years. There had been plenty to celebrate. The early lightening victories in Europe. The grand parades and rallies. His promotion in the Hitler Youth. A new world order that had been promised by the Fuhrer. A new world order that would have Germania at the centre of it. A place in the sun for all Germans in a society free of Jews and communists and its other enemies.

Martin considered. However, it had come at a cost. His sister for one. Then there were his old school friends and families killed in the bombing. The huge German losses in Russia he'd learned about, listening into forbidden foreign radio stations. And now uncovering the truth about the mass killings in his camp. Would it be the same for other concentration camps?

A few years ago, Martin had eaves dropped once on his father's telephone conversation and had even heard the island of Madagascar mentioned for the resettlement of Jews. There had been no talk of killing them.

One thing for sure, now he knew the true fate of the Jews in this camp, he had to help Rachael and Erika. If he could at least save the small boy. He knew he owed it to his sister although most probably she would never know. She might not even be alive.

*

Martin had made a full recovery by the following morning and managed to get himself released from the infirmary. The doctor being rather surprised, as most patients did their best to get a few days extra in the sick bay. On his return to the barracks, he made his way past the army clothing store. His mind ticked over. He knew he had to pick the ideal time when the corporal in charge went for his lunch. Today was his chance, while his troop still thought he was in the infirmary. Once reporting back to his superior, it would be hard to break away from the daily duties.

Martin kept to the side wall of the stores, out of sight from the sentry tower. The area around wasn't busy, so he crouched behind some large steel containers and watched the entrance. At midday, the stores corporal emerged and shut the door. He fiddled with the lock, and then after a furtive glance each way, placed the key above the door frame.

Martin allowed a few minutes and then moved to the entrance. He reached for the key and quickly let himself in and locked the door. Apart for a small window and a bare lightbulb, the place was dark and musty.

Martin knew that finding a spare Hitler Youth uniform in a concentration camp clothing garrison store was going to be a long shot, let alone the right size. Especially when Hitler youth were not regular members of the garrisons.

His eyes scanned boxes and racks marked up with belts, boots, gloves, caps and much more. A seven foot tall double cupboard against the wall drew his attention. The white card fixed to its door stated UNIFORMS.

He opened the door and quickly thumbed his way through a variety of large, medium and small SS tunics. He sighed. Nothing of use there. The top shelf above his head looked a better prospect. It had *YOUTH* scribbled in chalk on the inside of the compartment.

Martin lifted down the heavy bundle and sorted the uniforms. He sifted through and then held one up. A Hitler Youth tunic with trousers. Although it looked on the big size he couldn't believe his luck. Then it began to make sense. Perhaps stores preparations for when the Hitler Youth would take over most of the garrison force while the older men would be used at the front line to hold back the allies. The shoes, cap and shirt he found after rummaging through the rest of the cupboard.

Suddenly he froze. Voices outside the window. Shit! The storeman could be back early? The talking with some laughter continued and then faded. Guards having a smoke, Martin thought.

He tidied up quickly and then stripped off. With difficulty he pulled on the Hitler Youth uniform. It was a ridiculous tight fit but he eventually managed. Then his own uniform back over the top. The shoes he stuffed inside his tunic under the arms. They wouldn't bulge so much there, although he might have trouble saluting if a higher ranked officer approached. Then again he wasn't unduly worried. This time of the day, the officers would be at lunch. The guards too, would be no threat. Of course they were alert to pilfering but only carried out random checks on prisoners.

Martin carefully opened the door and checked both ways. Then he slipped out, relocked the door and replaced the key. He made his way to the female prison block.

The guard at the compound entrance asked him his reason for visiting.

Martin clicked his heels and said, 'Rottenführer, Martin Borch reporting under orders for the SS- Erstaufseherin to escort prisoner 300241 to clean her office. The guard held out his clipboard for Martin to sign and then waved him through while sniggering and making crude lesbian remarks under his breath.

As Martin approached the prison hut, it all looked very quiet. In the middle of the compound, the woman's body in the prisoner's striped smock, still hung from the gallows. Martin eyed it with caution. In his mind, what he had dismissed for clear cut justice only a day ago was now possibly bordering on murder. He climbed the hut steps and pushed open the door. Immediately the stench hit him.

Inside from nowhere, two SS guards appeared and pointed their pistols.

Martin's jaw dropped.

'What do want?' One of them barked.

Martin stood to attention and half saluted. 'Rottenführer, Martin Borch reporting under orders from the SS- Erstaufseherin to escort prisoner 300241 to clean her office.'

The guard with the Himmler type spectacles grinned and showed a set of tobacco stained teeth. 'If she was in this hut, Jew 300241 or any Jew including the little runt we found in hiding has gone up the chimney with the rest of the rags.'

Instantly the other guard shouted. 'Shut up, Gunther. We are not allowed to say, remember?'

'Ya, ya. We are not allowed to say,' he mimicked. He sat down on a stool and took out a hipflask of brandy from his tunic. Gunther took a swig. 'Half of Dachau is covered in ash and we are not allowed to say,' he joked. 'As if the people outside don't know from the stench.'

The other guard repeated, 'I said shut up, Gunther, and put the booze away.' He turned to Martin. 'All the prisoners in the hut have been sent to the punishment block. We're looking for hidden contraband and weapons they were supposed to be hiding.'

'Gunther said sarcastically, 'Ya, ya, of course, I forgot. They've been sent to the punishment block.'

'But what for?' Martin said in astonishment. 'What happened?'

'One of the Jew bitches confessed to smuggling gunpowder while under special treatment.' Gunther winked at Martin. 'Special treatment. That means having her fingernails pulled out.' He took a swig and then grinned showing his stained teeth again.

The other guard shook his head. 'One day, Gunther, your mouth will get us all into trouble.'

He'd heard enough. Martin clicked his heels. 'I will report back to the SS- Erstaufseherin and tell her the situation.'

Gunther leered. 'You tell your SS- Erstaufseherin not to worry. There's lots more girlies in the camp to clean out her orifice.' He put a hand jokingly to his mouth. 'Sorry, I meant her office.'

The other guard yelled again. 'Gunther, for Christ's sake!'

Martin stumbled down the hut steps in a daze. He had to get away from the stench. As he breathed in fresh air, his eyes welled up with tears. He looked over to the hanging body slowly twisting in the breeze. The realisation of what was happening, what he was part of - slowly began to creep over his body; like crawling leeches sucking at his guilt.

CHAPTER NINE

Near the end of 1944, Karl knew the war was going badly for Germany. Unbeknown to the others, he'd been preparing for this eventuality as the Americans moved nearer, penetrating the Wehrmacht's disintegrating front line.

He'd amassed quite a haul in bank notes of various denominations together with diamonds and gold teeth. These had been stolen from the camp depository where they'd been held after being collected from prisoners, alive or dead. The syndicate he was head of including the depository guards and accountants had done themselves proud. Himself especially, with a bulging suitcase he kept in his wardrobe.

However, one day Karl was confronted by a surprise visit from SD Reich Security. Rumours had been rife through the camp about his stealing from the prisoners. The three men from Gestapo Security wearing black SS uniforms had obviously been tipped off. They ordered Karl to take them to his sleeping quarters and asked him to open the wardrobe which he always kept locked. Karl lied to them and said he'd mislaid the keys somewhere. They immediately padlocked the handles of his wardrobe with a chain and stuck a warning note on the door stating – OUT OF BOUNDS – PROPERTY OF REICH SECURITY.

They told Karl they would send for a local locksmith. Karl had to think quickly. It was around lunchtime. He apologised for losing his keys and asked them if they would like to dine with him in his office while they waited. He highlighted Fois Grais and fresh lobster were on todays' menu with a rather good Riesling. The portly Gestapo Kriminalkommissar in charge hesitated, he looked at his watch and realised the locksmith might be a time. Knowing as well, the long car journey back to Berlin had a shortage of good restaurants and they might not dine until tonight, he accepted Karl's offer. He curtly ordered his two subordinates to check out the remaining garrison lockers and report back an hour later.

While a young attractive SS Aufseherin in her smart grey uniform and cap, escorted them to the commandant's office, Karl discretely handed her a note.

Twenty minutes later, a young orderly was waiting on them and pouring a good German wine. The portly Gestapo Kriminalkommissar, with a heavily stained serviette draped over his chest, was already on his second glass of Riesling and wrestling a large lobster mounted on a platter of fruits de mer. As he twisted off legs, cracked shells, sucked white flesh from orifices while making a revolting noise, in-between scoffing down the odd oyster and talking with his mouth full, of his family and how good a cook his wife was.

At that point, Karl was relieved to receive his planned phone call concerning a breakdown with one of the crematoria and excused himself, leaving the Kriminalkommissar to chat with the attractive SS Aufseherin while he was away.

Karl made his way back to his sleeping quarters. He knew the other two SD Gestapo would be over at the garrison block. For how long he didn't know. He had to be quick.

Moving the wardrobe away from the wall, he levered off the thin plywood rear panel using a fork from the canteen. He took out the suitcase with the incriminating contents and placed it under the loose floorboards with his other stash. With the rug back in its place, Karl re-sealed the back of the wardrobe using the same panel pins and a heavy paperweight to drive them home. With one last look to make sure everything was as it should be, he made his way back to the lunch.

An hour later, after a few minor confiscations his subordinates had found in the garrison lockers to justify their journey and expenses, this included some pornography in addition to a few recreational morphine phials and three bottles of schnapps; the Kriminalkommissar eased his satisfied full stomach into the staff car with his colleagues.

Waving any prosecution this time, he gave a Heil Hitler salute and then sped off into the cold winter mid-afternoon.

Karl breathed a sigh of relief. From now on he had to be careful. He knew one of his subordinates must have reported him, knowing there was a large amount of incriminating evidence in the wardrobe. It could have been his chief physician Dr Joachim Eisele.

According to rumours, the slim thirty-eight year old Dr Eisele with his duelling scar and pointed features was having an affair with the SS-Oberaufseherin of the female camp, Greta Binz. She was in charge of the women's medical section.

She'd proudly display the jewellery presents Dr Eisele had given her. Her favourite charm being the Hünenkreuz, a silver medal of purity with crossed swords and a small swastika at its centre. It replaced the one she'd been given for joining the BDM as a young girl. The one her stepfather had torn from her on the way to the closet.

She'd wear the medal with pride as she strutted, riding whip in hand, along the rows of inmates at rollcall.

Dr Eisele had informed Greta Binz. As chief physician he had the authority to award the medal to the most pure and conscientious member of his medical team. On the back he'd had it engraved with Greta's rare blood group - AB Negative. Of course the real truth, that he'd taken it from some feeble-minded girl with the same blood group at the time she was arrested, he kept to himself.

Karl had also heard rumours about other presents that were made for Greta Binz in Dr Eisele's workshop. A lampshade cover from the skin of inmates with tattoos for one, and a necklace made from human eyeballs. How true that was, he couldn't say. He considered Eisele and Binz a pair of out and out monsters from what they got up to. They were seen together quite a bit.

Karl had met the notorious thirty-two year old Greta Binz in 1944 on a visit to the neighbouring female block. She had arrived from Dachau Concentration Camp recently and had been newly promoted to SS-Oberaufseherin. The meeting with her and officials of the Reich's Office of Medicine, was to discuss the new sterilisation programme for some of the chosen female inmates. It was further rumoured she'd had lesbian relationships with female prisoners. Many of them became her servants and were awarded special privileges, although that didn't stop her shooting them when she would fly into a rage at their slightest misdemeanour.

*

Because of the camp's quiet location in the backwaters of Dachau, news from the front in early January 1945 was sometimes scant and unreliable. However, most of the garrison at Pullhausen Concentration Camp guessed things weren't going well. The Allies were getting nearer every day. It was then Karl received orders from Reichsführer Heinrich Himmler to evacuate the camp with its prisoners. They were to be moved away from the front to Bolzano, a transit camp at a distance about 190 miles.

Karl knew it wouldn't look good if he was captured as a commandant of a concentration camp. He knew he had to distance himself from the others, especially those fiends, Eisele and Binz. Karl considered himself a professional in his work. Work that was vital to the future of Germany although unpleasant at times. However Eisle and Binz took their work to a level of sadism and cruelty and made no attempt to hide the fact.

Karl had never wanted to make waves. Dr Joachim Eisele had a niece that was married into the Heinrich Himmler family. Himmler was a powerful man, second only to Hitler. Karl knew which side his bread was buttered.

Dr Karl Borch with his chief physician, Dr Joachim Eisele, was holding a meeting in his office with all the other camp doctors present.

'Gentlemen, I'm afraid the news is not good. The Americans are getting close, so we will have to leave the camp.' Borch looked worried as he fingered the brass button on his field grey tunic. Looking immaculate in his uniform with his highly polished black boots, he continued, 'The evacuation will be phased over the next two weeks. Nearly 6,000 prisoners will have to be moved to Bolzano transit camp about 190 miles away. The garrison here will be escorting them, so no one will be left at Pullhausen.' The Commandant nodded to the doctor and said, 'Your department chief, Dr Joachim Eisele, will fill you in with more details.'

Dr Joachim Eisele stood up in his SS-uniform and returned the nod with a thin engaging lopsided smile. He informed them. 'First of all, team, I would like to thank all of you for your excellent work and participation in our euthogenics programme. Your help in pioneering the party's ultimate goal, to produce a master race from the subjugated peoples considered just acceptable from our European and North

African conquests, will be invaluable. The work carried out in this camp is an important advancement to enable us to change the physical features of other races in line with our Aryan look so we may embrace them into our Third Reich.'

The physicians applauded, while Dr Joachim Eisele clapped as well and then waited until the noise had subsided. 'Next week, all of us with myself, will be traveling to the camp at Bolzano. We will set up a temporary medical centre there and carry on where we left off. We have to make sure we take all our medical records, scientific papers and equipment with us. Anything we can't carry must be destroyed.'

A few of the doctors looked stunned with the news. They had no idea the situation was that serious?

It was no surprise to Karl Borch although he was in a tricky situation. He'd employed Dr Eisele with his anthropological studies and research, while using inmates for human experimentation. Karl knew deep down, most of the work was unscientific and had no regard for the health or safety of the victims. However, if the war swung the other way, and he was called to account for this research, he might be included with Eisele and Binz for war crimes.

He knew he should be exonerated from the human experiments. His work dealt with the day to day running of the camp and its organisation. Eisele on the other hand, performed the dissections for the euthogenics programme on the living and the dead, preparing specimens in the camp laboratory for shipment to Berlin. However, it still wouldn't look good, if he was taken prisoner as a camp commandant.

He already had false papers and a passport. They'd been taken from a German political prisoner with his similar looks and height.

Now he had to take his chances. He knew he'd be shot as a deserter if the SS caught him. He wouldn't fare much better with the Russians. He'd seen the propaganda photographs in the newspapers that had got through. Red army retribution against the SS left little to the imagination. He had no desire to be burned alive with tank fuel. If he was going to be captured, let it be the Americans.

The first thing he had to do, was erase the blood group SS tattoo under his left armpit.

In his bathroom, alone with a bottle of brandy, a cut throat razor and some bandage dressings. Karl slashed away at the ink numbers until they were a frenzied bloody mess and unreadable. If he was wounded and needed blood, the metal dog tags around his neck supplied the information.

Karl decided he would make his escape during the journey to Bolzano transit camp.

*

A week later on the morning they were leaving, it was freezing cold. Holding a suitcase containing all his plundered valuables, with false identity papers hidden in the lining of his jacket, he boarded the back of a lorry with five other doctors. Huddled together to keep warm, their journey would take in some of the back roads, as this would give some forest cover against the possibility of an air attack, which had rendered the trains too risky, since the Russians now dominated the skies.

With a halfway stop at Garmisch, the doctors climbed down and sauntered their way towards the café in the square. Dr Borch made his excuse for wanting his suitcase. A change of shirt because the one he was wearing needed washing. That wasn't far off the truth. The constant sweet smell and the fine white ash from the crematoria chimney, impregnated clothes and uniforms. Something he wasn't going to miss.

Telling the others he would meet them for coffee, he made his way to the café washroom. Locking himself into the cubicle, he frantically changed out of his uniform into labourer's clothes and then put on a beard and a moustache while finishing his disguise with a peasant cap with the earflaps pulled down near his eye line. He took out from his suitcase an old canvas shoulder bag. Pushing the suitcase behind the toilet cistern, he stopped for one last look in the mirror. Then he peaked through a small crack in the partially open door. It was clear.

Dr Borch had his directions and plans. He'd studied the map several times. Walking slowly with a slight limp and a heavy stoop, he made his way out of the square and into the woods. With water, food and a compass, it would take him around a day to get to the small town of Konstanz near the Swiss border. He had to get there by evening at the latest. It was too cold to stay out overnight. Karl decided to keep off the main roads to avoid any military convoys in the area.

At Konstanz, he would try and get a labouring job in the surrounding countryside as a farm worker. Bribe the owner if he had to, for a roof over his head in a barn or an outhouse with meals thrown in. He had the money. Then see out the end of the war in Konstanz. Wait until it had all cooled down. Start afresh, hopefully nobody would recognise him. Perhaps set up a medical practice there?

An hour later he'd covered around six miles through woodland, keeping a distant road in his sights. Then Karl heard the rumble of a convoy. Suddenly there was shouting and a hail of machine gun bullets rained down on him. Karl dived into a clump of bushes.

Someone shouted in German. Then other voices. He crouched and held his breath. Two Waffen SS passed him so close he could almost touch them. They were all around.

'SS, shit!' He cursed under his breath. He couldn't give himself up. They'd shoot him. Karl had the SS blood group tattoo scar under his arm. The wound was still fresh from where he tried to erase it. With his German accent, they'd look for that for sure to check if he was a deserter.

Minutes went by, along with more shouting, and then the voices became distant. Eventually he heard the rumble of a convoy moving away. Karl waited another twenty minutes until he was sure it was clear.

He moved off keeping low, still following the road at a distance. It was then he saw a shape in the trees above. Karl stopped and crouched. Maybe the SS were waiting for him. Trying to flush him out. He took out the binoculars from his bag. After he focused, he realised it was the remains of a parachute caught in the high branches with a body dangling.

Karl checked each way and then moved towards the airman who was dangling five feet off the ground. It looked surreal, him hanging there. He prodded the airman for any signs of life. The body swayed back and forth. As it slowly twisted, Karl saw the blue face with the tongue sticking out and the parachute cord tightly wrapped around his neck. He muttered, 'Poor Bastard, nearly made it. Strangled by his own cord.'

Karl was about to move away and then stopped. He looked at the body. It must have happened recently, it wasn't smelling. Perhaps that's what the SS were looking for? They may have seen him come down?

With a knife he reached up and cut the cords. The lifeless pilot crumpled to the ground. Karl carefully reached inside the pilot's tunic pocket and rummaged, and then withdrew what appeared to be a lucky rabbit's foot, a compass, some Reichsmarks in small change, a photo of a woman with two children and two identity cards.

Karl hesitated with the photo. The young mother was smiling while she sat and held her youngest. The eldest also smiling, sat cross legged by her side. Karl scrutinised the pilot ID card. It showed Dr Karl Eder was a Gefreiter Private First Class Airman in the Jagdgeschwader 53 `Pik-As` squadron based at Landsberg-Ost. The other card stated he was a doctor and had qualified at Dresden Medical School.

He smiled with satisfaction. Karl couldn't believe his luck finding ID with his first name as well as being a doctor. Karl presumed in earlier times the doctor would have probably been ground based, helping with the wounded in some field hospital. However, these days with pilots being scarce in numbers, his superiors must have decided he would be put to better use killing the enemy rather than healing the wounded.

On his map, Karl saw Landsberg-Ost was near the village of Penzing about fifty miles from here. Another photo showed the pilot standing by a Messerschmitt Bf 109. The Messerschmitt's in that squadron had a distinct yellow engine underbelly.

Karl knew his Luftwaffe. He studied in the early thirties to become a pilot. The problem being, not only was he colour blind, but also violently airsick as soon as he was lifted off the ground. With that in mind he turned his attention to medicine. A decision he sometimes now regretted.

Without hesitation, Karl pulled off the pilots dog tags from around his neck. Then Karl removed his own farm labourer's clothes and tore off the dead pilot's uniform. The shirt, tunic and trousers were slightly too big for him. It didn't matter apart from the trousers. With a belt he hoisted them up. The pilot's boots were also big, but he could double up using socks. Now he had to hide the body.

To his left he saw what looked like the remains of a mortar crater from some previous engagement. It was partially filled in with leaves and branches. Probably camouflage material that had been discarded, but it would do. Karl dragged the body and hid it in the crater as best as he could. No one would know until the smell might cause someone to pause if they were passing. By then, hopefully, he would be long gone.

Now if he was caught by SS he had an excuse. A downed pilot, and if they found the parachute so what. He had to get a story together of how his Messerschmitt was shot down and roughly where. Karl looked at his map and then decided. He would say his starboard wing got riddled with canon fire from an American B24 Liberator, returning from a daylight raid on Munich. Karl knew there'd been attacks from radio reports. Tell them, as he drifted down he saw his plane plunge towards Lake Constance, which was also local. Very convenient. No crash site or remains. Last thing to do was deface the photograph on the pilots ID card. It really didn't look like him. The face needed some changes.

Karl grabbed a leaf and using some spit, he rubbed away gently at the black and white photo until it slowly began to fade. He'd learnt the trick from the Jews in the camp. Those who realised their fate if they had time, would rub out family members in group photos who'd not been rounded up yet; so as the SS and Gestapo wouldn't recognise them.

Pleased with the result, he gathered his things together. At least now, if he was caught by the enemy and taken prisoner, he'd be just another shot down pilot with the name of Dr Karl Eder, a Gefreiter in the Luftwaffe; not SS Dr Karl Borch, Commandant of Pullhausen Concentration Camp.

Checking the map and his compass again for the Swiss border and the town of Konstanz, Karl swiftly moved off keeping low, still with the road in sight. An hour later as it was getting dark and colder, he heard another convoy.

This time the voices sounded British. Hundreds of them seemed to be sweeping the woods with the convoy as backup. There were foot soldiers everywhere. Karl made a mental note of some crossroads he could see. Then he feverishly sorted his bag and pushed the stash, containing money, diamonds and the stolen passport of the camp prisoner, into the dense undergrowth nearby.

Karl crouched and waited. Suddenly the bushes parted, and three British soldiers levelled their Lee-Enfield rifles at him. The British 21st Army Group had arrived. Karl saw it on their tunic sleeves. A Lance Corporal and two Privates prodded him to get up.

The Lance Corporal barked at him in German. Karl raised his hands. 'I Speak English.'

The Lance Corporal jeered, 'Do you hear that, Boys? We've got ourselves an English speaking Kraut.' The two others laughed. 'Tell you what, Herman, you're dead lucky you being Luftwaffe. Some Yank units round here have been shooting SS and Wehrmacht on sight. They'd liberated one of your concentration camps on the way. They're not in a good mood.

Karl was very grateful he was wearing a pilot's uniform.

CHAPTER TEN

Karl was escorted to the road and shoved into an army lorry with fifteen other prisoners. With three other lorries' containing captured Germans, the journey to Frieburg prisoner of war camp on the German border to France took five hours. After a three day stay at the camp, it was an overnight train journey across France to Le Havre, and then across the English Channel, with over three-hundred other prisoners crammed into large barges to arrive at Portsmouth.

Karl with the others, was deloused and taken under escort by train to Kempton Park Racecourse and held in a command cage. While there, he was interrogated and had his security risk assessed in line with his ranking by the Prisoner of War Interrogation Section PWIS. Being Luftwaffe, Karl was classified as high security because of his supposed knowledge of ariel photography. They considered, if he escaped he might also have the ability to commandeer a plane and fly back to Germany.

The PWIS interrogated Karl on military matters to get an idea of his loyalty to the Nazi regime. Convincing the board he wasn't an ardent Nazi and had no strong feelings either way, he was issued with a grey patch on his uniform. A grey patch meant that a prisoner, especially Luftwaffe, although high risk was not a hardened fanatic like the SS.

The following day, because of his high risk Luftwaffe classification, Karl was taken by train under military police escort to Grizedale Hall in Cumbria. This was a large stately home known by the Prisoner of War Interrogation Section as Camp-one. To deter escape, Camp-one was surrounded by Grizedale Forest, with Lake Coniston on one side and Lake Windermere on the other.

After a medical examination and being photographed, a balding early forties intelligence officer, Major A.P. Henderson, along with two personnel from the PWIS, interrogated Karl for two days. During breaks he was offered sandwiches and coffee, even pastries. They asked him about his family and hobbies, his job before the war - where he'd learned to speak good English. He told them his father had been a strong influence, having worked in London at the Savoy hotel before the First World War. Then came questions about the books he liked to read and his favourite films - his tastes in music and art - what sport he followed.

Karl knew he was being softened up in a friendly atmosphere; they were trying to gain his confidence. No doubt the probing military questions would come later. But at the moment he answered them freely; and all the time a stenographer was taking notes at a desk behind him.

For Karl, the alarm bells began to sound when they asked him his views on National Socialism - the Nazi treatment of Jews. What he thought of Adolf Hitler. Then questions about his training, where he'd learnt to fly. They pinned a map to a wall. Where exactly in Germany was his airfield - how many planes and personnel - the whereabouts of strategic troop and tank movements. Karl nonchalantly looked at the map and gave his name, rank and serial number - the minimum information he was allowed to give as laid down for prisoners of war by the Geneva Convention.

Major A.P. Henderson sighed. He knew he wasn't going to get any more information out of him. He ticked the Grey Box and stamped Karl's file, for de-nazification, dated January 26th 1945.

After his interrogation, they moved Karl to the POW barracks in the surrounding forest. They let him keep his Luftwaffe tunic but painted a large white POW on the back.

That afternoon, Karl was escorted by military police to Nissen hut number-four. As he entered, around forty prisoners looked up. Some of them were squatting on the edge of their beds, others were lying in bunks. A few were grouped around crude wooden tables and chairs playing cards and chess. Elsewhere conversations were going on.

They stopped when they saw him and then huddled together and spoke more softly.

In the middle of the austere room was a wood stove. Karl thought, the winters here could be bleak if this was going to be the only source of heat. As well as burning wood, his nose detected a strong smell of stale sweat and tobacco.

Just at that moment, a blonde German named Lutz entered the hut and took out a military Waffen-SS whistle from the breast pocket of his uniform. A long drawn out piercing shrill stopped all the talking. Lutz, an unsavory looking individual with high cheekbones and sharp features, wore a Hauptmann Luftwaffe tunic with two wings and one bar. The whistle dangled from a lanyard as he looked at the piece of paper he was holding with Karl Eder's details. He smiled at Karl and then at the others.

With the group's undivided attention, Lutz, even with his boots on, had to straighten his five foot-nine-inch frame to make himself more impressive as he introduced Karl to the rest of the men. Lutz made it very clear he was in charge and known as the Lagerführer of the camp. It was his job to liaise with the British and enforce discipline when it was required. With the others looking on, he gave Karl the induction speech.

Because of his former rank and excellent English, Lutz was billeted in the luxury of the stately home, Grizedale Hall. No doubt there were other reasons why he was given this status, especially with the looks he was receiving from behind his back while addressing Karl.

It was obvious; Lutz was not liked, probably because he was some kind of informant.

Lutz proceeded to tell Karl, with a smirk of pride, some of the opportunities in the camp. The opportunities varied from lessons in learning English and shorthand by a local lady who visited once a week under guard, to forestry and farming while on work detail. Karl also learnt Lutz was in charge of the work detail.

'Would you like to work, yes?' Lutz asked. He saw Karl hesitate and added, 'Of course you don't have to. Under the Geneva convention it is not compulsory for Luftwaffe including the rank of Gefreiter, as yourself,' he said mockingly. 'Most of the men choose to do it, as it passes the time more quickly.' Lutz added with a sarcastic tinge, 'And the one thing we do have here, Herr Gefreiter, is time.'

'As long as it's not directly helping the allies, what are the benefits if we work?' asked Karl.

'Ah! Spoken like a loyal German,' said Lutz mockingly, 'but never-the-less, a sensible and realistic one.' Lutz then went through the perks of what a working prisoner received. 'If you work, you will receive the same rations as British servicemen.' He pulled out a packet of British cigarettes and lit one, then offered to Karl. As the others were watching, he thought it better to refuse.

Lutz continued, 'If you volunteer for work detail you will receive, as well as your canteen meals - cigarettes, chocolate, jam, cake, cheese, tea and of course coffee.' He paused to inhale his cigarette and then said with a laugh, 'And how us Germans love our coffee, eh?'

Karl cast a nervous glance over Lutz's shoulder at the others. One of them nodded to confirm it was OK.

'Count me in, when do we start?'

'Tomorrow, I will have you detailed for local farm work. After morning roll-call you will move off with the others.' With his leather boot, Lutz ground out his half-smoked cigarette in a wasteful gesture while the others looked on. He turned to them and smiled, 'Good-day to you all.'

After he'd gone, some of them spat on the floor and mumbled insults. One prisoner moved swiftly to the doorway to act as a lookout. Another one shouted, 'Quick, he's been under there too long.'

Four of them using rags and clothing as padding, wrestled the hot stove off the tin plate that was used to catch the ash. They kicked the plate to one side to reveal a hole just bigger than a football. 'Hurry, get him out of there.' The same person who shouted seemed to be their leader. He was an early thirties dark haired man who stood around six-foot in his boots and flying jacket. A previous flying mission had left him with a distinct scar on his chin and part of his left ear was missing. They called him Felix.

With the others looking over, Felix knelt and offered his hand down into the hole. Karl watched in astonishment as a muddy arm grabbed hold and was then hauled up. The man, wearing only shorts and covered from head to toe in dirt and filth, collapsed on the floor breathing hard and calling for water.

Felix cradled his head and administered the water using a shaving mug. The man, spilling most of it, gulped and spluttered it down then called for more. After a while, they helped him to stand.

Swaying a bit, he slowly walked around the room to get the feeling back into his legs. Karl was amazed at the power of water, how quickly it could resuscitate, bring someone back into the land of the living.

Now the digger had to get himself to the latrines before the British guards spotted him. They had a water pump there for showering. Four latrine buckets full of mud had to be disposed of as well, all before evening roll call.

With the all clear, the digger slipped out holding a fresh set of clothes. The others lined themselves up, and in turn took a handful of mud and stuffed it inside their torn pockets. Then they casually wandered outside in groups and nonchalantly spilled it out, bit by bit, from the bottom of their trouser turn-ups.

Grunting and puffing they positioned the stove back over the tin plate. Then Felix came over to Karl and introduced himself. With a click of his heels and a stiff arm Nazi salute, he said in near perfect English, 'I'm Oberstleutnant, Felix Kappel, head of the escape committee.'

Karl returned his greeting with a similar click of heels and a Nazi salute.

'Your English is good,' Felix said. 'We try and speak it while we're here, so it comes natural. To condition us when we breakout.'

With four other committee members standing with him, Felix explained to Karl their plan. 'We've set the date for the camp concert night in two weeks' time. It's going to be a mass escape for all the men in this hut after the show. They've been digging for three weeks and not far from coming up through the wooden floor boards into the supply warehouse.'

From his tunic pocket, Felix took out a crumpled piece of paper with a crude map. He whistled to the lookout to keep alert and then continued in a low voice. 'The warehouse stores the long canteen forms we require to make a bridge across the two barbed wire fences. Getting to the fences at a distance of thirty-feet without cover is going to be our biggest obstacle.'

Karl looked at the map and suggested, 'Couldn't you carry on and tunnel under the fences, or just break into the warehouse under cover of night?'

Felix smiled. 'We're ahead of you. We considered those alternatives, but the extra digging required and the time it takes, increases the risk of us being caught. Then there's the intense security around the warehouse with the constant sweep of searchlights. Makes it easy for them to spot us breaking in from outside.'

Felix took out a fancy silver cigarette case and offered one of his Woodbine rations to Karl. As Felix flicked his Leitz lighter, both men inhaled. Then he continued, 'Using the warehouse as cover, we can time it right. It's the nearest place to meet up before we escape. In-between the searchlight sweeps we can make our move.'

Felix pointed on the map to the dotted lines of the tunnel. 'Look, you see, once we've come up into the warehouse through the floorboards, we can cut a hole in the wooden side that faces the fence. The hole will be blind to the view of the sentry tower. Then under cover of night and concert party noise, we'll lay the canteen forms on the wire fence to make a bridge and crawl across, making our escape into the surrounding woods. After that, it's every man for himself.'

For a moment, there was silence. Karl looked at the map once more, then Felix. He smiled. 'Sounds good, count me in.'

Felix slapped him heartily on the back. 'Wunderbar. I am so glad you will join us, Herr Karl,' he joked. 'If you had said no, we'd probably have killed you anyway, being a new man and left to tell a possible tale. The English are very good at their bribery. We couldn't take a chance you see.'

With a half limp smile Karl said, 'I'm glad I made the right decision.'

Felix took a long draw on his cigarette and frowned. 'We do have a slight problem though. The British guards patrol the fence day and night, so we have to be careful, however,' he broke into a smile, 'there is a possible silver lining, as the English say. At the previous concert party to improve moral, Major Henderson had allowed the guards to draw straws to decide who could watch the show and who remained on duty. There was a relaxation in security around the perimeter fence. We just hope he repeats the same goodwill gesture.' The committee nodded in agreement.

*

The tunnel was ready, and on the night of the concert, the whole camp consisting of over three-hundred and sixty men were sitting eagerly in the canteen. They were waiting in anticipation to be entertained and have a good laugh. They hadn't seen a lot of laughs and wanted cheering up.

Each of the escape group had a little money, not much, only what had been smuggled in and shared out, and a fake ration card.

Karl didn't want to go. He hadn't told anybody. He'd rather stay where he was and get a square meal a day, than risk getting caught and face solitary confinement for a stretch. Worse still, if he managed to get back to Germany, the Nazi war criminal investigators might be hot on his trail, and then of course there were the Russians. Get caught by them and it was an instant bullet in the back of the head or a train ride to Siberia. He would've liked to have seen his son but that was out of the question now.

Karl had made up his mind. The only thing to do was to twist his ankle - limp badly and tell the others to go on.

Only the guard towers with their search lights were manned that night. The rest of the British camp garrison were sitting along both sides of the canteen walls.

As Felix was head of the escape committee, he'd decided to pair himself off with Karl after the breakout. He reckoned, because they spoke good English, they stood a better chance together of making it to the coast than the rest of the men.

Being the last of the escape group, they planned to make their move after the men had completed the final song and dance sketch with the grass skirts and coconut brassieres. As scheduled, Felix would come out on stage and thank everybody and then announce to finish off the night, tea and cake would be served at the canteen counter.

It was an added bonus that the men in Karl's Nissen hut were the only ones organizing and acting in the concert party. Along with the performers, they had permission to help out as scene shifters and work the gramophone and lighting in the partitioned-off kitchen. The kitchen, at the rear of the canteen makeshift stage, also doubled as the dressing room. A back door from it led to Karl's hut just opposite. All they had to cover was a distance of twenty-feet. But it was in full view of the sentry tower.

Major A.P. Henderson, also attending the concert, had briefed the guards not to be trigger happy. There was going to be some activity in and out of the canteen tonight with prisoners moving scenery stored in Nissen hut No.4. He told the guards on duty to relax a little. 'At least all the prisoners are under one roof,' he'd joked with them.

Oberstleutnant, Felix Kappel, had gone over the escape plan with the men. In groups of two's and three's they would slip out the back door of the canteen kitchen and walk slowly, no running, to Nissen hut No.4 in full view of the guards. Then one would walk back again carrying a bit of scenery prop as an excuse. They were relying on the guards not counting or keeping check on the numbers of men who went backwards and forwards. This would continue, gradually depleting all the prisoners from the canteen kitchen until, the only men remaining were the Hawaiian act, with himself and Karl. Whoever was last man in the hole it was essential to tie the rope to the stove and pull it over the opening.

The concert party finale had been timed for nine-thirty. With six remaining men on stage, the evening had gone according to plan. The first groups had moved the stove in the Nissen hut and then climbed down into the hole and crawled along the tunnel, finally making their way up through the warehouse floor. The floor boards had been carefully loosened prior to the concert night and kept in place in case of discovery. Once inside the warehouse, all there was to do, was punch out a small side area of the wooden slats that was blind side of the sentry tower, big enough to climb through and pass the canteen forms, and then lay them on top of the two barbed wire perimeter fences to make a bridge to crawl across.

The crowd rocked with laughter as the Hawaiian dancers supported by an old HMV gramophone, danced on stage sprinkled with sand. Wearing paper grass skirts and lopsided coconut bras, sliding one foot in front of the other while jerking their heads backwards and forwards like Wilson and Keppel, finished off the evening with an Egyptian dance routine.

To make himself heard over the deafening noise, Felix nudged Karl and cupped his hands and said, 'Haven't seen that snake of a Lagerführer, Lutz.'

From the canteen doorway they both scanned the crowd and looked worried.

'Nor have I,' Karl said. 'What do you think he's up to?'

'I don't know, but he can't be trusted,' Felix said looking serious. 'If he smells anything he'd grass on us just to look good with the Major. He's got him in his confidence.' Felix leant in closer, 'They've got some black market going on together. POW rations being sold in the local village and the rest of it. Just remember, Lagerführer Lutz would sell his own mother down the river for a couple of Reich marks.'

'Do you want me to go and check out, see if he's sniffing around?' Karl said.

'No, I'll go. He knows me. I often run into him having a quick smoke outside the hut when I'm on lookout.' Felix joked, 'I keep him talking while the others move the stove back and clean up. If he sees you he might get suspicious. You stay here and wait until I get back. OK?'

Karl nodded and gave him the thumbs up.

Felix stepped outside and made his way to the hut. He saw the lights inside were on. As he reached the doorway he ducked down. He spotted Lutz crouching by the stove. Thankfully the last group through had pulled the stove over the hole. Nobody else was in the hut.

Lutz was examining the stove. It was cold. Something Felix had hoped nobody would notice. The stove was lit every night, even in the summer for heating tea and coffee. Lutz was thinking. *Why not tonight?*

He rubbed his fingers in the dirt and then to Felix's horror, Lutz picked up a small piece of solid mud. He rolled it in his hand with a suspicious look. He put his hand under the stove and pulled out some more clumps of mud. He looked around and over his shoulder making sure he was alone. Then he stood up.

Bracing himself, he grabbed the stove and with an almighty grunt he dragged it away.

Lutz stared in disbelief at the wooden board temporarily jammed in the hole from the last man in the tunnel. He crouched again and touched it, still not able to comprehend. Lutz leant over and pulled at the board; suddenly it came free sending him spilling backwards. He got up and stared into the hole with astonishment.

Felix watched him as his face slowly changed and he knowingly smiled. Lutz pulled out his whistle and put it to his lips.

With his attention diverted, Felix had crept behind. As he swung the heavy tea kettle, it smashed into the back of Lutz's head and he cried out as the blow catapulted him into the hole. The brittle snap of his neck as he hit the bottom echoed through the hut.

Felix put a hand to his mouth and nervously mumbled, 'Oh God, what have I done?' He looked at the doorway expecting to see British guards running in with their rifles pointing, but there was nothing. All was quiet apart from the distant concert music and bursts of laughter.

With no time to waste, Felix dragged the stove back over the hole. Then panic gripped him. He thought what to do; can't use the tunnel anymore, to risky. Just hope the others had made it through. Felix walked out of the hut. He looked up at the sentry tower and saw under floodlight they were chatting and smoking. They ignored him as he made his way back to the camp concert.

The finale was loud and noisy with everyone singing to a scratchy Lili Marlene record that was playing. The men had changed out of their Hawaiian costumes and were waiting with Karl in the kitchen for Felix to come back with the all clear.

As he walked in he shook his head, they could see it was bad news. Felix spoke to Karl in English so as not to alarm the others. 'I had to kill Lutz, he found the hole,'

'You killed him,' Karl said in amazement. 'What about the body?'

'It's in the hole. There was nowhere else to hide it.'

'So what now?' Karl said. The other men looked at Felix expectantly.

'It's too risky for the rest of us. We'd have to get him out of the hole first, and there's no room with him in the hole. If we're seen that would jeopardize the plan for the others already through.' Felix told him, 'We've got to give them time to get away as far as possible. If we get a chance, we can make an escape another time.'

Felix explained in German to the others what had happened. The POWs threw their arms up in despair.

'But if they find Lutz they'll shoot us or hang us,' Karl said worried.

'No they won't,' Felix assured him. 'If he's in the hole they'll think he escaped with the others; and if they do discover the hole, then it'll look like he fell while trying to escape.'

'But the tunnel entrance, it's in our hut.' Karl said concerned. 'They'll know we were in on it if it's discovered.'

'If they have us in for interrogation that's where we have to keep our heads,' Felix insisted to Karl. 'All we have to say is, if we knew about the tunnel and the escape then why are we still here? We'll just say the others never told us about it, they couldn't have trusted us.'

Karl told him, 'You'd better explain it to this lot,' nodding to the POWs. 'Everybody's got to have the same story. I just wish I shared your optimism.'

Felix looked serious, 'I just hope the last man replaced the floor boards in the warehouse.'

Because the concert party had been such a success, and flushed with one too many brandies, Major Henderson decided to cancel the usual evening roll call until the following day. His logic being, once again, there couldn't be a problem as all the POWs had been under the same roof.

*

In the morning, something was wrong. No one could put their finger on it at first. It was too quiet Major Henderson thought. He always had his office window open first thing. He looked at his watch. It was four minutes past seven. The morning roll-call was late.

The Major looked out of his window. Where was Lagerführer Lutz? He should have blown his whistle by now. The guards with their roll call sheets had assembled outside the huts in front of the flagpole. They were getting restless. In hurried conversations, Lutz's name was mentioned several times with shaking heads and shoulder shrugs.

Just then, one of the soldiers who'd been on night watch, produced an air raid whistle and handed it to the Sergeant Major.

With bulging cheeks that pushed against his waxed mustache, he produced a long drawn out shrill which immediately brought forth moans from inside the rows of Nissen huts.

This was the usual morning wakeup call as British guards went from hut to hut banging on the doors shouting, 'Achtung! Achtung! Raus! Raus!'

The POWs, reluctantly as usual with a lot of muffled swearing and cursing in German, got themselves into line outside their huts so they could be counted. With hut No.4 there was an immediate problem. Eight men stood in line instead of forty-three.

The Sergeant Major stepped down from his podium and walked over to them. He barked at Felix, 'Where's the rest of your men?'

Felix looked around and shrugged his shoulders. 'I thought they'd been seconded for some early morning work detail. When we woke up they were all gone,' he told him innocently.

'All gone, what do you mean, all gone?' he barked back. The Sergeant Major waved two guards over and went inside the hut with them. After a couple of minutes he came out with the guards following. The Sergeant Major looked bewildered. He looked at Felix and his men.

A Corporal marched over with a fistful of roll call sheets and stamped his black polished boots to attention. He saluted the Sergeant Major and offered him the sheets with a resounding, 'Huts five to number-nine, all present and correct, Sir.'

The Sergeant Major looked at him and said wryly, 'Thank you, Corporal Oskins. I wish I could say the same.'

At that moment a jeep drove up. A worried Major Henderson climbed out still buttoning his tunic and holding his cap. Before dressing properly he'd driven the half-mile from his stately home barracks in panic. Major A.P. Henderson had a lot of responsibility and a lot to answer for if things went wrong. As far as his military career was concerned, he was at the last chance saloon.

He'd messed up with his battalion at Dunkirk; responsible for a lot of British servicemen killed. Retreated too early and got his men lost in a minefield. At his court-martial, his only saving grace, apart from his mental breakdown, was his father-in-law, General Douglas Fielding. He sat on the bench with two others from high command. No doubt, with more feelings and concern for his daughter than the man standing nervously in front of him, and after nodding and conferring for ten minutes with two other generals, Major Henderson's court-martial was dismissed on the grounds of diminished responsibility.

As far as his military career was concerned he was finished, and he knew it. The only thing they could do with him now, so he could keep his pension, was to get him out of the public eye. Have him sit out the rest of the war at some backwater desk job - looking after POWs.

'What's up, Sergeant Major?'

He stood to attention and saluted. 'Err - a slight problem with today's count, Sir.' He looked at the roll-call sheet for hut number-four. 'We have some prisoners missing, Sir.'

'Missing, what do you mean, missing?'

'There should be a count of forty-three for hut number-four, sir. But there's only eight, Sir.' He nodded to the men in line.

'Where's Lutz?' he said annoyed.

'I don't know, sir. I thought perhaps you might know, Sir?'

'Me, why me, for God's sake?'

The Sergeant Major shifted awkwardly. 'I thought perhaps they might have gone on some early morning work detail you and Lutz arranged, Sir.'

'I arranged nothing, Sergeant Major. If I had,' he said sarcastically, 'you would have known about it.' Major Henderson walked briskly over to Felix and his men. 'Where are the rest of you for this hut, Oberstleutnant?'

Felix shrugged his shoulders again. Karl and the remaining six POWs looked vacant. 'I told the sergeant, Sir, they were gone when we woke up. Just guessed,' Felix said looking hurt and concerned, 'we weren't included in some work detail, Sir.'

The Major came up close and eyeballed Felix. 'Where's Lutz, what have you done with him?'

At that moment all hell broke loose. The air-raid siren started up and three perimeter guards came running up.

Out of breath they stood and saluted and then one of them said quickly, 'Sir, we think there's been an escape. They must have gone over the wire. They've broken into the supply warehouse and used the canteen benches to get across.' The private stopped and cast a glance at the small group in front of hut number-four and then looked at the other groups, then back to the major. 'Do we have any men miss...?' The private tapered off; from the glum faces he knew he was asking the obvious.

'Yes we do have men missing, Private,' the Major shouted. 'Now start looking.'

By lunchtime, with the remaining camp locked in their huts using temporary buckets for latrines, Major A.P. Henderson and his garrison of thirty-two men had launched a search of the camp and the surrounding Grizedale Forest. The Major wanted to keep the escape under wraps as long as possible before notifying the police and his superiors as well as the locals. That's all he needed, the press getting hold of it and driving the village population of Grizedale into a blind panic.

At least if he caught some of them it wouldn't look so bad. He could wipe some of the egg off his face. It could be seen he'd made an effort. But the chances of that as the day wore on, looked pretty slim. With a quick inventory, the supply corporal had calculated they'd stolen ten canteen forms and four rolls of flagpole rope.

Later, alone in his office, Major A.P. Henderson sat with his head in his hands mulling over the escape possibilities. No doubt some of them knew the area and the layout.

Most Luftwaffe pilots had studied detailed maps of England during their training. It didn't take much to work out, with Coniston Water on one side of Grizedale forest and Lake Windermere on the other. With the canteen forms and rope they'd planned to make a raft and get to the coast.

If that turncoat Lutz was with them, he could've had access to a radio transmitter, pinched one from the signals office and taken it with him. Lutz could have planned the whole thing over months. Arranged a submarine to pick them up; then back to Germany. They'd be heroes of the Führer at his expense. He could just see the front pages of the Daily Mirror.

Major Henderson shut his eyes, his mind was working overtime. Then he raised his head with a sudden realisation. Innocent or guilty it didn't matter. He could blame them. Show his seniors he'd caught the ringleaders at least before they could get away. All he had to do was fake it. Plant things on them like a drawn map. Some stolen ID cards. Notes about the escape plan. Where it could be easily found. Under their bunks. In the books they were reading. In the lining of their clothes. Get them under arrest first. He moved to the half open door and barked out, 'Sergeant Major, arrest Felix Kappel and Karl Eder immediately and place them in solitary confinement.'

CHAPTER ELEVEN

By late February 1945, eighteen year old Martin's conception of Nazi ideology was being severely tested. He hadn't heard from his father in months. He knew Pullhausen Concentration Camp nearby had been evacuated along with its prisoners including half from his camp. The remainder at Dachau were being used for factory and quarry fodder.

With most of Germany in ruins and the Americans only fifty miles away from Dachau concentration camp, Martin and his friend Carl were glad to be supporting the garrison. They were both excited. This was their chance to do something meaningful, something positive for the war effort, instead of helping out with the mundane jobs of stores inventory, book-keeping, polishing boots and running errands. They'd seen some of Goebbels propaganda films showing Hitler Youth fighting the advancing Russians using bazookas and grenades; afterwards, the Führer awarding them the Iron Cross.

When Martin and his friend had been promoted, the acting Commandant, Gottfried Weiss, had made it clear, the crematorium and its surrounding area including the railway sidings were still strictly out of bounds. Their duties were to maintain the perimeter fence and the guard towers. Shoot anybody in a striped uniform trying to escape, and keep a look out for the Americans. They were given K98 Mauser rifles. Martin and Carl knew how to handle guns; it was part of their Hitler Youth training.

In groups of four they were placed under an SS guard who showed them the sentry duty routine, including safety rules on how to clean their rifles. Billeted in the SS barracks, eating and drinking rations out of tin cups and plates, felt like being real soldiers. It was as if they were at camp again.

One afternoon, Martin witnessed the true reality of Dachau. He heard shots around the back of the kitchens. When he went to investigate he saw an SS guard with three Hitler youths. One of them was Carl. On the ground was a dead Jewish prisoner; another one wounded was trying to crawl away.

Carl was holding a pistol, a Luger P-08. He was walking around the wounded Jew and pretending to shoot. 'POW! – POW! Where do you want it, Jew-boy?' he shouted. The others were laughing. The guard looking on was having his ten-minute break, leaning against the wall having a smoke.

Martin asked him, 'Why have they been shot?'

The SS guard told him, 'They were caught stealing potato peelings from the dustbins.'

The older Jew, already with a bullet in his shoulder, tried to sit up. The other two youths were mimicking Carl, pointing their fingers at the Jew and shouting, 'POW! - POW!'

The Jew pleaded with them. He told them in broken German, 'Please, we are given permission from Kapo. In bins, we can have. Yes?'

Carl walked around him, making the terrified prisoner strain to turn his head, thinking he may be shot from behind. Carl asked him again, 'Where do you want it, Jew boy?'

Suddenly, they all stopped. Two prisoners appeared carrying sacks, then froze rigid when they saw the situation. They immediately took off their caps and bowed. Carl fired a shot in the air and shouted, 'Vamoose, You Pigs.' They dropped the sacks and fled.

Carl returned his attention to the Jew in front of him. 'I asked you, old man, where you'd like it?'

The Jew just looked at him, not quite understanding. He said something back in Polish, but it was drowned out by the shot as part of his skull was blown off.

While blood pumped furiously from the gaping hole, the others cheered and the guard smiled. He put the cigarette to his mouth and clapped. Carl nudged the lifeless body with his foot. Then, showing-off to the others, he spat on the Jew as they patted him on the back.

*

One morning, Martin was summoned to the signals office. An SS orderly gave him a piece of paper from a wire message. It stated his mother in Berlin was very ill. She had contracted cholera from contaminated drinking water. The doctor had given little hope she would last out the month. Frieda was being looked after at her mother's home by her two sisters as all the Berlin hospitals were full.

Martin hadn't had leave at Christmas to see his mother. This was due to three-quarters of the garrison being called to the front in an effort to stall the allies. He'd been told he was needed more than ever to fill the gap that had been left. However, with this news he went straight to his commanding officer and asked for three days compassionate leave.

With a nod from his commanding officer after a telephone call to the Commandant, Martin was on his way by lunchtime all packed, traveling in the back of a supply truck to Leipzig via Nuremberg. From there it would be on to Berlin. The journey would have been quicker by train but now it was too risky. The allies dominated the skies and a puffing steam engine was an easy target.

With an overnight stop at Leipzig, the journey had taken twelve hours to Berlin. The supply truck he was traveling in made a stop on the outskirts of the city at a food depot. Martin was told none of the trains were running due to power cuts but some of the trams still travelled into the city.

Boarding an overcrowded tram, Martin stood all the way to the station at Berlin Heidelberger Platz. Looking through the window he was transfixed with the devastation. He hadn't been in the city for over a year.

With no more trams running, he decided to walk the remaining few kilometres to the city centre and to his grandmother's house in Leipzigerstrasse. He would have preferred the indoor comfort of a tram as it was a typical cold late February day with a fine drizzle.

As Martin trudged through the rubble with his backpack he could see most buildings were shells without rooves. Many walls were daubed with slogans. *Victory or Siberia. You can damage our homes but not our hearts.* Martin grinned at a sarcastic one. *It took Hitler twelve years to achieve this.*

Making his way onto Potsdamer Strasse, the main route into the city, he saw Hitler Youth and old men of the Volkssturm hauling burnt out lorries' and trams to block roads. Martin reasoned they were making barricades against the Russians. An invasion of the city looked imminent. The overpowering stench of death and putrefaction including damaged sewer pipes gagged at the back of his throat.

Passing what was once Kurfursten Station, Martin could see its complete destruction looked recent. Makeshift ambulances with painted on red crosses and a fire engine parked themselves between mounds of twisted girders as rescuers picked their way over piles of rubble listening for cries of life. Others carried stretchers and canvas bags collecting bodies and body parts. It was then he spotted a smart leather boot at the side of the road. Martin peered in close and then shrunk back. The owner's foot was still inside it.

Further along, he came to a wall with a nailed on board filled with stuck on messages. Martin's curiosity made him read some. *Willy are you OK? Gertrude and her family are dead. It was a direct hit. God keep you safe... Rita, are you and Klaus OK? Max, Otto and Harriet are missing. Leave a message. Girta... Has anyone seen a seven year old boy with blonde curls? Leave a message, Elsa his mother...*

Martin carried on. The people he passed seemed to have vacant faces. No more stopping to chat with friends with a snappy Heil Hitler. Now the tide had turned, he reasoned most people were concerned with trying to stay alive and where to find the next meal.

On the other side of the road he came across a long queue of women filling buckets at a standpipe. Others when their turn came, stripped to the waist to wash themselves. Martin looked away, he felt embarrassed.

As the Potsdamerstrasse passed over a tributary of the River Spree, he slowed to look into the black inky water. The bodies of two women floated slowly under the bridge with their skirts splayed out. Moving on he noted every single wall and building was damaged with bullet and shell holes.

Further along, he could see a crowd gathered around a dead horse in the road. An elderly man with a knife was hacking away at its hind quarters while some women eagerly looked on.

Approaching the station at Potsdamer Platz, Martin stopped dead in his tracks. At a road junction a body hung from a tree. The young boy with the blackened face and protruding tongue had a placard around his neck. It read, *I am a deserter. I went back home to hide.* Others walked past him without taking a second look.

Martin had seen enough of death at Dachau Concentration Camp. He'd finally learned the realisation. To speak out, make some defiant gesture would have been a firing squad or a bullet in the back of the head. He'd learnt to detach himself. In the camp they were the enemy. The Jews, the communists, the Russians, the gypsies and the homosexuals. However, this was different. The boy hanging there was wearing a Hitler Youth uniform. This was one of their own.

It was the heavy drone of aircraft that made him look up. Martin could see the shell bursts of the anti-aircraft guns. Then the air raid siren went off. The wail made people run for cover. Martin stood confused looking for shelter. Someone shouted to him and pointed to a flight of steps leading to a cellar. People were running for it. Martin followed. Just as he began to descend the cellar steps, a bomb blast knocked him down the concrete stairs. As he tumbled he cut his head on the sharp corner of something. Martin ended up on his back.

He slowly raised himself on one elbow. His head was throbbing and he was seeing double. Blood from a cut poured down the side of his face. He fumbled in his pocket for a handkerchief. The others, around fifteen of them, sitting on the crude wooden benches looked away. Martin realised it was his uniform. The SS-Totenkopf armband and the skull and crossbones deaths head on his cap. Because he belonged to a concentration camp SS division they were nervous.

Hauling himself up, he staggered dragging his backpack to the only vacant part of a bench. The bombing had become more intense. Three more explosions rocked the cellar with dust and small bits of plaster falling on everyone. A woman started weeping while two others shivered with fear. The bombs seemed all around them. Martin lowered his head and closed his eyes. As he dabbed his cut, the stench was getting to him. At least in Dachau, the garrison had a shower every three days when the hot water was working. He realised these people hadn't washed in weeks.

To make it worse, a woman excused herself. She crouched down over some newspaper. Clearly having diarrhoea, she finished and cleaned herself up with some rag she had in her handbag, then discarded it through the grill of a grating.

Martin cupped his nose. Although he'd been indoctrinated to believe it was the filthy Jews who smelled, however, this time he had to admit even Jews smelt better.

After what seemed an eternity of continual bombardment with rocks and bricks cascading down the cellar steps, the all clear sounded. The relief on people's faces was evident. They began to smile and mumble to each other.

His cut had congealed a little. Martin tied two of his knotted handkerchiefs around his head and climbed the dusty stairs with the others. As the cold air hit his face he was met by a mound of rubble. Martin climbed over and helped some of the women. It was dark, his watch showed 7:25 pm.

In the street he stood transfixed for a while. Most of what was left of the houses was now levelled. Fires lit up the remaining haunting shells. Shouts and pleadings punctuated the earie silence with the frantic ringing of a fire engine bell somewhere in the distance.

Hoisting his backpack he continued along Potsdamerstrasse stumbling amongst the fresh rubble from the air raid. Martin had cycled this once smart looking street as a boy. Not in his wildest dreams could he have imagined it would look like this.

He passed some members of the Volkssturm. Their armbands stood out against their drab jackets. They were lifting two bodies into a cart which was laden with more bodies. As he approached, the three elderly males backed away. One of them said something and pointed to Martin's uniform. They feared him and removed their caps in respect. Martin nodded to them and then carried on.

Within half an hour he'd reached Leipzigerstrasse where his grandmother lived. Turning the corner he saw her house. Although the windows had been blown in and replaced with boards, some roof tiles were missing and a partly demolished chimney stack, the rest seemed untouched. An oasis amongst a pile of rubble Martin thought. As he wrapped on the door using the old iron knocker, his two aunts appeared, their red eyes and stained mascara said it all. He broke down at the door and wept.

Martin stayed on for his mother's funeral. He managed to wire his camp. Told them his mother had died. With roaming bands of SS looking to shoot deserters, he thought it best. He didn't want them reporting he'd gone AWOL.

A few days later, a service was held amongst a small band of remaining relatives. Martin's father hadn't appeared. He hadn't seen his father for months. For all he knew his father could be dead or captured.

Later the same day he kissed his grandmother and two aunts goodbye, and managed to get a return lift in a supply truck back to the concentration camp.

CHAPTER TWELVE

The guns in the distance had rumbled for the last four days. Now it was distinctly louder. The Americans couldn't be far away.

On the 26th April, there was a buzz around the camp. The commandant along with a few of his SS regular guards had been seconded to the front line. Now in charge was SS Obersturmführer Heinrich Wicker with a skeleton garrison.

The workshops had stopped sometime back. Lack of raw materials and no power had confined prisoners to their lice ridden huts. Morning and evening roll call was the only time they got fresh air or saw daylight. Electricity in the kitchens was off, and food was being cooked over wood-burning stoves. With no running water due to a broken main, a small supply was sourced and brought into the camp by trucks.

The day before at morning roll call, the guards hanged a French Jew. Someone had placed the Croix de Lorraine resistance flag made from a cut-up shirt and some paint in one of the hut windows. Hut 41 wanted to show the advancing liberators they still had spirit. As the SS guards burst through the door they jumped on the first prisoner they could grab to make an example of.

The hanged body, clad with its striped rags and oversized cap, swayed and twisted in the breeze.

It was on the Sunday morning of the 29th they first saw them. Martin with three others was on duty at the main gate. Two Americans had driven up within a hundred yards and then climbed out of their jeep and just stood there. After a while they climbed back in and drove off.

The guards in the tower reported the incident to the new commandant.

A few hours later the Americans were back again in force with two divisions of the US Seventh Army including the 42nd Rainbow Division and the 45th Thunderbird Division.

At the gates, a surrender party met the American Brigadier General Henning Linden and his men. This consisted of SS Obersturmführer Heinrich Wicker, a few SS guards and a Red Cross representative carrying a white flag. The SS Obersturmführe was dressed in full military regalia sporting his medals. When he clicked his heels and raised his arm with a, 'Heil Hitler,' the salute wasn't returned.

During the day, helped with the aid of prisoners that could walk, American soldiers made their way through the camp and uncovered atrocities. Now and again, German guards were singled out and shot or beaten to death at random.

Martin had been on duty up in the watchtower with three SS guards. Some incensed American soldiers fired their rifles up at them and immediately a white flag appeared. The Americans ordered them down. They all had their hands up.

Martin was shaking uncontrollably.

Not far away a group of prisoners had surrounded a German soldier and was beating him to death with his own rifle. It was mayhem. Shots were being fired with screams and shouts.

An American corporal with some other GI's stood in front of Martin and yelled something in broken German. It was all happening in slow motion for Martin, the fear, the sights. The shock of it had made him go deaf in that instant.

The American pointed in the distance to the railway yard and shouted again, his face twisted with rage. Martin saw his mouth moving and the froth of anger, but no sound. Then he opened up with his M1 carbine killing the three SS guards with him. Martin knew he'd be next. He closed his eyes, shaking. He couldn't plead, his jaw was frozen in fear. He clenched his fists, waiting, his whole body shivering.

After what seemed an eternity he opened his eyes. The angry corporal with his group was gone. Martin thought he'd been spared because of his age. Then someone prodded him in the back. An American with his rifle was forcing him to walk with a large captured group of Germans. The soldier was shouting, *'Raus!–Raus! Move you Nazi bastards.'*

The camp inmates that had the strength were lashing out at them. Martin raised his arms to try to protect himself from the blows. He knew this was his last day. He wasn't going to get out alive. Then he saw his friend Carl. Carl, with his face all bloody, badly beaten, was on the ground. Five emaciated prisoners, one with a pistol loaned from an American sergeant standing nearby, surrounded him. The prisoner with the gun was walking around Carl pointing and shouting, 'POW! – POW!' Carl saw Martin and shouted weakly for help. Then the prisoner put the pistol at Carl's head and shot him.

Martin was herded past the scene with the rest of the SS garrison. They eventually came to a long high wall at the rear of the camp that separated the crematorium from the huts.

With around three-hundred captured Germans, he was forced at gunpoint to stand with his face against the wall with his hands up. Martin was jabbed in the back by an American with the muzzle of his M1carbine. With shouts of, 'Hände hoch - hände hoch,' he did as he was told, stretching up and trembling.

It was then he relieved himself, he couldn't help it. The American stepped back as urine splashed down onto Martin's boots. The American laughed and carried on down the line counting the Germans.

The sound of a lorry turned his head. Out the corner of one eye, he saw soldiers climb down carrying a heavy-duty machine gun with its tripod. Martin knew his guns from the books he'd been given at Hitler Youth camp. It was a 0.5 calibre M2HB with 110 round bullet belts. Without bringing attention to himself, he subtly looked behind. The Americans were setting up the machine gun at his rear.

Martin suddenly realised, he was at the end of a firing squad.

This was finally it. There was nowhere to run. He couldn't run. His legs were numb and wet, as if set in cement. His heart began to pound. Martin began to make a pitiful mewling, a pleading sound. Then he heard the sergeant shout behind him, 'Ready - aim - fire!'

Amongst blood curdling screams and cries of pain, soldiers to the left of him began to topple. Martin screwed up his eyes and clenched his fists, ready for death. This time, he shit himself, but it didn't matter. No one was going to find out. The *Rat-a-tat-tat* of bullets, and bodies sliding down a blood-splattered wall, was getting nearer.

Then, silence, apart from the sporadic moaning of some still alive. The smell of oil and cordite from the machine gun as well as human excrement hung in the air.

Martin was in shock, for a second he thought he must be dead. He looked to his left and saw some remaining Germans standing. Martin tentatively turned his head and realised, they'd run out of ammunition. The Americans were changing the bullet belts. His stay of execution would only be a brief one. He thought of making a run for it, but the fear rooted him to the spot. A couple of minutes passed. It was like standing on the gallows wearing a noose, waiting for the trapdoor to open. Once again the sergeant shouted out those fateful words. 'Ready - aim - fire!'

Martin knew this was it; he braced himself ready.

'Nein! - Nein! Halt! Please halt! - Don't kill him.'

He heard the shouts behind. Then muffled talking. It seemed an eternity. He stood there shivering in shock, not knowing, wondering.

'Raus! – Raus! Move!' Suddenly he was yanked by the collar and pulled out of the line. He stumbled over some bodies and got up in a daze. The corporal prodded him with his carbine. 'Get over there.' He gestured to a group of American soldiers who had a female camp inmate with them.

Martin thought the worst. He'd been singled out to be tortured. Given to the mob for their bit of fun like his friend Carl. Perhaps it would've been better to be shot, over and done with. The corporal continued prodding him along until he got to the group.

While the Americans looked on, the shaven headed inmate, wearing a striped smock showing the badge of a political prisoner, hobbled slowly towards him. Whoever it was, looked a walking rag. She was covered in filth and smelt terrible. He wondered if she had a concealed gun or knife - had asked the soldiers for permission to have her little piece of revenge.

Suddenly, she said those words he would never forget, 'Martin, it's me, Magda.'

He looked at her but it didn't register. Then his sister's features began to leach into his brain. 'Magda, dear God! Is it really you? What have they done to you?'

She held out her dirty trembling hand. Martin slowly took it, and dropped to his knees. He held her hand against his face. He started to weep, rocking backwards and forwards, the tears streaming down his face. 'Oh, dear God, what have I done? What have we all done?'

The American soldiers shuffled uncomfortably.

Then the machine gun started up again, but Martin couldn't look.

Afterwards, two soldiers with pistols made their way along the wall taking care of any twitching bodies.

A cigar chewing colonel, his leg up on the front bumper of a jeep with a rifle resting across one knee, joked to his men when he looked at Martin. He shouted to him, 'You are one lucky, Kraut. I'd have you sitting beside me in a crap game, any day.' The other Americans laughed. Then he said to Magda, 'If he's your brother, we'll put him in the compound with the others for classification.'

As Martin was escorted away, he looked over his shoulder at Magda. She raised a thin arm and waved.

CHAPTER THIRTEEN

Greta Binz, while on the run as a war criminal in late 1945, had read in the newspapers about the capture of Dr Joachim Eisele. Somehow he'd escaped the hangman. Diagnosed with schizophrenia and diminished responsibility, he'd been sentenced by a Nuremberg court to ten years for war crimes. Greta had smiled to herself. Joachim was clever, he could fake anything.

From the severe sentences handed out to other SS female guards with her similar rank, Greta knew she could expect no mercy and would probably receive the death penalty. Then again, if Joachim could fake schizophrenia to escape the hangman's noose, so could she.

With this in mind she did her best to keep out of the public eye and got herself a job as a Jewish farm worker just outside the small town called Weiden which was fifty miles east of Nuremberg. With the roads full of refugees and displaced persons and wearing typical grubby peasant clothes, she didn't look out of place.

Greta, using the name Ruth Bleiberg who'd been a dead Jew from her camp, also used Ruth Bleiberg's stolen corresponding identity papers while living in one of the converted barns as she carried out farm labouring work for food and shelter.

A few weeks later, the farmer's daughter recognised Greta's face from a newspaper and, seeing the size of the reward, contacted the authorities. Greta had an idea she'd be shopped. She'd seen the farmer's daughter snooping around her things. Fortunately, the morning the Americans came for her, she'd spotted the military trucks approaching and managed to hide her Jewish identity papers along with some valuables in a disused well at the rear of the barn.

None of that was any good to her now. The allies would see through her disguise straight away; the farmer's daughter did. What she hid might be useful one day, even in years to come. That way she'd have something to fall back on if she was ever free again, or alive come to that.

After being captured by the allies, Greta Binze expected to be hanged as a war criminal. However due to her psychiatric assessment, she faked schizophrenia and the psychiatrists had swallowed it. Slipping into the only character she could think of, Greta went back to her childhood years when she was locked in the confession closet. In the defendant's box at her trial, she collapsed and beat her fists on the wooden partition, pleading with her parents to be let out. Then she began sobbing and shouting passages from the Bible. *The ungodly are cast into a lake of fire and brimstone as an eternal punishment. And the beast was taken, and then with him the—,*

This was until, one of the three judges interrupted and beckoned for the military police to have her escorted from the courtroom.

With her medical reports in front of them, and after conferring with one another, she was sentenced to life imprisonment as a war criminal.

*

Greta Binz knew she was being constantly watched. The Institution for the Criminally Insane in Nuremberg had in 1954 recently installed the latest in security technology, close circuit television.

Although this new technology was financed by the occupying Americans, with a small mention in some of the Nuremberg newspapers; to show how well the Western forces were improving conditions in Germany compared to the Eastern sector; it still meant that Greta couldn't let her guard down.

Her large cell had just been redecorated. She'd wanted powder blue but her psychiatrist had twisted her arm and convinced her, white would look much better. So as usual, she went along with him. Greta looked at her watch, 'Come on, You Two, breakfast is ready!' she shouted. 'Hurry up or you'll be late for school.' She picked up the two child plaster mannequins and positioned them so they were sitting in front of her. She dished out the toast and cereal. 'Manfred, sit up straight and take your elbows off the table.' She pushed his arms and Manfred gave her one of his stares. Greta ignored it. She looked over to her daughter, 'Ursula, stop slurping your milk, and have you done your homework?'

Greta moved the head so Ursula nodded. 'You've got your examinations coming up next year and I want you both doing well and going to a good German School. Not one of those state schools full of kids from foreign labourers and the like.'

They looked at her glassy-eyed, not quite understanding.

'Manfred, I've cleaned your football boots and your kit is washed and ironed, so don't forget to take it with you.'

Manfred wasn't taking a blind bit of notice. He had his eyes focused on *The Adventures of Tintin,* the comic book in front of him.

'Hello, can anybody hear me, it's your mother talking; do I exist?' She looked at them both. 'Obviously not.' Greta heard the sound of the school bus pulling up outside. She yanked them up, 'Come on, you two, off to school now.' She helped them into their school blazers and ushered them to the door.

The big yellow bus was patiently chugging. With her guttural German, Greta could make the sound of an engine quite realistic. Then she kissed them off on the head and they were gone. She shouted, 'Walk, don't run,' and then tossed the mannequins into a cupboard.

Greta started putting the plastic cups and plates into the sink. They were always used when she'd forgot to wash up the china ones; that was her excuse anyway.

Suddenly Greta turned to the telephone and made the noise, 'Tring - tring, tring - tring.' She mumbled, 'I expect it's mother as usual.'

Greta's mother phoned on the dot every morning at 8:40 a.m. 'Hello, Mother, I knew it was you.' Knowing the cameras were on her, Greta had to get into schizophrenia mode and change character for her mother's voice.

'Of course it's me. Who else would it be? Unless it was that boyfriend of yours? Gonna sleep belly to belly with him, was you? Oh! The boys - the boys, she's discovered boys. The boys come next, like dogs sniffing out a bitch on heat. Like sniffing and slobbering. Trying to find out where that smell is. That... s...m...e...l...l... Now you pray, my child, bow your head. Ask forgiveness for your sins, or you'll stay in that closet.'

Greta dropped to her knees still holding the receiver.

Her mother, started chanting down the telephone. 'Oh Lord, help this sinning girl beside me see the sin of her days and ways. Show her that if she had remained sinless, the curse of blood every month would never have come on her.'

More than once as well as phoning, her mother had visited Greta's cell. Always the other side of the door. Waiting, listening, ready to chastise. Greta made it look good in front of the cameras. She would stand by the door and talk loudly to herself as if her mother was really there. Greta whimpered, 'Let me out the closet, Mama. Oh Mama, I've found the way.

Jesus came to me, Mama, while I was in here. I'll be a good girl, Mama.'

'You stay in there, girl, till your father comes home, then you'll get the strap.'

'Please, Mama, I'll be good, open the door.' Greta pressed her ear against the receiver and whined, 'Please, Mama, let me out.'

After some time, Greta got up from her knees and replaced the receiver. The telephone wire ended abruptly before it reached the wall socket. It wasn't connected.

She composed herself and picked up Ursula's stuffed Dalmatian puppy. As she looked through the security bars of her cell, she hugged the cuddly toy affectionately.

*

It was nearly 5:30 p.m. Greta had made tea for Manfred and Ursula. They sat at the table with invisible orange drink and cakes. 'Daddy will be home soon, You Two. Finish your homework and you can stay up and play with him for a while.'

They ignored her and stared transfixed at the opposite wall.

The psychiatrist pressed the buzzer and spoke into the security box to the guard. 'Werner Becker, to see patient, Greta Binz.'

At that moment, a yellow bus with three armed guards pulled up. The back doors opened, and then five prisoners linked by chains, wearing striped prison clothes climbed out. The prisoners stood behind the psychiatrist who were all flanked at rifle point. Another much louder buzzer went off with an amber flashing light and the steel door slid open.

The psychiatrist waved to Gunther the security officer in acknowledgment and then an inner door with steel bars disappeared into the wall. Werner Beck knew the drill; he put his money, keys and watch into the tray and then Gunther got out of his chair and did a brief body search, always apologising as he'd done for the last eight years. After a brief exchange of pleasantries, he left Gunther in peace with his evening newspaper.

The tall good-looking, early forty-something psychiatrist, with chiselled features and dark wavy hair, made his way to the door stating, ALL VISITORS TO CHECK IN. At the desk, he signed the logbook with his name, date and time.

Horst, the guard on duty, handed him his visitors pass and the security key. Werner clipped the pass to his coat.

Visitors had to be escorted at all times, so Horst picked up the desk phone and dialled the extension. 'Herr Fischer, the psychiatrist, Werner Becker is here to see you.'

Although Herr Fischer, a short portly balding late fifties man with a thin trained moustache, was governor of the institution, he still liked to keep a close personal touch with the inmates, as he called them. Herr Fischer and the psychiatrist had known each other for the last eight-years, since Greta Binz had been admitted in 1946 as a 34 year old.

'How is she this evening?' Werner inquired.

'She's waiting for you, Werner, to come home from work as usual,' Herr Fischer replied with a grin.

They walked up a flight of steps to Block A, and along a corridor to the fifth cell with the steel door. Amongst the smells of disinfectant, bleached linen, alcohol and waxed floors, they watched her for a while through the cell door spy hole.

'She's far more responsive since we moved her out of the padded cell,' Herr Fischer highlighted, 'but we still make sure there's no sharp objects anywhere. Only plastic cups and saucers; same goes with knives and forks.'

The psychiatrist nodded in agreement, 'Best to be safe than sorry. What about restraints?'

'We only have to put the jacket on when she's having her medication. Greta always makes a fuss when she's having her electric shock procedure. I'm sure the treatment room reminds her of the abuse she suffered as a child in the closet.'

'Maybe we can do something about that,' the psychiatrist said. He took out his notepad and scribbled. 'I'll work on her when she's having therapy.' He looked up from his pad with an idea, 'Perhaps soothe her with some background music?'

'We could give it a try,' Herr Fischer responded, 'It certainly can't hurt.' Herr Fischer picked up the clipboard hanging on the door. 'This morning the usual phone-call scenario with her mother - she got all upset, thought she was back in the closet.' He thumbed through some pages, 'Oh, she wanted a white coat, on the small side. Said it was for Ursula, you know that mannequin, to take to school for her cooking lessons.

The orderly gave her one from the laundry room, He asked me first. I didn't think there was any harm.'

'At least we've got her schizophrenia down to three characters,' the psychiatrist said, 'including being my wife.' He rolled his eyes while Herr Fischer chuckled. 'Let me in and I'll take a look at her.'

'OK, Werner. I'm off home now so let yourself out with the key and then ring for the orderly. He'll escort you back to reception. I'd like to stay but it's our wedding anniversary and the wife wants me to take her to a show.' They both laughed.

With his security key, the psychiatrist opened the cell door and stepped inside. It was safe. With a camera in every room and twenty-four hour monitoring, he didn't have to worry much. 'Darling, I'm home.'

Greta appeared from the little kitchenette wiping her hands on the striped apron. 'High, Werner. You're early.' She walked over and gave him a peck on the cheek. 'I'm making us a nice fish pie for dinner. Give me twenty-minutes. Can you lay the table and open the wine? I bought a screw top at the store instead of those awkward corks, also tell the kids to wash their hands for dinner.'

'OK, Darling,' Werner Replied. He'd done this charade countless times. It got her in the right mood for therapy which was to follow. However, he'd often wondered who was mad, him or his patient. He laid the table with the plastic cutlery. 'Have, you two, washed your hands for dinner?' Werner said loudly looking at the mannequins so Greta could hear.

Manfred and Ursula ignored him and stared at the wall.

The two child mannequins had come from the fashion department of a high street store, school clothes included. They'd been Werner's idea. He'd attended a lecture at the University of Berlin given by the eminent psychologist, Dr Frans Hoffman. Studies had shown, sociopaths and psychopaths behaved well and responded to role-play therapy in a social bonding family environment. Something that was usually lacking in their childhood and important character forming years. To be sure they were safe, they'd tested similar mannequins. Smashed them up with various household objects, to see if they would splinter and could form a possible weapon, on herself or on others.

Greta glanced at the kitchen wall clock. It was 6:25 p.m. In five minutes as always, the bell would ring announcing the start of the evening shift. This heralded a big exodus on all floors with the new shift taking over, including reception and the surveillance room.

She closed the women's magazine with the fish recipe and slipped it back into the rack with all the others. The Institution allowed Greta magazines. It was one of the perks as a lifer. Her favourite was **Stimme der Frau**. Every now and then, there was a free sample inside.

'Are you sitting ready?' she shouted from the kitchen, 'I'm dishing up.'

'Yes, Darling,' Werner replied.

Greta appeared with a tray and pie dish. She sat it down on the place-matt in the middle of the table. 'Mind, it's very hot,' she said. With her oven gloves, Greta removed the lid. Then, one-by-one, she spooned out portions of invisible fish pie onto the plastic plates.

Werner sniffed his plate, 'Umm, Darling, it smells gorgeous.'

'Now tuck in,' she said. 'Werner, did you pour my wine?'

'Sorry, Darling, I clean forgot.'

He pretended to go and fetch it when she waved him to sit down. 'I'll get it, Werner. Don't let yours get cold.' Greta got up and hesitated; 'Now where did I put that cork screw?' Then her face brightened, 'I know, I left it in the kitchen.'

Behind Werner, with a soundless first time throw, Greta found the target. She'd practised during the security shift changeovers. While she was away, she did the same in the bedroom.

Werner pretended to eat his invisible fish pie and said loudly, 'This tastes really good, umm.'

Suddenly the 6:30 p.m. shift bell went off. He looked at his watch, the time was moving on. *Get this nonsense over as soon as possible, then start her therapy schedule,* he thought. Werner looked at Manfred and Ursula; heads positioned with their glass eyes still staring at the wall. His attention wandered to the radio. Some music was being played.

Then a puzzled expression came over Werner's face. *It was unusual for Greta to forget, even though this was just role-play.* He shouted over the radio music, 'I thought you said the wine bottle was a screw–'

Shluck! Werner heard the sound and felt the instant pain. For a fraction of a second he looked down and saw the end of the free sample from **Stimme der Frau Magazine**. The knitting needle gift, the one fixed to the inside of the back page, which mailroom security had failed to find and remove. It was now sticking through the back of Werner's neck and out his Adams apple. Werner coughed. A large bubble of blood appeared from his left nostril while looking at Greta in disbelief, not quite able to comprehend.

She was grinning at him. 'Want some more pie, Werner? There's plenty left.'

It was all in slow motion. He looked down to the blood spurting in jets onto the white tablecloth, then to Manfred and Ursula sitting quietly staring at the wall. Werner coughed a lot of blood and made a gurgling noise. He tried to get himself up.

Greta kissed him affectionately on the head. 'You feeling OK, Werner?' She was still grinning at him.

He tried to say something to her, but she was becoming blurred and distant.

Werner had probably forgotten all about it. In the state he was in, no one could blame him for not remembering – knitting needles come in two's.

The second one slammed home, right next to the other one. A darts player would have been proud of the grouping. It woke him up for a second. This time he clawed at it like a zombie – jerking and gurgling with eyes rolling around like marbles in a pouch. There was one final spasm, and then he slumped forward onto the table.

'Guess, Werner, you've had a hard day? I'll do the washing up.'

Werner's tongue lay in a puddle of blood on the plastic plate, like a pigs head on display in a butcher's window.

She stroked his forehead thoughtfully with a glazed look in her eyes. The 6:30 p.m. radio news jolted her back to reality; what she should be doing. Greta looked up at the security camera, the one she'd covered with her first time throw using the tea towel. Now there wasn't a lot of time; around three or four minutes at the most while the surveillance room changed shift.

Greta unclipped Werner's pass and took his cell key. She found his wallet and gave a low whistle after quickly counting 2,300 Deutschmarks. Then she rolled him onto the floor. Pulling him by the legs, she dragged him into the bedroom. A trail of blood marked his route. With great effort, she hauled him up onto her bed. Greta covered him over with the sheets and bunched them up to cover his face. She looked pleased at the result. She slipped on the white coat she'd been given from the laundry room and fixed the visitor's pass. In the mirror, she adjusted the hairpiece from Ursula's mannequin. *The bedroom camera, quick,* she thought. Greta stood on a chair and removed a pair of panties off the lens, and then dashed back into the dining area. With a broom she flicked off the tea towel from the other camera.

With Werner's briefcase, she looked the part - a visiting doctor that had forgot to sign in.

Horst and Gunther would be off duty now, and due to cost cutting, replaced by evening contract security.

Greta looked at her two children. 'Goodbye, Manfred, goodbye, Ursula.' She waved to them, but they were too busy staring at the wall. Using the key, she opened the cell door and gave one last look. Then she clicked her heels and said, 'Heil Hitler.'

The guard had just settled in front of the security monitor with his coffee. He nodded at the screen and mumbled to his colleague, 'Looks like Greta on block A is having an early night again.'

CHAPTER FOURTEEN

Greta thought Nuremberg was looking like a city again now it was November 1954. The last time she saw it in 1945 there was devastation and ruins as far as the eye could see.

With the money she had stolen from the psychiatrist during her escape, she travelled by train and bus to the farm on the outskirts of Weiden. After eight years she was hoping the Jewish refugee identity papers under the name of Ruth Bleiberg were still hidden in the disused well.

It was a clear cold night as she made her way to the rear of the barn. The beam from her torch found the well cover. Trying to remove the cover, the farmer's dog started up with some fierce barking. Greta saw the farmhouse lights come on, and then the owner appeared with a shotgun. There was nowhere to hide.

As he approached with the dog close to his heels, the only thing she could do was climb inside and drag the cover over. The smell of stagnant water was overpowering as she tried to hold her breath. A rotting corpse came to mind. She'd smelt many of those back in the camp.

In the darkness, she could hear him swear about foxes and the like. Greta waited until his footsteps retreated and then switched on her torch. She found the loose brick, and there untouched for eight years were the identity papers in the name of Ruth Bleiberg. A wave of relief swept over her. This was her passport for the future. Next to them lay the silver neck charm - The Hünenkreuz Medal of Purity that Joachim had given her. Greta slipped it on. She fondled the silver medallion, running her fingers over the German cross with its diagonal swords. For a few seconds she thought of the past. The good times back at the camp when she was important. When that Jewish filth backed away in fear or bowed their shaven heads in front of her. The distant barking dog cleared her thoughts.

She lifted the well cover and checked. Then she climbed out and made her way back along the country lane to Weiden, and the hotel room she had booked for two weeks. Now Greta was all set for the next part of her plan. This involved her old friend Dr Joachim Eisele and Monika Huber, the laundry women who changed the beds while she was in the prison institution.

*

Greta had recently read in the newspapers of the release of Joachim Eisele. It was a small column with no photograph. She considered, interest on Nazi criminals had decidedly waned over the years to her good fortune. Even the news of her own escape with the murdered psychiatrist had been swiftly relegated from the front pages of newspapers to mere obscure inside pages. The major power talks in East Berlin and a confirmed sighting of Adolf Hitler in South America, held the public interest at the moment.

Greta telephoned the prison where Joachim Eisele had been held. She'd posed as his long lost sister and asked them for his current address. They told her he was staying at a hostel in Langwasser, a district of Nuremberg in the south eastern part of the city. The area was well known for its red light district and very seedy. It had a mixture of refugee camps and temporary housing developments. A halfway house for excons wouldn't have looked out of place.

Using a public phone booth at Langwasser Station, Greta telephoned the hostel number.

She detected the smell of stale urine as her roving blue eyes stopped and took in the very descriptive graffiti daubed on one of the panels. As the dial tone kicked in she waited, and then an old man's voice.

'Hostel.'

'Oh! Can I speak to Doctor Eisele, please?'

'Doctor who?'

'Doctor Eisele, if he's there?'

'No Doctor here, you've got the wrong—'

Greta interrupted, 'Err, Joachim Eisele?'

'Just a minute, I'm the manager here, I'll check my list.'

Silence for a few seconds and then, 'We've got a Joachim here.'

'Yes that's the one. Could I speak to him, it's quite urgent?'

Greta could detect the hesitation.

'Well, you've come through to the reception phone, I don't usually...'

'As I say it is urgent.'

'Ok then, just this once. I'll go and knock on his door.'

She heard footsteps retreat and then a sharp couple of knocks. Silence for a while followed by a muffled exchange. Footsteps approached and then the clatter of a receiver being picked up.

'Hello.'

'Joachim, is that you?'

'Yes, who's this?' Former SS Chief Physician Dr Joachim Eisele, just released from prison after an eight year stretch for his part in war crimes against humanity under the veil of medical research, was now reduced to living in a halfway house with no job or money and clearly in a bad mood. This, together with standing in a freezing hallway in his vest and underpants and being woken up at ten in the morning, didn't help the situation.

'It's Greta. Long-time no see.'

'Greta, who?'

'SS-Oberaufseherin Greta Binz of Pullhausen Concentration Camp, remember?'

Silence for five seconds and then, 'Jesus Christ, Greta, How'd you get this number?'

'There was a small column in one of the Nuremberg newspapers on your release with a brief history of your trial. So I phoned the prison, posing as your long lost sister and they gave me this number.'

'So, what do you want? You're a war criminal on the run. I read what you did to that psychiatrist. I shouldn't even be talking to you.'

'Now - now, come on, Joachim, you could be more friendly.'

'I'm not in a friendly mood. I'm living in a shit hole with no job or money and most of it's your fault.'

'Don't blame me, Joachim. I served eight years as well before escaping. We both did things we regret. Still, most of those Jews deserved it - what with their constant bloody whining. It was just our rotten luck that some of them survived to give evidence.'

'Spare me the history lesson. So, like I said, what do you want?'

'To meet. Got a little business proposition for you.'

'No thanks. Last time I worked with you in that camp, I spent the next eight years sewing mailbags.'

'Come on, Joachim, you want to make some money don't you? Make some quick money as well.'

'What do you mean?'

'Not on the phone, too risky. Meet me in the Rialto café round the corner from you on the parade. Say, at three this afternoon?'

*

The Rialto was empty apart from an elderly couple sharing an apple strudel and talking about their grandchildren. Greta and Joachim had ensconced themselves in a rather tatty cloth seated booth by the wall, well out of earshot. They ordered two teas and a couple of slices of cheesecake.

Considering the eight years spent in prison since 1945, they both looked well, apart from their pasty skin colour which was to be expected.

Forty-two year old Greta Binz was now heavily made up to look like Ruth Bleiberg, the Jewish women in the photograph of the identity papers she was holding. With her long dyed brown hair and a centre parting that framed an older face, her tall stature looked considerably slimmer as a result of the prison years. Joachim on the other hand, tall and lean at forty-eight with his pointed features and thinning blonde hair, had also lost some weight but still retained his thin engaging lopsided smile.

'So that's the plan, Joachim, what do you think?'

He was wary. 'You honestly reckon you can get away with impersonating this Monika Huber, your old laundry lady from the prison you were in?'

'Look, I'm telling you, we look exactly the same. People could mistake us for twins. Even my old psychiatrist said so.' Greta nibbled at her piece of stale cheesecake and then said all serious, 'Listen Joachim, we got friendly when she used to come into my cell every week. I got her confidence. Monika told me things. She seemed a bit of a loner and never married. She used to say her mother was her only friend. Monika lives with her mother in this large house on the outskirts of Nuremberg. Apparently the house is all paid for, but they can just about afford to run it. That's why she works the laundry job.'

Joachim was getting interested. 'And you say this house is worth fifty-thousand deutschmarks?'

'Yes, I checked out the house prices from agents.'

'Are you sure this Monika lives all alone in the house?' Joachim questioned. 'There's no other family?'

'That's what she told me.' Greta swigged her coffee. 'The mother, Eva her name is, was taken ill around four years ago. She became very frail and had to be moved to a local care home. I've staked out this Monika for the last couple of weeks. Followed her by bus from her house to the care home. She visits her mother there five times a week. It's called the Saint Egino Care Home just off Mannertstrase.

Joachim smirked. 'You'd think the silly bitch would sell the house. Down size or something?'

'She can't. The house is in her mother's name. She only gets it when her mother dies.' Greta grinned at him. 'And then we get it when good old Monika dies. That's where you come in.'

'But to kill *both* of them. The mother *and* the daughter?' Joachim said, looking worried. 'You reckon you can impersonate this Monika? Sell the house pretending it's her? Do you think we'll get away with it?' Joachim looked at her with a frown, still unconvinced.

Greta rolled her eyes. 'Joachim, this is our chance to get into the big money.' Then she suddenly grabbed his jacket lapel and dragged him closer. With her nose in his startled face, she said angrily, 'Or do you always want to live in some fucking halfway house for ex-cons looking for part-time work if you can get it?'

Joachim pushed her hand off his jacket and said, 'Listen, Sister, the reason I never danced at the end of a rope at my trial was because I was careful. Before I was caught I'd prepared my defence by falsifying medical research papers using Commandant Dr Karl Borch's name. I made him look as though he was the main perpetrator in the camp's experiments. So if we're to be partners, we have to be just as careful. This has to be thought out cleverly. No hitches. Remember, you're still wanted. To be seen with you would be a risk.'

'Don't worry, Joachim. I've got a new name with identity papers. I've changed my image. I'm a Jew now.' Greta smiled. 'Slightly ironic, don't you think?'

*

This was the fifth time a blue Volkswagen had followed Monika Huber. She'd stepped off the bus from seeing her mother at the home - just a hundred yards away from where she lived in a quiet street in the suburbs of Nuremberg.

It was 7:30 p.m. and dark with a distinct chill in the air. The evening rush hour had gone, and the busy road she had travelled on was now quiet. On her previous journeys, Joachim had used a telephoto lens from the car so they could study her clothes, makeup and hairstyle. Unbeknown to Monika, she had her double sitting next to Joachim in the car, ready to step into her shoes.

Walking with her head down, she had no idea she was being followed. As Monika Huber started to turn off the main road into her street, the Volkswagen slowly pulled up alongside her.

With no traffic or pedestrians around, Joachim seized his chance. The window came down, as Joachim in disguise with a beard, leaned out and asked her for directions. 'Excuse me,' he called in a posh voice, 'I'm looking for Nuremberg Airport. Am I on the correct road?'

Monica Huber looked over and saw the man holding a map. As she approached him, she saw the female passenger and felt reassured.

'Do I keep to this road?' He thrust the map towards her and pointed to a spot with his finger.

She squinted and leaned into the car window to get a better look. It was the last thing she ever did.

It took a split second; the knife concealed behind the map, slashed at her throat.

Monica Huber instantly coughed a large amount of blood. She looked at the man in disbelief, not quite able to comprehend what had happened. It was all surreal. She looked down at the blood spurting in jets onto her coat, and then her eyes wandered to the grinning man, to the map, all bloody. She began to stagger.

Joachim's hand reached out and grabbed her coat lapel as she began to slide down his car door.

She hung there. To an outsider it still looked as if she was having a chat to someone in a car.

Greta climbed out and slowly walked around to the other side. She put her arm around Monika's shoulder and supported her, as if they were chums. It looked like they were both chatting to the driver. Greta held her up until she was sure it was all clear. Then Joachim climbed into the back of the car and unzipped the body bag.

Within forty seconds, Monika Huber lay sealed up on the back seat covered with a blanket. Then they drove the short distance to where she lived and pulled up in the alleyway at the side.

Using the street light, Joachim quickly sponged the blood off the car door and then carried on nonchalantly, whistling as he worked cleaning the windscreen and mirrors.

Plastic sheets had been laid to save the upholstery and minimise possible forensics, but to be sure, the hired Volkswagen was booked in for a valet the next day.

When all was finished, they took the keys from her handbag. Letting themselves in they breathed a sigh of relief. The first part of the plan was over, and now they had a new home.

'I like the kitchen.' Greta walked around, opening and shutting unit cupboards.

Joachim called to her, 'There's a laundry room.'

Greta walked through a small doorway to see a sink, washing machine and tumble dryer.

Joachim had found a large laundry basket. As he held up the lid, he grinned at her. 'Guess where Monika's going to stay?'

Greta sniggered, 'We'll have to charge her rent.'

At that, they collapsed laughing out-loud. Joachim, his face contorted in mirth, wiped tears from his eyes. Greta carefully dabbed her mascara, trying not to smudge as she hitched with laughter. Then they quietened down.

'And guess what I've found?' Greta took his hand and led him out down the hallway. With her free hand, she pushed open a door. 'Look, a double bed.'

Joachim grinned as Greta put her arms around him.

'Now,' she said, 'have those prison years curbed your urge? Or does an old lag still like to shag?'

Joachim kicked the door closed and manoeuvred Greta to the bed.

*

The hole nearly dug, had taken over one and a half hours. The silence as the spades stopped was overwhelming; only peppered by the light night-time traffic and the hum of pylon cables.

It was three in the morning with a very slight drizzle. The late November weather had been kind to grave diggers on this early Sunday. The muddy field just off the autobahn yielded not too many stones, not too soggy either. The added weight of water at the end of a shovel could double the time and be very tiresome.

At nearly two-foot six-inches deep, Joachim's foot rested on the shovel. 'That's enough,' he gestured Greta to stop. She willingly dropped her spade. Their panting began to slow down. Perspiration billowed in the car headlight beams.

Suddenly a rustling sound behind them. They both instantly froze. Ears pricked up like a fox - waiting, then nothing. 'Must have been some animal,' he said to reassure her. 'Calm down. No one can see us here; we're well covered by the ridge of trees.' With his spade, Joachim patted the sides of the hole while Greta rested.

She poured herself a coffee from the thermos. 'Do you want one?' she said offering a cup.

'Something a bit stronger I think.' From his inside pocket, Joachim took out a hipflask; his head went back and then came forward with a wince as the brandy found its way. His arm moved into the car beam to check the time. 'We're doing OK.'

Their boots were heavy and clogged as they laboured their way back to the car.

A scuffle and screeching in the distance turned their heads in alarm.

'What the fuck was that?' Greta yelled. She looked at him in panic.

'Take it easy,' he said quietly, 'probably, an early morning snack for a fox or something.'

They went back to business as they lifted Monika's body from the car boot.

Greta couldn't look at the face. Although, like Joachim, she'd seen and dealt with death many times at the concentration camp, this was different. The dried blood around the gash in the neck, looked as though she was smiling.

He saw she was looking queasy and offered the hip flask.

Greta sat on the edge of the car boot and sipped the brandy, then handed it back to him.

'You OK now?'

She nodded, 'I'm OK. Just come over a bit funny.'

Joachim waited until she was ready to carry on. Then it was back to business. They took a leg each and pulled the body, the arms trailing out behind as if being prepared for the last crucifixion. The smell of damp earth was beginning to clog their senses.

At the edge of the grave, they laid the body down. Then Joachim, with some exertion, rolled it over until it toppled into the pit. Thwump!

Monika Huber lay face up in her last resting place. A sad pitiful figure as her eyes reflected off the headlights, glassy and staring; hair matted to her face from the slight drizzle. *A discarded doll at the bottom of a toy box,* Greta thought.

Joachim glanced at his watch. 'We'll have to get a move on. Don't want to meet up with an early morning labourer doing his farming rounds.'

They were at the car boot again. Their legs buckled under the one-hundred-weight bag of builders lime. Each holding an end, they staggered, stumbled and cursed in unison until they reached the side of the pit. Together they tossed the heavy parcel onto the high piled mud.

The spade came down with a *slash!* - cutting the bag. Joachim scooped out and carefully spread the grey dust over the body, like a loving mother tossing icing sugar on her child's birthday cake. It was beginning to work already.

The fine-drizzle reacting, bubbles forming on the face. The mouth open with its last fixed grin.

Joachim smiled. *It was a lonely place to finish up*, he reflected. *No warmth here, none of the comforts of a quaint village graveyard. No relatives walking over you on some significant date to leave a bunch of flowers, or tidy up from time to time around an elaborate headstone. This was the outer reaches.*

'OK, let's get the mud back in,' he said to her. Joachim glanced at his watch again, 'We'd better hurry now.'

The panting and wheezing quickened. Steam came off their thick winter jackets and floated its way across, caught in the slanted car lights. The first rim of daylight was appearing. Joachim looked up worried; he wiped his sweating forehead leaving a muddy scuff.

Greta's mouth was dry, it tasted of copper. She wished she'd brought more water. The smell of the muddy field had become nauseating. It was filling up her brain.

Eventually he waved for her to stop. The remaining earth that didn't fit was thrown around, as if it never had belonged. Greta busied herself giving the last final pats. Fussing here and there, flattening down mounds, making sure it all blended with the rest of the ground.

The early morning drone of distant traffic was becoming noticeable

The boot lid slammed shut and then it was back behind the wheel. Joachim switched the ignition on. Rurr-rurr - rurr - rurrr rurr. It wasn't going to fire. He tried again, Rurr-rurr - rurr - rurrr - rurrr.

'Fuck,' came the whisper, 'come on, You Mother.' *The damp? The drizzle? The headlights on all this time?* Thoughts swam through his mind.

Joachim waited. Greta by his side closed her eyes and crossed her fingers, both hands. He tried again. The engine turned over a couple of times and then fired up.

'Thank God,' she said and collapsed in a sigh.

'I always had faith in Volkswagens,' he said to her with a grin. His foot padded the accelerator and then brought it down to an idle.

With the windscreen wipers on slow, they reversed along the small track and then out into the country lane. Still with a smile, Joachim's hands gripped the wheel so hard that the whites of his knuckles showed. Now he was on a high, his head was spinning. Joachim was enjoying himself. What with prison, he hadn't had a good time in ages. At least not since his camp days, where he could shoot a Jew if the whim took him. He turned the music up louder.

'Calm down - calm down,' she muttered. Then she looked at him with a smile. Greta started laughing. They both started laughing, finishing with a punch in the air.

For the first time that night, they began to feel hungry. 'Let's find ourselves a breakfast? I could eat a horse.' Joachim looked at her for acknowledgement.

She nodded, 'A good breakfast and a nice hot bath'll do me.'

CHAPTER FIFTEEN

Ursel, the middle-aged day carer came into Eva Huber's room. The door was always left open so they could keep an eye on her, to listen out if she called or wanted help.

'Didn't see you at lunch, Eva. So I've brought you a sandwich and some soup. How are you feeling, My Love?'

'Soup...soup...,' Eva uttered looking vacant.

'Yes, that's right. I've got you some soup. I'll put your bib on. Don't want you staining your nice cardy, do we?'

'Soup...soup...'

'Yes, it's tomato. You like tomato? Yummy-yum.'

The care lady sat with Eva and patiently spoon fed her. She broke up her sandwiches and dipped them in the soup. Eva wasn't wearing her dentures. She never did. They didn't fit any more and were too painful. When they finished, she dabbed Eva's mouth with a tissue and cleaned some small stains off her sleeve.

'Would you like some squash, My Love?'

'Squash...squash...' She always repeated things she liked.

'I'll top you up.' The carer smiled. 'There you are.' She put the half full plastic beaker on the side by her wheelchair.

'I'll be in later with your medication, My Love. So I'll see you then.' The care lady gave her a wave and a smile but there was no response. Then she disappeared out of the door.

Little old Eva Huber, at seventy-nine, had been at the Saint Egino Care Home for the last four years. Prior to this, her daughter Monika had looked after her mother when she became frail, and the symptoms of senile dementia started taking hold. Eva's late husband had a connection with a member of the care home board. They'd been in the army together. Monika had exploited this, managing to get her mother a place in the home while just using her pension for her keep. That meant Monika, to her relief, didn't have to lay out any extra money.

Now with thinning white hair and bandaged legs, Eva was forever locked in a world of her own. However, the staff liked her; she was one of their favourites - easy to handle at washing, feeding and toilet times.

The Saint Egino Care Home was set back on Mannertstrasse near the river Pegnitz in the northern part of Nuremberg. First used for disabled soldiers after the war, it had now become a full-time care facility for the elderly with dementia.

Eva had her own spacious room with large picture windows and a door that led out onto a large inner garden. In the spring and summer, weather permitting, they'd wheel her outside so she could see the blue tits clamour around the bird box.

Unlike Eva, some of the other patients had no visitors; but the staff did lay on socials, and there was always a Sunday service in the dining room with hymns taken by the local Reverend. In addition, a choir visited twice a month, and a lady came to play the piano every Saturday afternoon during tea.

On this late Tuesday afternoon, Eva had been wheeled back from the lounge and was dozing by the window. Her medication previously administered was now taking effect.

The contract cleaner paused in the corridor. He knocked twice on the quarter open door. There was no answer. The cleaner looked sideways, left and right, and then walked softly into Eva's room. The door closed quietly. The hand still gripped the handle in apprehension for a moment. Waiting for a stir, a movement, a sound, but everything was silent apart from the slight snore of Eva.

It was the cleaner's first day at the sanatorium. Wearing the auburn-coloured wig for nearly three hours had made the head itch. In fact, by now, the hands were absolutely dying to give it a good scratch. The panty hose also felt so uncomfortable. It was the first time Joachim had ever worn one.

Never having had a feminine pair of looking legs at the best of times, and shaving them first thing before coming to work, had made him grateful that the blue housecoat he received in the morning, along with the bucket and mop, was long enough to cover everything up.

By 5:15 p.m. it was now dark on this early December afternoon. There was a fine drizzle and the rain sheeted against the windows in blustery gusts.

Joachim paused and listened, and then moved over to the bed and picked up the large green pillow, still looking in the direction of the door. Then, walking slowly and soundlessly towards Eva, he approached her from the rear while his big hands moved into position. The right one came over Eva's head gripping the pillow; the left one moved in to support the back of her neck.

Suddenly someone tried the doorknob and then, voices. Some dialogue exchange. The sounds trailed off. Joachim held his breath while his hands trembled slightly from the surprise. He strained to listen, but only the slight snore of Eva filled the room. Then his feet positioned themselves to get a firm balance. He looked at his watch, waiting for the minute hand to come round, as if counting away the few remaining seconds of life.

Then the pillow slammed into Eva's face.

It didn't take long, about three minutes in all. Joachim's neck muscles bulged, while both hands, pushing and supporting, shook with the pressure. Suddenly they stopped. The grip relaxed. His heart was pounding, breathing in sharp snatches of air, trying not to be heard. Eva's head fell forward to one side. He repositioned it as if she was sleeping and then closed the staring eyes.

Out from the plastic bucket came the new green pillowcase. A quick exchange was rendered, finally patting and fluffing it into shape on the bed.

Joachim moved to the door, quietly opening, peeking out, looking right and left. When all was clear, he left the door partially open as before and then walked off down the corridor to finish some remaining chores.

Halfway home, Joachim's car stopped at a roadside ditch. It was dark, there was nobody around. The window came down and his hand protruded holding a carrier bag full of women's clothes. His arm swung out and the bundle disappeared down the embankment. Then he wound the window up. There was a pause. The window came down again and a pair of women's shoes were ejected with some force and mumbled cursing.

Behind the wheel, Joachim lit a cigarette and inhaled deeply, savouring the first chance to relax that day. Then the car nonchalantly pulled away, windscreen wipers on slow, its tail lights gradually disappearing into the late evening drizzle.

*

'Err...hum...Shall we start?' Herr Birte Köhler looked at his silver-chained fob watch, and then at Greta with a senior partner smile of the correct dim wattage gauged for such an occasion.

As he sat in a high-backed leather chair, he drew authority from his dark blue suit with matching waistcoat. The sophisticated brass and green-shaded desk lamp illuminated the dark walled panelling of the solicitor's office, including the last Will and Testament of Frau Eva Huber.

Eva's death certificate had recorded a stroke. Not a hint of foul play was discovered. Joachim was relieved when nothing was reported in the newspapers. Greta in her disguise as Eva's daughter was summoned by the care home to identify the body. Suffering from a bad head cold, an excuse for a nasal voice, and with a scarf wrapped tightly around her face, including a large bobble hat well pulled down, she signed for most of Eva's possessions.

Now at this moment, sitting across the desk from Herr Köhler in the offices of solicitors, Köhler, Köhler and Stenzel was former SS-Oberaufseherin Greta Bintz of Pullhausen Concentration Camp and doing a very good job of impersonating Monika Huber. She'd made herself up especially to match Monika's passport photo, the document she had to provide as proof of beneficiary. The signature when called for was exact. She'd practised and practised in the time leading up to the reading of the Will.

The solicitor opened up with, 'I would like to bring the reading to order, on this the seventeenth day of January in the year nineteen-fifty-five for the last Will and Testament of Eva Girda Huber in accordance with her wishes.'

Greta sat there listening to Herr Köhler with all his countless solicitor's jargon including - without prejudices, perpetuity periods, power of trustees, power of attorneys - peppered with testimonials and attestations, and of course not forgetting the many herewiths and aforesaids until finally, he eventually came to the nitty-gritty part. 'And the full sum of monies worth fourteen-thousand six-hundred and forty deutschmarks together with the aforementioned property, shall be left to my daughter Monika Ursel Huber.'

Greta was in a daze. She shook her head slowly. Her mouth opened and closed, then opened and closed again like a fish in an aquarium tank. She started to say, 'I can't believe she had that amount of spare cash in...'

After checking out the accounts they could find, without causing too much interest, Greta and Joachim had calculated the old lady had just under five-thousand deutschmarks in savings. They hadn't reckoned on the savings account held by the solicitors in accordance with Frau Eva Huber's wishes. Like many old people she wanted to make sure she had enough money for her funeral. Now it made sense why the old lady had nominated Köhler, Köhler and Stenzel as executors of her Will.

Greta's head was spinning. With the available cash and the sale of the property she was going to be rich beyond her wildest dreams.

Herr Köhler sat back and pinched the sides of his nose where there were a couple of angry red patches from his glasses, and then casually sifted through some documents on his desk. He glanced at his watch and looked a little startled.

As if on cue, Herr Köhler pressed the intercom on his desk. 'Can you tell Herr Schmidt I'm sorry for the delay, I'll be with him as soon as possible.' He then rose and extended his hand to Greta. 'I'm grateful for your time under these difficult circumstances.'

Greta was thinking, *you can't be as grateful as me, Herr Köhler...*

After a formal handshake, he opened the door for her. 'My secretary will see you out. She has prepared a statement for our costs including funeral expenses. As I said before, the fees have already been deducted. If you have any more questions or queries, please feel free to contact us. Many thanks, Miss Huber.'

Further along the corridor in another office, Greta met a smiling secretary. After the exchange of signatures and receipts, the glass front door of the solicitors practice closed behind her.

*

Greta and Joachim knew they had a bit of luck riding on their newfound situation. Monika Huber had few friends. After she had been killed, they sent her resignation letter to the prison institution. Not socialising with work colleagues at her untimely end had helped to minimise contact with people.

Keeping a low profile and with the aid of a wig and Monika Huber's clothes, Greta still managed to falsify her signature at the bank while dipping into the available fourteen-thousand six-hundred and forty deutschmarks the mother had left.

For a while, they temporarily ensconced themselves in the house, however, they knew it was risky to continue living where they were.

On one occasion, an elderly neighbour did approach. Greta's handkerchief immediately covered her face, stifling a cold. After a brief muffled exchange, she quickly excused herself.

Soon after their little scare, they quickly sold the house in early April for just over forty-one thousand deutschmarks. Then within a short time, they were renting a chic double bed apartment in a fashionable mews on Sulzbacherstrasse.

It had taken three weeks for the cheque made out to Monika Huber from the sale of Eva Huber's house, to wing its way from the appointed solicitors through the letterbox onto their doormat.

'Not bad for a couple of days work,' Greta said to Joachim as she let him hold the cheque.

He looked at it. Joachim had never held a cheque for forty-one thousand deutschmarks. He rubbed it across his nose, as if smelling it. All that money on a single piece of paper.

He immediately wanted his fifty-per cent share. It wasn't that he didn't trust Greta. He was just being careful. He knew all that money could change you. The temptation could make you do things you wouldn't ordinarily do. Joachim wanted his own separate bank account. Greta of course agreed and told Joachim to open one up and she would transfer half his share once her account had been credited.

With the sale of the property and savings, it had worked out to 26,320 deutschmarks each, which included deductions for funeral costs, and then rent and deposit for the new flat, and living expenses already laid out.

Greta approached him. 'Well Joachim, they say one good favour deserves another.' She slowly removed her coat and unzipped her skirt. It fell to her ankles as she stepped out. Greta wore his favourite, suspender belt and stockings with no panties. She put her arms around his neck.

Joachim's hands went to her buttocks.

'Now isn't this better than those girlie mag's of yours?' she said, pressing herself against him.

As his fingers probed, he was hardening as expected.

CHAPTER SIXTEEN

Two months later, Joachim was on the phone to his mother. Greta heard him. He was talking rather loudly. He cupped his ear to Greta and mimed she was deaf. 'OK mum, I'll come and see you tomorrow. I said I'll come and see you tomorrow. That's right. I'll get the train to Munich, be with you around lunch time - yes lunch time.' Joachim put the receiver down and rolled his eyes.

'What's up?' she said.

'It's my mum, poor thing. She might have to go into hospital for treatment.'

'Nothing serious I hope.' Greta pretended to looked concerned.

'It's her ulcerated leg. It's got infected.' Joachim looked worried. 'She's seventy-eight and still going strong - bless her. I'm all she's got. Do you know, she was the only one to come and visit when I was in prison?'

She put a hand of sympathy on Joachim's shoulder, 'I'm sure she'll be all right.'

'I said I'd go and see her tomorrow, spend the afternoon with her.'

'Of course you must, Love, she'll like that.' Greta couldn't have given a monkey's toss, but she patted his shoulder because he looked upset.

The following day, while Joachim was away at his mother's, she decided to treat herself and go shopping in Nuremberg. For the first time in her life she was going to push the boat out. The morning would be spent weaving her way through the stores along the fashionable Königstrasse and then finish up with a late lunch at the Lanserhof Hotel. This was something she could only have dreamed of doing a few months ago.

She'd been to Königstrasse a number of times, but only to browse. Now she had money, there was a spring in her step. Shopping meant something, it was purposeful.

By late morning, Greta was clutching four fancy bags labelled Dior and Balenciaga. Flicking through the pages of fashion magazines in prison had sealed her love for these designers. It had also passed the time and the awful monotony.

As she pushed her way through the heavy swing doors of the Lanserhof Hotel, Greta took a deep breath. It looked bloody expensive - and it smelt bloody expensive. She eyed up the suited Maitre d. He was standing on the podium in the exclusive roped off area with the afternoon menu open in front of him like an orchestra conductor with his sheet music.

'Just the one, Madam?'

She nodded as the Maitre d' clicked his fingers.

Passing faces looked up at her as she followed a waiter to a fancy decorated middle table.

Leaving Greta with the menu, he came back after a few minutes and flipped his pad.

It had been a long time since she could peruse a menu without having to worry about the prices. 'I'll have a glass of champagne and the Foie gras, followed by the grilled Dover sole.'

The waiter made his notes, nodded indifferently with a, 'Thank you, Madam,' and then strode off and eventually disappeared through the swing doors.

She sat back and surveyed the diners. It was easy to pick out the business tables from the special occasion tables. Male domination and the lack of smiles gave it away. Although the restaurant was nearly full, the service was surprisingly quick as the waiter set down the fluted glass and the gussied-up Hors d'oeuvre of duck liver. The presentation looked fantastic with the gleaming silverware either side of her plate.

Greta sipped her champagne and nibbled at the Foie gras. She sat back and took it all in. The regal looking silk drapes over the bullion windows. The soft pink Rococo chairs and matching table clothes with the tulip folded serviettes. The fancy cutlery. She knew she deserved this. She'd worked hard to get it. Greta was one-step ahead at the moment and liking it. Prison was just a horrible dream.

Three minutes later, the waiter came back with a polite nod and asked, 'Is everything to your satisfaction, Madam?'

Greta returned the nod with a, 'Yes thank you.'

After the Dover sole, came a crème brulee that was to die for. Greta finished up with a 15-year old cognac in a heavy crystal brandy glass accompanied by coffee and mints. Twenty minutes later she caught the waiter's eye with a writing gesture.

Within a moment he was back carrying a small silver tray with a smart leather wallet and a small plate of complimentary mints. The wallet, emblazoned with the Lanserhof Hotel motif in gold, was discreetly shut with the bill inside. The waiter left while Greta checked the amount.

Sixty-two deutschmarks including service charge! Greta's first reaction was of shock. She checked the bill again. It was all correct – nothing there that shouldn't be. Now how to pay. She checked her purse and then realised, she didn't have enough. Assuming it was going to cost around thirty deutschmarks, she'd only brought fifty with her. The rest had gone on her shopping earlier. Fortunately she had her cheque book. The only thing she could do was write one for the remaining balance.

Leaving aside change for a tip, Greta laid her payment across the wallet and caught the waiter's eye again.

He came over with a smile and then frowned and said, 'I'm sorry, Madam, we only accept cheques from our account customers.'

Greta felt herself going red in the face. This was so awkward and embarrassing. 'I'm sorry, that's all I've got.' She swallowed and looked at him.

Looking stern the waiter said, 'I'll have to have a word with the manager.' He raised his arm to the Maitre d' who immediately came to the table.

After an exchange with the waiter, the Maitre d' picked up the cheque with distain. He asked her, 'Is there any way you can get the remainder of the balance in cash?'

'The cheque will be honoured. I do have my bankbook to prove I have cash in my account.' Greta removed it from her handbag and held it up with an anxious look.

The Maitre d' waved it away. 'I'm sorry, Madam, the Lanserhof Hotel has a policy to accept cheques only from customers who have an account with us.' Looking at the cheque again he said, 'We do have a Bank Deutscher Länder across the, road if it helps?' He glanced at his watch. 'They should still be open, Madam.'

Greta lightened. 'Yes... yes of course. I'll go straight away.' She rose and gathered her bags.

The Maitre d' checked her. 'That's okay, Madam. You can leave your bags with us. We'll make sure they're safe.'

Greta hovered and then realised it was their insurance that she would return. 'Yes... of course. I won't be long.'

Getting a few looks from the commotion as she hurried past the tables, Greta made her way out through the front door onto the street. Immediately the cold air hit her face and the warm cosy feeling from the brandy was gone.

The Maitre d' was correct. Across the road was a Bank Deutscher Länder. She checked she had her passport - Greta always carried Monica Huber's passport with her for security just in case she was stopped. Although disguised as Monika, she still had to be careful. The police were still looking for Greta Binze the Nazi war criminal and now an escaped murderer to boot.

Greta pushed her way through the heavy swing door and found a table to rest on. She fumbled with her cheque book and wrote one out for cash. Then she queued at the counter until her turn came. The young female bank clerk smiled as Greta asked, 'I'd like forty deutschmarks please?' At the same time she pushed her bankbook with the cheque forwards.

The clerk surveyed the items and noted the bank address. 'As this is not your branch, do you have any identification?' She smiled again expectantly.

Greta slid her passport towards her.

The clerk flicked the pages and studied the photograph and then handed the passport back. She counted out three notes and the rest in coins and slipped them under the grill. After hitting a few keys on her ledger machine, she tore off the printed slip and filled in the bankbook with the new balance. Then her red ink stamp thudded down finalising the transaction.

Greta thanked her and was about to leave when she hesitated. Something was wrong. The new balance in her bankbook. It stated twenty-deutschmarks. Above Greta's withdrawal, the clerk had made the book up showing another withdrawal of 26,260 deutschmarks. 'Excuse me, there must be some mistake.' Greta showed her the bankbook. 'This withdrawal.' She pointed to it with her finger. 'I never made that.'

The clerk looked puzzled and then checked the ledger slip. 'It's correct madam. Our records show the withdrawal was made yesterday at your branch, the address on the book.'

'But that's impossible, there's some mistake.' Greta said anxiously. 'I've had my bankbook with me all the time.'

The clerk tapped the account number into her ledger machine and the mechanical keys noisily thumped out a printed form. The clerk tore it off and handed it to Greta. 'It shows madam your account is a joint one with two signatories. A Joachim Eisele?'

Greta stared at the printout. 'No... It's a mistake. I'm the only account holder.'

Looking at the printout the clerk added, 'We have two signatures on record, Madam, with an agreement signed by yourself a week ago to have a Dr Joachim Eisele as a joint account holder.'

Greta raised her voice, *'No – no, I never allowed him to be an account holder.'*

The deputy manager at his desk behind the clerk looked up. He immediately rose and came over with an air of authority in his navy-blue pinstriped suite.

After a brief exchange with the clerk he took over. 'I suggest, Madam, you take this up with your branch manager. We have other customers to attend to.'

'But there must be some mistake, I never allowed—'

'He interrupted. 'Thank you, Madam. And good day.'

Greta looked at her bankbook in disbelief. She looked up and was about to say something, but the deputy was already busy in conversation with another one of his staff.

She hesitated, her mind was swimming. There had to be a mistake. Greta couldn't concentrate. She had to get back to the Lanserhof Hotel and the pay her bill. They had her shopping as insurance.

*

Fifteen minutes later, clutching her bags, Greta was back on the street heading for the post office. They usually had a payphone there. When she got inside the booth she pulled her diary and thumbed the address list until she came to Joachim's mother. He had asked her to make a note in case she needed to reach him in Munich as he would probably stay overnight with his mother. Greta fed the slot with two ten-Pfennigs and then dialled the number.

The familiar whine of a misdialled or incorrect connection permeated her ear. 'Shit.' Greta redialled and got the same tone. The hairs on the back of her neck were beginning to stand up. She was getting a bad feeling about this.

Greta dialled the operator who also tried the number for her. However, the same non-connection bland tone was all that could be heard.

Panic began to seep into Greta's brain. She took the tram home to Sulzbacher Strasse. Frantically fumbling with the key to let herself into the apartment, she immediately picked up the hall phone and dialled the number again. She pressed the receiver bar, but the dull clicks only made the non-connection tone worse. Then she raced to his bedroom. They'd used separate bedrooms because he'd snored and after a shag it was nice to get back to your own space and independence. Greta flung open Joachim's wardrobe. It was completely empty. For a second, she rationalised – *why would you take all your clothes just for an overnight stay at your mother's?*

Joachim's wardrobe was the final straw. The terrible truth had finally dawned. He'd turned her over. *'You cheating fucking bastard,'* she screamed and screamed, thumping the side of the wardrobe with her fist. *'I'll get you - you cock-sucking mother-fucker, if it's the last thing I do - if it's the last thing I fucking do—'* Greta continued thumping the wardrobe with tears rolling down her cheek. Suddenly she stopped. Another feeling of panic swept over. 'The biscuit tin, for Jesus Christ!' Greta raced into the kitchen and reached up to the top of the dresser. Clutching it in her hand she knew before she wrenched the lid.

The spare petty cash tin they shared. It was like staring into an empty chasm. She shrieked, *'You Mother! My three-thousand deutschmarks!'* The lid clattered to the tiled floor.

Greta sat on a kitchen chair shaking with rage. She hit the table with her fist. Then she cooled down. She had to clear her head. Think straight, what to do.

Obviously, can't go to the police or the bank. They'd want to see proof of identity. Ask questions. How she got the lump sum in the first place? Who was her partner? Then there was the social security. Why was she still receiving a single persons allowance with all that money in the bank? So as not to arouse any suspicion, she was still registered and drawing benefit in Monika Huber's name. In fact, she'd forgotten to go and collect the last two weeks cheques.

Greta put her head in her hands. How was she going to trace that slimy bastard and get the money back? In the meantime, how was she going to pay the rent and bills even food.

Greta lifted her head with realisation. Her last bank withdrawal. It was going to be for a surprise holiday for both of them. She'd hidden 300 deutschmarks in the pocket of one of her leather jackets.

Inside her wardrobe with a sigh of relief she withdrew the envelope. He hadn't bothered to look there, the bastard. She calculated, with the three-hundred and Monika Huber's benefit back pay she could get by for now. However, it wasn't going to last long and the sooner she started looking for that *son of a bitch* the better.

Greta made her way back into Joachim's bedroom. There had to be something that could give a clue to where he'd gone. Greta knew he was clever. To get away with what he'd committed as a camp doctor for only an eight year sentence, when other SS had been executed for less. Joachim had told her how he'd falsified the names on anthropological and euthogenics documents so as to evade some of the blame before he'd been caught by the Allies.

'Old, Mr clever Dick. What have you forgotten?' she said to herself as her eyes roamed his room. Then she decided; the only thing was to search the place.

He'd already emptied his wardrobe and drawers. She quickly lifted the mattress and then got down on her hands and knees. From under the bed, Greta pulled out his collection of car magazines and some porn. She flicked through one pile and then another other pile. Greta suddenly stopped. A Touropa holiday brochure revealed itself.

Greta sat on the bed and slowly thumbed the pages. Halfway in, her hand froze. A circle had been drawn around The Clipper Holiday Apartments in Rimini on the Adriatic Coast of Italy. 'Yes, you Bastard,' she muttered under her breath.

Greta looked at her watch. It was gone six o'clock. Too late to ring now.

The next morning, Greta picked up the telephone and dialled the number on the holiday brochure.

'Touropa holidays.'

'Good morning, I'm phoning on behalf of Herr Joachim Eisele's booking. I'm his secretary.' Greta knew what was coming next.

There was a pause then, the young woman's voice said, 'Do you have a booking reference number?'

'I'm sorry, it's just that...he's my boss and he did ask me to ask you if there was a possibility he could extend his accommodation stay. He asked me yesterday, but I forgot all about it. I'm out the office for two days so I haven't got access to the reference number. He's booked to stay at the Clipper

Holiday Apartments in Rimini on the Adriatic Coast of Italy. It's in your Touropa holiday brochure.'

'I can't really check anything without a reference number you see because–'

Greta interrupted, 'I would be grateful, stops me getting chewed out because I forgot.'

'Well I...OK...what's his name again?' she said with an overworked sigh.

'Herr Joachim Eisele's,' Greta replied.

'How do you spell that?'

Greta said, 'E-I-S-E-L-E.' She heard the receiver put down with an angry clunk.

The assistant went to the filing cabinet and searched the folders and then came back. 'He's booked for two months up until the end of July, and if he wants to, he can extend up to the end of August?'

'OK, many thanks,' Greta replied. 'I'll let him know and get back to you if he's interested.'

'Have the booking reference number with you next time, it makes life easier,' she said with a hint of sarcasm.

Greta put the phone down and mimicked, 'Have the booking reference number with you, it makes life easier – why don't you shove a plum up your arse, Bitch.'

Greta reasoned as she mumbled, 'At least the silly cow confirmed where he was staying and for how long.'

*

It could have proved difficult, but thankfully Monika Huber had applied for a five year passport three years ago. Greta remembered being told in the institution. Monika was going to take her sick mother to Rome on a pilgrimage to see the Vatican and hopefully the Pope. She thought at the time it was an expensive holiday for a cleaner, until Monika had mentioned her mother would be paying.

Greta wondered how Joachim could have got hold of a passport in such a short time using his real name, especially with his past form. Probably had someone make him up a false one. He had the money now to contact the best people for it. However, Joachim was clever. Clever and dangerous; she had to remember.

Four days later, after sorting her remaining finances to buy some holiday clothes and sourcing the cheapest accommodation and flight on offer, she finally arrived at Rimini airport on a British Vickers Viscount. That was also care of Touropa holidays.

The customs officer never even glanced at her passport at Rimini airport.

As she stepped outside the terminal, the midday heat hit her. It had to be around seventy-five degrees and not a cloud in sight. The travel agent had told her to expect this, and to be hotter for the first week of July.

Greta made her way to the taxi rank, and showed the first waiting cabdriver the address of the Hotel Garitonni on Via Ennio Coletti. She'd got a last minute cancellation for a two week bed and breakfast booking on the other side of town from where Joachim was staying.

The travel agent had shown her the town map, and her first choice had been the Clipper Holiday Apartments where Joachim was staying. However, she'd told the young lady in the smart Touropa Holidays uniform, they were rather expensive and picked the hotel she was travelling to now.

The lunchtime taxi drive to her hotel took thirty-five minutes. When the driver asked for four-thousand lire, Greta's face dropped. She had to confirm with the cabby she'd only booked for a one-way trip, just in case he was assuming she was going to use him for the return journey and wanted money up-front. The over-weight unshaven driver with his hand held out, shook his head and confirmed in broken English, 'Solo trip only.'

When she handed him the coins and not a lire more, he mumbled something in Italian, swung the taxi around with tyres screeching, giving Greta the full wrath of his disappointment, and sped-off.

The small grey walled reception office of the Hotel Garitonni where she checked in, smelt of stale cigarettes and garlic sausage. Behind the counter, the young good-looking Italian in the white short-sleeve shirt and tie, flashed a smile as he asked for Greta's passport.

She'd forgotten about that.

He assured her in his perfect English that it was a legal requirement to hold passports for up to three days. Greta didn't make a fuss, she just handed it over with a return smile. But it meant she had to be careful.

She couldn't move on Joachim until she had her passport returned in case of a quick get-away. If she had to cut-short her stay, she'd need to make her exit as inconspicuous as possible. Make an excuse at reception that her mother had suddenly been taken ill or something similar; good enough to draw a bit of sympathy without drawing attention.

Clutching her key and a holiday pack containing a map of the area, excursions and boat trips, she took the lift to the first floor. She found the door to number seven and let herself in.

There was no point in doing anything until she'd done herself a make-over.

After Greta unpacked, it took just over two hours with the scissors and the blonde hair dye. The short bob with the side parting suited her she considered in the mirror. Then came a good even spread of quick tan sun lotion followed by a pair of large white over-the-top sunglasses and a sombrero to finish off. 'Your own mother wouldn't recognise you,' she said to her reflection, 'let alone that robbing bastard.' She also knew she had to change back again to a near resemblance of Monika Huber to satisfy the passport for her return trip.

It was around six, early evening, still with plenty of light outside. A good time to try out her new look she thought, and get familiar with the surroundings.

The apartments where Joachim was staying were situated on Viali Ortigara opposite the main beach. Outside her hotel she hailed a taxi and showed the driver the address. With the sombrero well pulled down, she climbed into the cab and took the twenty minute ride to the Clipper Holiday Apartments.

As instructed, the taxi pulled up on the opposite side of the road. Greta could see an upmarket apartment block with large balconies. Joachim certainly wasn't stinting himself. He didn't have to, with her money as well tucked away in his little bank account.

Across the little square was the Alcatraz Bar. Perfect for nursing a beer or a coffee while she staked him out.

She was about to move on when a swish looking black Mercedes-Benz pulled into one of the parking bays stretched out along the busy road. And there he was, getting out of it with a young woman. Greta ducked down, a natural reaction, then thought *that was stupid*, bringing attention to herself. She didn't have to, he would never recognize her. The car had hire plates. Joachim was probably giving himself a little treat of things to come.

He shut the car door and paused. He looked around nervously, taking stock. He was in smart casual wear. They were both carrying shopping bags labelled Giorgini. *A fashion shopping spree on my money, especially now you've got double bubble*, Greta thought.

The pretty, tanned Scandinavian girl with long fair hair, came around from the side of the car and kissed Joachim. It was definitely a thank-you kiss. He embraced her, and then arm in arm they sauntered off to the entrance of his apartments... *no doubt for a good old, thank-you shag*, Greta thought.

*

Three days later after her passport was returned, Greta set off early morning by cab just as the Alcatraz opened. She settled herself by the window. Three coffees and two croissants later, Joachim appeared, without the girl, just after 11:30 a.m. He was dressed for the beach in his T-shirt, shorts and sandals, carrying a rolled beach towel under his arm.

Greta paid her coffee bill, and at the same time watched Joachim cross the road and browse at some magazines and newspapers racks displayed on the pavement. After he purchased a German newspaper and a tube of Spanish wine gums, he headed for the beach, with Greta at some distance behind.

At one point to her horror, with only thirty-feet between them, Joachim stopped and turned around. He looked at her briefly, then shielding his eyes he scanned past her, as if checking for anybody following. Satisfying himself all was clear, he crossed the road and made his way along the front until he stepped onto the sand and took a seat at the thatched Hippo Bar.

A Scandinavian waitress in her mid-twenties came out, and manoeuvred her way through the half dozen or so people sitting at tables, to serve Joachim. She glanced at the serving counter to make sure, and then stooped and kissed Joachim passionately while he fondled her arse. It was the same girl he was with three days earlier. Greta thought to herself. *You certainly don't waste any time, Joachim, but then who could resist you with all that money?*

It was a clear sky again and up to around the middle-seventies in temperature. Greta had taken a seat under a brolly at one of the promenade cafes a short distance away.

By 2:0 p.m., it had reached nearly eighty-degrees and Greta was on her second beer. The beach had thinned out a little with people going for lunch.

The thatched Hippo bar lay quiet while the fat middle-aged owner slid off for a break, leaving the cook in charge at the counter reading a newspaper. The Scandinavian waitress approached him shyly and had words, and because it was quiet, the cook gestured saying, 'Okay, just twenty-five minutes that's all.'

That was enough for Joachim and his pretty little Swedish number. Within minutes they were frolicking on one of the sun loungers.

Ready to make use of her lunch break, she had already discarded her top and was spread-eagled on Joachim, kissing him and giggling. After ten minutes, it was time for a dip. They both eased themselves up from the sun lounger.

Greta watched while they put all their valuables underneath the lounger and covered them with a towel. Then hand in hand, still laughing and giggling, they walked down to the water's edge.

This is it, Greta thought. *It was now or never.*

While they were chest deep in the sea with her legs wrapped around his waist, Greta made her move. With the sombrero pulled down, she stopped on the beach near the lounger to shake sand from her sandals. She ducked down, and her fingers feverishly searched underneath the towel until she felt a bundle of keys. Her spirits lifted when she saw the Clipper apartment tag with the door number 8 etched-on.

She knew she didn't have a lot of time, perhaps another fifteen-minutes with them in the sea at the most. Then back to the sun-lounger, where they may or may not check under the towel. If they flopped down into a lovers smooch straight-away, all randy and dripping, even better. Maybe half-hour before they discovered what was missing. Perhaps another ten- minutes searching in the sand. At the outside, she knew forty-five minutes was her max.

A uniformed man behind an expensive marble reception counter raised his eyes as Greta paused. 'I'm here to see Mr Joachim Eisele,' she said. 'I'm his sister.'

The middle-aged man scanned his register. 'That would be number eight on the second floor, Madam. He looked behind at the racks and then said, 'There's no key so I believe he's in.'

She thanked him and moved to the lift.

'Umm, just a moment, Madam.' He leant across the counter to her. 'Visitors must sign the register. It's our fire policy.'

Greta came back and took the pen and signed herself Eva Eisele. She beamed. 'Just want to surprise him. He doesn't know I'm here.'

At that moment the lift pinged and Greta moved quickly towards it.

On the second floor she made her way down the smart hallway until the door of number eight faced her. Greta fiddled with the key and the lock snapped open. She eased herself in and instantly smelt the remains of Joachim's morning fry-up.

Now, where to start?

She needed cash, a few hundred deutschmarks would be handy right now, but knowing Joachim, he wasn't going to leave a lot lying around.

The first door Greta opened was the bedroom. On her hands and knees she checked the first twin bed and then the mattress, but no luck. Then she noticed, over in the far corner the small chest of drawers partly covered by a large linen basket full of washing. On pulling the bottom drawer, her face lit up when she saw his pistol. Something made her look down to one side. She saw a pair of sandals she hadn't noticed before - and they had feet inside them.

Suddenly there was a sharp pain in her head with coloured dots, and then came blackness.

CHAPTER SEVENTEEN

Joachim put the base of the lampshade down and felt through her pockets. He searched through her holiday shoulder bag and placed her purse, diary, his set of missing keys and a map of the area onto the bed. The purse revealed another set of keys, a few lire notes and some small change. Joachim went to his balcony and came back with the washing line. He tied her hands and feet tight behind her back so they were pulling against one another, then he stuffed a handkerchief inside her mouth.

Greta came round laid out on his rug. The blurring in her vision slowly began to sharpen until she could focus on Joachim. He'd made himself comfortable with a chair, sitting there looking down at her, while holding a large steel carving knife. The back of her head was sending slow waves of pain to the front of her head. With each wave, it felt someone was squeezing her head an extra turn in a cider press.

He put the knife to her eye, just in case she screamed, and pulled the handkerchief from her mouth.

'You awake? That's good,' Joachim said. 'How did you find me?'

'I found the holiday magazine,' she quickly said, nervously looking at the blade out of the corner of her eye.

'Who knows you're here?'

'No one, I swear.' Her answer came without hesitation.

Thwack! He hit her across the face so fast she never saw it coming. Her head snapped to one side and white dots exploded in front of her eyes, and she tasted blood as her lower lip burst, the inner lining had been cut by her teeth.

He looked crazy.

'I spotted you a few days ago and earlier on the beach, Greta. Even through the make-over and *that* Spanish hat.' He smiled as he picked it up and flicked it across the room. 'Figured it was only a matter of time for you to make your move, and here we are.'

Greta was shaking; she blinked as she looked at him and tasted blood.

Joachim leaned over and bellowed into her face, *'Who knows your hear?'*

'No one–no one, please, honestly.'

Joachim looked at Greta's frightened face. The bitch knew too much, could incriminate him. Because she'd been shafted for her half share, she could grass him up to the police with an anonymous phone call. Tell them he'd killed Monika and her mother. She could disappear and revert back to that Jew

Ruth Bleiberg identity while he'd be in the frame holding all that money. She could drag him down. He had to get rid of her, and quick.

'Please, nobody else knows I'm here, please believe me?' she blurted out with her lower lip swelling up. Greta felt blood spilling down her chin in a small stream.

Joachim put the tip of the carving knife onto her lower eyelid again. It dimpled the sensitive area and pushed up her eyeball in its socket. 'Tell me who else knows you're here, and don't hesitate. If you hesitate, I'll know you're lying and I'll flip your eye right out of its socket onto the floor. I can do it. Believe me?' He leaned in, pushing the knife painfully deep until a tear of blood appeared on her lower lid where he'd nicked the skin. 'So who else knows?'

'Please God, nobody. But, there's a letter.' Greta gulped. He still had the knife to her eye. 'There...there's a letter, left in my hotel safe. As insurance, in case something like this should happen.'

Joachim pressed the knife again. 'What's in the letter?'

'There's a copy in my diary.'

He looked at her warily with his cold blue eyes, then reached over and picked up the large size diary from the bed. Joachim flicked through the pages and then stopped at the neatly folded letter. With it was a passport photograph of himself. *She must have found the spare copies. Shit!*

As he read the letter, Greta watched his face. Joachim's expression changed to a look of deep concern, as the descriptive story of the murders he had committed and the inheritance deception with his current holiday address, unfolded, clearly typed before his eyes.

He pressed the knife again. 'Where's the safe? What's the hotel?'

'It's on the resort map, the Hotel Garitonni on Via Ennio Coletti,' she cried out. *'Please don't hurt me, it's the truth.'*

'We'll see about that.' Joachim picked up the map and found the Via Ennio Coletti with his finger. It was across the other side of town. He'd have to take the car. 'Where's the safe, in your room?'

'No, it's in a little lobby off reception. The key's on the ring.'

Joachim picked up her bunch of keys; it was notably the smallest one, flat and crudely cut. 'What's the number of the safe?' He threatened with the knife. 'And don't lie, you lie to me and you'll know pain, believe me.'

'Number seven, number seven, the same as my room number,' Greta gulped, *'I swear.'* Her frightened eyes still followed the knife he was holding. 'The letter with the photo is addressed to the police. Also I've got six-hundred deutschmarks in the safe. It's yours if you want it. Just let me go, I promise you'll never see me again.'

Joachim smiled, 'I've got enough money to keep me going, Greta, thanks.'

'Look, you need me to open the safe. There's only around thirty safe boxes. You'd be spotted straight away going to my safe box. They know me by sight at reception. I'm on nodding terms with them. I'd have to go with you.' Greta was stalling for time. 'Another thing, if I don't return the key within seven days they automatically open it with their spare.'

Joachim took the pistol from the bottom drawer; the last thing Greta had smiled at before he'd knocked her out. With the oil rag, he slowly buffed-up the barrel of the Walther PP and thought, he'd have to try on his own first. Get past reception without being seen. Too risky to take her with him, in case she made a bolt for it or tried to attract attention. Don't want to be spotted. If it does look like hassle, then he'd have to take a chance and go to the safe with her. Conceal the gun, hold it to her back, pretend he's her boyfriend.

He hit her round the face again with the back of his hand, *'You fucking bitch, for giving me all this trouble.'* She flinched at the sting and fresh blood oozed from her lip.

Before she could say anymore, he stuffed the handkerchief back in her mouth. With the knife, he cut off a length of washing line and gagged her with it. As it cut into her mouth to keep the handkerchief in place, he tied the knot at the back of her neck. It was then he noticed her silver chain. Joachim pulled off the medallion charm. He looked at the silver German cross and smiled in thought for a second. 'You know, Greta. I can remember when I gave you this. The Hünenkreuz Medal of Purity.' Joachim lost himself in thought. 'I took it from some halfwit girl on her way to prison. She'd reported to the Red Cross what she'd seen at the Lodz ghetto. The stupid Bitch.' He dangled the purity medallion in her face. 'Can you believe it? She even had the same blood group as you engraved on it.' Joachim rubbed his thumb fondly over the medal. 'So in love, weren't we?' Then his face changed to serious. 'However, all relationships have a clock attached to them. They all end in time and unfortunately for you, ours is now.'

Against Greta's protests, while she kicked and moaned through her gag, Joachim pulled off her other remaining jewellery consisting of two rings, a pair of earrings and two bracelets.

'The least identification the better where you're going,' he said to himself as he dragged her with great effort to the large wardrobe, and then bundled her inside.

As the wardrobe door slammed shut, she realised this could be her coffin.

Greta heard the front door slam and the Mercedes start up. She knew she had around forty minutes. Around twenty-minutes for him to drive to her hotel.

Greta began to flex the muscles of her thighs and calves. She strained and threw her head back baring her teeth as fresh blood from her swollen lip leaked out the sides of the handkerchief down her chin. As her bound feet kicked against the wardrobe door, the cords on her neck stood out. But it was no good, she was too scrunched up to get any leverage. Hot pain bloomed suddenly in her right calf, tightening it.

She had to be careful. She rested for a while.

Greta managed to turn her weight to one side, and then she kicked backwards at the door. But that was no good either, not enough room to give it a full good thump. The wardrobe rocked away and then steadied itself. After three more futile attempts, she knew the door was a non-runner.

She lay back breathing hard. Her wrists were sore. Every time she kicked, the washing line pulled. It was when Greta rolled slightly; she noticed the tiny slither of light at the bottom in front of her. Thumping away she'd hit her head against the rear panel. Then she realised. *Of course, you prick,* she remembered. Cheap wardrobes had ply or hardboard backings. They faced the wall so it didn't matter.

'Got to get it away from the wall,' she muffled. Greta threw herself from side to side, rocking it and hoping, with enough noise someone might notice and call the landlord, even the police. She positioned herself and gave another hefty kick at the panel, then winced as her wrists jerked at the same time. *'Fuck you!-You mother,'* she mumbled again. It rocked heavily to the point of nearly toppling over.

A nightmare thought flashed. *If it falls on its back, I'm well and truly done!* She took a breather and tried again. Greta screamed with exertion, the rope cutting into her mouth as she flung herself from side to side rocking the wardrobe until suddenly, she lost all sense of orientation as it toppled over and smashed onto the marble floor tiles. The noise was deafening.

Someone must have heard. She breathed in deep snatches through her gag, listening out, waiting for a neighbour to thump on the door, call out!

Thank God, she'd landed right. She could see a strip of daylight above her from a damaged corner. With difficulty, Greta wriggled and turned herself onto her stomach, then kicked back, yelling with the pain as her sore wrists jerked. The thin ply backing held on by panel pins, burst out with each thump until both her feet were poking through. She wriggled herself around with the extra given space, and then kicked out the other end. Finally, she flipped herself over.

Greta lay there staring at the bedroom ceiling. She was still in her wardrobe but at least with no lid.

If he came back now, it would be her coffin. She imagined his last act as an undertaker, making sure she was at peace before re-fixing the lid. Then manoeuvring the makeshift casket on a two-wheel suitcase trolley down the outside fire escape. Into the boot of his Mercedes. Tying the boot lid down around the end sticking out. A story at hand if he was approached. Hoping to sell it at the local flea market tomorrow.

Then her final trip to somewhere untraceable. A secluded cliff top. Some quiet bridge or jetty. Probably smashing the ply so it would fill up quickly. She doubted if Joachim would cross himself as he watched her burial at sea. He certainly never crossed himself at Pullhausen when inmates died on his polished steel medical table.

Now lying on her back, she knew this wasn't the best position. Greta twisted herself around, swearing as she banged her head and face in the process, until she was resting crouched on her knees. From there with great effort, as the rope cut deep into her wrists, she raised her top half, and then painfully banged her head again while she rolled head first over the wardrobe edge and flopped onto the marble tiles.

Greta lay there exhausted breathing in snatches. Then she froze. The adrenalin was surging back into her. She was thinking how long he'd been gone? Her head jerked to one side as she strained to listen. Traffic noises outside! Was he back? He'd been gone, it seemed an eternity.

Greta waited, then nothing. She had to get untied and quick, if she was to stand any chance.

She started to inch along on her back, the rope cutting into her wrists as she winced with each small push her legs would allow. Greta continued pushing until she slid out of the bedroom into the hall. At the far end, she could see the front door. *Make it to the door, push yourself upright against the door and turn the handle. Get outside, get seen.*

Greta moved nearer, bit by bit. The only thing that mattered now. Her whole life shrunk down to this very act of survival. Then she stopped.

Shit, the lock? The bloody lock was too high. She could see the handle clearly now. Even half-standing upright, no way would her tied hands get to that.

Greta didn't want to waste any more valuable time, she turned back dismissing the idea, muttering three fast *fucks* to herself. The clock was ticking. She had to get back down the hall. *Get into a room. Hide or something. Better still, find something sharp. Get yourself free and with any luck stab the fucker at the same time.*

Greta slid along past two closed doors until she came to one a quarter open. She nudged it and it creaked wider. Lying on her back it took a few seconds to get some orientation. It was the lounge.

She took in two large rugs and a coffee table. Greta stopped and stared for a second. On the coffee table was an expensive looking bronze paperweight of a couple having sex. *That was Joachim's style.* There was a sofa and across from that a drinks cabinet. Behind its glass doors sat a few bottles including brandy and liqueurs with an assortment of glasses. Greta moved in further over the rugs, rucking them up as she went past the sofa. Then she saw the electric fire set in a marble style mantle-piece. Over in the far corner, a tall floor lamp with a fancy soft shade stood next to a French polished sideboard with sophisticated figurines laid out on top. It all looked very upmarket. It complimented someone who could afford the finer things in life. A far cry from Joachim's halfway prison house when she first met him again.

'Fuck,' she muffled out. She lay on her back looking at the white ceiling. It was the most comfortable position. Her wrists all bloody and chaffed, screamed out their pain. The chances of finding anything sharp were looking remote. She could imagine Joachim searching the rooms in panic then realising with a smile she was still a prisoner. His little fly all exhausted now. More tangled up than ever in his sticky web. Then a thought occurred, the electric fire? The switches were low. She could reach them at a push. Lay something to burn near the bars. She could move away quick. Hope people might see smoke coming out under the door, smell burning.

Then it dawned. What if nobody came? End up a charred mess. Pleading to a grinning Joachim to put her out her misery. As the worst scenario, the prospect of a slow death from being barbequed, soured any further plans with the fire.

Then Greta had an idea, she looked at the drinks cabinet. *The glass doors?* She pushed off and slid her way across until her feet were in range. Wincing as the rope cut into her wrists, she turned her face away and with a few heavy thrusts, kicked out the glass. Greta manoeuvred herself around the glass shards on the floor until she had her back to the cabinet. Straining her neck to look behind with the bit of slack she had, she slowly began to saw through the rope using the jagged bits still attached to the frame, cutting and nicking herself at the same time.

She could feel her wrists getting looser. Now and again she would stop and strain hard trying to force them apart, then back to the sawing, until, with a sudden ping of ecstasy, the rope parted.

Greta rubbed her wrist's, they were stinging badly with the rope burn. She pulled at the gag, both hands, until she levered it over her chin. She tried to untie her feet, it was difficult. The knot was too tight; he'd made a good job. She tried a piece of glass but like the wrists, it was slow going and she didn't have the time. Joachim could be back any minute.

The kitchen, get a knife. Greta slid to the nearest wall and then using her back, she pushed herself upright. Hopping out of the lounge into the hall, she spotted the glass-panelled door. She opened it and saw the knife-rack on the kitchen work surface. Using the smallest one, she cut her feet free and then slipped the stiletto into the back of her trouser belt. Greta went to the apartment door and tried to open it, but it was locked. No surprises there. Then she gave it a couple of half-hearted kicks out of frustration; it was too sturdy to have a go with her shoulder. She'd end up breaking her shoulder instead.

A quick look around revealed no telephone. No surprises there again. *The balcony doors*, she forgot about the balcony. Greta moved quickly to the lounge again. She tried the handle, pushed and pulled but he'd locked them. *Smash the glass.* Greta picked up the bronze paperweight from the coffee table and hurled it at one of the small bullion windows. It bounced off making an almighty crash and leaving only a small glass chip. The strong urge to keep trying was overtaken by the fact she didn't have the time to persevere with it.

Greta had to face it, there was no escape. She had to surprise him. Also this was her only chance of getting any money back. Whack him over the head and search the place.

She went back to the bedroom. She stepped around the bits of wardrobe and started searching where she'd left off. Then in one of the drawers underneath some shirts, a biscuit tin. Greta pulled the lid off. 'Bingo! You careless little fucker, Joachim,' she said mockingly.

Greta sat on the side of the bed. She didn't have time to count, however Christmas had definitely come. The tin was stuffed with money, in what appeared to be hundreds of Deutsche marks notes ranging in denominations from fifty up to 500 in value. She'd count it later when she had time. Greta shoved it back in the draw.

She carried on searching. She ducked down under the other twin bed and suddenly jerked back with a fright. She'd spotted a body. She gingerly peered again, and then slowly pulled out a blow up sex doll with astonishment. It was scantily clad with a half-cup bra, suspender-belt and fishnet stockings including orifices. The large box it came deflated in, clearly showing her name as *Luscious Leonie*.

Greta held it up with a smirk as it bounced around like a balloon. It was nearly as tall as herself. She tossed it onto the bed; it lay there with its legs open ready for action.

Now she had to sort out how to jump him, and quickly. He was going to be back any minute, and probably not in a good mood when he realised he'd been sent on a wasted errand.

Greta had lied. There was no duplicate letter or photo, not even a six-hundred deutschmarks freebie. In fact the safe box didn't exist. The Hotel Garitonni didn't have any. And the key on the ring? That was for her cheap suitcase.

Greta had to hide from him and quick.

Three minutes later she heard the front door slam. Then swearing, *'You lying slag, I'm gonna teach you–'* Then he reached the bedroom, *'SHIT! Fuck, wait till I get hold of you.'* Then he went to the lounge. Suddenly it went quiet. Greta froze.

Joachim came back into the hall. He called out, 'Now come on, Greta. I know you're in here. You can't get out. I made sure of it. Don't make me come after you.'

The only room he hadn't checked, the bathroom. Joachim held the pistol ready; he didn't want to use it unless he had to. It was far too noisy, might draw attention. He'd corner her, then use the knife to finish her off.

Joachim gently pushed the door open, in case she jumped out with her own weapon. She'd time to find one. The bathroom door creaked, as it swung wide. And there she was, hiding, silhouetted behind the shower curtain. *Stupid bitch,* he thought, *as if I couldn't see her. Still, it'll keep all the mess in one place and easy to clean.* He slipped the pistol into his pocket and pulled the knife slowly from its sheath strapped to his lower leg.

Then Joachim lunged forward in a mindless stabbing frenzy, grunting with each thrust through the curtain and falling headlong into the bath still stabbing a hissing *Luscious Leonie.*

The last thing Joachim saw was his blow-up doll wearing Greta's clothes.

THWACK! She hit him smack on the back of the head with the heavy bronze paperweight. Then she hit him again and again.

Finally, Greta put a finger to his neck and checked; just to be sure he was dead.

She tugged away at the deflated doll until it was free of Joachim and then put her clothes back on.

Greta sat on the toilet seat. What to do next? She could take the money and do a runner. How long would it be before Joachim's body was discovered? Two to three days at the most. The problem was the concierge had seen her. Even in disguise it was risky. The taxi drivers would remember her. Then her description would be all over the place. In newspapers, posters at airports and sea ports. They'd be on the lookout that she may have changed her appearance. Greta thought hard. There was only one thing for it. She had to get rid of him. Fake an accident. Then she wouldn't be connected to him in any way.

Greta moved back into the bedroom and found the contents of her shoulder bag and jewellery. She put on her rings, earrings and bracelets. Greta picked up the medallion, the Hünenkreuz Medal of Purity. She said to the empty room, 'So in love. You're right, Joachim, all relationships have a clock attached to them. They all end in time as you said. Unfortunately, *your's* is now, not mine.'

She slipped the medallion back on, and sat on the edge of the bed with her map, to pick out a few local clifftop beauty spots highlighted with a camera icon. One of them seamed ideal with a hotel listed a short distance away. She could pre-book a taxi from there. Greta was hoping by 12:30 a.m. it would all be finished. She could then take a leisurely stroll to the clifftop hotel and hover around out of sight until the taxi arrived. Then back to her own hotel. After that, the world was her oyster.

Greta let herself out of the apartment and found Joachim's hired Mercedes. The registration number was on the keyring. She also checked the location of the fire escape. It was at the rear of the building as the arrowed signs stated, and down two flights of stairs. Greta had to use the fire escape. That could be tricky. She had to wait until dark to find out.

By late evening she was ready. Greta had cleaned up the flat. Put the wardrobe back against the wall, found a screwdriver in the kitchen drawer and removed the damaged drinks cabinet doors. The unit looked as good as new, as if it never had doors. That all went down the communal waste chute along with bits of plywood, broken glass and a punctured blow-up doll; and then she cleaned out the shower bath. Joachim was suitably dressed for the occasion with a cap covering a head wound.

With a peak outside the apartment door and holding up Joachim with his arm around her shoulder, she dragged him along the hallway with his head slumped forward and the cap over his eyes. Greta knew the meaning of a dead weight as she wrestled with him down the fire escape stairs. It seemed an eternity as she struggled with him along the basement passageway, until she pushed up the bar of the fire escape door and stepped out into the street.

She was met by a humid Italian July night. Greta caught the smells of pasta and coffee from local restaurants still serving late diners.

She'd parked his Mercedes as near as empty parking bays would allow. It was only a short walk to the car with him, but even in the dark they both looked very conspicuous.

Just then, within twenty-yards, a couple turned a corner and approached.

Fuck!-fuck!-fuck! Greta said in her mind. 'Come on now, Steve,' She laughed, 'you always get plastered on holiday.'

The couple slowed-up and started smiling.

'Come on, Steve, not far now.'

The early thirties Italian woman spoke first in broken English. 'You need an 'and?'

'Oh no, it's okay,' Greta replied with a smile, 'our hotel is only up the road.'

'But 'e looks 'eavy. My boyfriend will 'elp you.' She motioned to her glum looking partner and he stepped forward reluctantly, with a look that said he wished his girlfriend would keep her mouth shut.

'No-no, please it's okay, honestly. I've done this loads of times on holiday. My husband likes a drink, trouble is, he doesn't know when to stop.' Greta laughed.

'But 'e is to 'eavy for a woman to carry on 'er own. Ricardo, 'elp the lady.'

He stepped forward again mumbling something in Italian with his arms out ready to support.

Greta, trying to grin through it all, protested again, holding her free hand up to stop him. 'No, honestly it's alright. I can manage,' she laughed. 'It's only a short walk - look, see up there.' She pointed to an imaginary spot, and their eyes briefly followed her arm.

Suddenly, Joachim slipped a little from her grasp. Greta with great effort hoisted him back to a better hold. 'Whoops! Nearly lost you then, Steve,' she said to him, laughing it off.

'But I insist, you might 'urt yourself. Ricardo, do not just stand there, 'elp the lady.'

Greta had had enough. Her patience was in tethers and had finally come to an end after a long traumatic day. She exploded and screamed at them. *'Listen, you Two Fucking Wop Dego's. I do not need your fucking help for the tenth time. Now both of you, can do me one big favour and take your greasy dego selves and fuck-off! Do you understand that?'*

She stopped them in their tracks. They both stood there with their mouths open.

With that retort, Greta hoisted Joachim for a better hold and then carried on walking with his feet dragging on the pavement. After a couple of minutes, with great difficulty, she turned to look, and saw with relief they'd gone. With another fifty-yards to go, she finally made it to the Mercedes.

At last, with him sitting in the passenger seat slumped forward out of sight, she breathed a long sigh of relief. With the map spread out in her lap, Greta started up the car and slowly pulled out of the parking bay and headed for the clifftop sea view.

The journey of twist and turns along the cliff top road was uneventful. When a bend came up, she would grab Joachim with her right hand just in case he might topple onto her.

By 12:20 a.m., the headlights had picked out one of the very nasty extreme sharp turns high up on the headland overlooking the sea. She eased on the accelerator and pulled into the visitors lay bye with the pay and view telescope. At this point, the metal safety barrier stopped and was replaced by a low two-foot high wall. This was capped with wide coping slabs for seating and picnicking. Greta adjusted the driver's seat as far back as it would go and then climbed out.

At once, the smell of the sea and the crashing waves below filled her senses. As expected, the place was deserted.

She looked up at the stars. It was perfectly clear with very little wind, even at this level. Out on the horizon a few fishing boat lanterns faintly twinkled, while to her left, the lights of Rimini lit up a dark landscape.

Greta walked around to the passenger side and opened the door. She looked at him for the last time, all crumpled up and lifeless. What could have been? She'd once fancied Joachim, could have settled down with him. With all that money, they could have had some great times together if he hadn't been so greedy and done the dirty. He just wasn't satisfied with his lot. It must have burnt a hole in his brain seeing her share lying there. Easy pickings he probably thought. However, prison had made her very streetwise and she'd learnt from the concentration camp days and living with him, how devious he was. They say devious minds think alike. Only, she'd been one jump ahead, and he was dead now. A lesson to be learned. A good teacher should always know the extent of his or her student's progress.

'Come on, Joachim, let's get you in the driving seat.' Greta bent down and with a lot of effort, hauled him over her shoulder. She staggered with him around to the other side of the car and rolled him off in front of the steering wheel. She went back and shut the passenger door, then came round to the driver's side. From her handbag she took the brandy from his drinks cupboard, unscrewed the top and tossed the half bottle into the car. A good excuse for crashing through a clifftop barrier. Then she removed her shoulder bag and placed it on the ground.

Greta sat on Joachim's lap and made sure she could reach the pedals. Then she switched on the ignition. She reversed back to the opposite side of the road to give herself a run-up. With the handbrake on, Greta did a practise exit as she swung her legs and jumped out. Then she climbed back in again and sat on his lap.

With the door half open, she looked both ways along the coast road as a last double check. And then over her shoulder she said to her very dead passenger, 'Well, this is goodbye, Joachim, it was nice knowing you.'

She revved up the engine and released the handbrake and then switched on the lights full beam. Then she started to accelerate.

Greta flung herself out and yelled in pain as she hit the road just as the Mercedes crashed through the wall and plummeted, then it hit a ledge and bounced and plummeted again and bounced and then smashed headlong onto the rocks and burst into a fireball.

For a few seconds, Greta lay there all quiet looking up at the stars. Her side ached and she had badly grazed her arm and knee but thankfully not her face. The cut lip from Joachim had congealed and the swelling felt as if it was going down.

Wincing, she rolled over and raised herself up. She picked up her shoulder bag. Limping slightly she gingerly edged forward and peered over the clifftop edge.

Nothing could be seen in the dark apart from a faint burning glow down on the rocks. No doubt, tomorrows beauty spot admirers would pick out Joachim and his Mercedes coffin. Certainly those using the pay and view telescope.

Greta brushed herself down and checked her watch. She was in plenty of time. With a handkerchief she dabbed her cuts and then slowly began to walk in the direction of the hotel for the taxi pickup. Once there she could find a washroom and with some makeup do a bit of touching up. With her large floppy sunhat pulled down over the white sunglasses, Greta was confident she could get back to her hotel unrecognised. She checked the money in her shoulder bag one more time. In his apartment she'd counted forty-five thousand Deutsche marks. More than enough for the troubles she'd put up with in Rimini. However, she still had to be careful.

*

Three weeks later, back in Nuremberg, while reading a newspaper in the comfort of her chic double bed apartment on the fashionable Sulzbacher Strasse, Greta's hand froze. The page two headline was quite specific.

WOMAN'S BODY FOUND IN FIELD
By Deutsche Post Reporter
Police were called to a field in the Kraftshofer Forest just outside Nuremberg near the autobahn, when a farm worker unearthed a large bundle while turning over muddy ground with his rotary cultivator. It was when he stopped the machine and approached the bundle that he made the grim discovery. Police immediately cordoned off the area and carried out an

examination. The bundle contained the badly decomposed remains of a woman wrapped up in plastic sheets.

At the moment the police are treating the incident as a suspected murder. The body had been covered in lime and all identification had been removed. A police spokesmen at the crime scene told reporters they were hoping her dental records would establish her identity and perhaps her last movements.

Anyone with information on missing persons is asked to contact Langwasser Police Station, Nuremberg 0911 668371.

Greta couldn't waste any time. She had to move away quickly and ditch the Monika Huber identity.

CHAPTER EIGHTEEN

At the end of the war Dr Karl Borch was released. As a former POW he was offered free transport back to Germany. He would like to have found out what had happened to his family. However, he was still a wanted man for war crimes and knew he had to be careful.

Still posing as Dr Karl Eder the former Luftwaffe pilot, he decided to stay in England. With his fake doctors identity papers he applied to the General Medical Council to be a general practitioner and went before a medical board. Because of the heavy bombing in Germany and the destruction of buildings where records had been kept, the council couldn't check his references. However, as there was a shortage of hospital doctors and GP's in Britain following the war, he was offered a compulsory year of pre-qualifying training at a London hospital. Karl accepted the offer.

A year later, qualified as a GP, he found work at a variety of hospitals, still keeping a low profile. After a few more years, Karl was offered his first residency post at an old people's home in London.

*

Greta Binz, still on the run, had bluffed her way into a care home in London. Since the capture of Adolf Eichmann, the Nazi hunters and the media had stepped up their interest in bringing other Nazis to justice. Greta decided it was too hot to stay in Germany.

With all the money she stole from Joachim, she decided to emigrate to England, although she had to grease some palms to arrange a new name and passport. This included being conned a few times with the promised passport and papers never materialising, and the forger running off with her money. For that reason, her funds had depleted to just a small savings account at the local post office.

Using her new identity, supported by hair dye and makeup, Greta Binz blended in well with the other care home staff and residents.

*

It was breakfast at the *Prince Regent Care Home For The Elderly*. The council run establishment just off the Edgware Road in London was originally a large Victorian town house.

However, last year in 1959 it had been given a much needed facelift. White walls, new yellow and brown carpet throughout, chintz curtains and recovered chairs were amongst some of the decor.

Klara Olinski, matron of the home for the last eight-years, helped the other two care workers Maureen and Gwen to serve breakfast. Then she rang her little bell. She kept it in her cardigan pocket and through experience, found it was a good way to get the residents' attention quickly. 'Now listen, everyone,' she said in her Polish accent. 'Today the fourteenth of June nineteen sixty is special because it's Ethel's birthday.' Matron pointed to Ethel and beamed a smile, while Ethel managed a half-hearted wave and grinned from her wheel chair. 'She's one-hundred-years old so let's all put our hands together.'

Forty-six-year-old matron Olinski, with her slim figure and light-brown short bob hairstyle, started them off with a slow and measured clap until most of them had the idea. After half a minute, the matron held up her hand to quieten them all. 'And to celebrate Ethel's birthday we will be holding a little party for her at three o'clock in the lounge.'

Wearing her matron's regulation green trouser suit, she quickly applauded Ethel again and then said, 'A reporter will be coming from the local newspaper to take photos at the party, so put on your Sunday best everyone. Oh, and before I forget, just to remind you all, there will be a new resident joining us this afternoon. Her name is Lila Bozeman. She's from a care home in Golders Green. She'll be with us for a few weeks while her own place is being renovated.' With a sympathetic smile she finished off and said, 'Ethel's party will be a good chance for you to meet her, so please make her welcome, that's all I ask.'

Later that afternoon they were all sitting grouped around Ethel and her cards. Ethel was slightly bewildered with the fuss and was slowly sipping a sherry in-between bites of birthday cake from a napkin. An elderly lady from the local church group had come along to play the piano for a couple of hours and was in the middle of her rendition of *Down at the Old Bull and Bush*.

The new resident, Lila Bozeman, was settling in after a morning of upheaval and travelling. Sitting relaxed, she clutched a glass of cheap champagne and was contented just to listen to the songs being played and take in her new surroundings.

The young reporter had sat with Ethel and clicked away with his camera, then jokingly coaxed her to give his readers an insight of how she had reached such a grand age.

'Eating fruit and a Guinness every day, young man,' she shakily told him amongst roars of laughter from the staff.

Making his notes, the reporter turned his attention to getting some group photos. 'OK, I want you all to get as near to Ethel as you can for a picture.'

With some help from the carers they shuffled into position around Ethel. Even Dr Karl Eder, the resident physician, who'd promised Ethel he'd pop in for her birthday, moved in closer holding his glass of champagne with matron, Gwen and Maureen.

'Now everybody, all say cheese.' The reporter mimed, 'C..H..E..E..S..E..' as the flash lit up the room making some of the residents wince. 'Let's have another one just to make sure.' He focused on them again and repeated, 'C..H..E..E..S..E..'

It may have been the flash that made one of the residents nervous or perhaps sparked off some epileptic fit, but suddenly Golda Bronstein started yelling, *'Oh my God! Murderer, murderer.'* She was pointing, *'It's the Beast! The Beast of Pullhausen! — the beast of Pullhausen!'* Then her eyes rolled underneath her dark glasses and she collapsed back into her chair unconscious.

Dr Eder with matron Olinski rushed forwards. The doctor felt her pulse while the matron shook Golda's arm trying to wake her. Then removing her dark glasses, the matron thumbed her eyelids open. There was no recognition. 'She's out cold,' she said to the doctor.

A few of the residents stared in disbelief while the doctor muttered, 'She's breathing OK.'

The matron slapped Golda's face to try and get a response and then said to the doctor, 'Looks like she's delirious, but at least she's coming round.'

77-year-old Golda, a short stout woman with wispy grey hair and a lined face with heavy features looked typically Jewish in her long patterned skirt with her shawl draped around her shoulders. Wearing dark glasses because of her eye problems, had made Golda seem aloof and difficult for the other residents to engage in nods and smiles with her.

Golda moaned and started saying something unintelligible.

56-year-old Dr Eder knelt down and shone his pencil light into each of Golda's eyes. With his stethoscope, he checked her breathing and then looked up at the matron. 'She's in shock.' He looked at the others. 'Did anybody see what happened?'

Matron Olinski glanced at Gwen and Maureen. They shrugged their shoulders in bewilderment.

Care helper Gwen Maddocks who was the nearest to Golda said, 'I don't know, Mrs O. One minute she's sitting there calmly having her picture taken then all of a sudden, the lovey goes into one. Starts pointing and yelling "Beast" or something. God knows what she saw.'

'Best thing is take her back to her room. I'll give her a sedative.' The doctor rummaged in his black bag and pulled out a strip of Temazepam tablets. 'These will make her sleep. Matron, it would be best if you can get one of the night staff to pop in on her from time to time. Then depending on how she is in the morning, I'll decide whether to send her to hospital or not.'

The balding doctor with light brown hair and blue eyes was still good looking for his age. At five-eleven, he was the tallest in the room and very distinguished looking wearing his dark blue suit and waistcoat. His Nordic looks wrinkled into a smile as he said to the residents, 'Enjoy the rest of your party, everyone.' Then he made his way out, while the carers lifted Golda into a wheelchair and followed behind.

Later that afternoon, Golda's best friend, Esther Heinemann, after having cleared it with matron, was in Golda's room. The door was half-open as always with residents that were poorly. This was to enable staff to listen out in case of emergencies. Just at that moment, while Esther leant over Golda's bed straining to hear what she was mumbling, one of the elderly residents entered.

Esther broke away startled.

'I'm Lila Bozeman.' She extended her hand. 'I just popped in to see how your friend was. I hope you don't mind?'

'No, not at all. Call me Esther, pleased to meet you.' They shook hands, then Esther said, 'Sit yourself down. It's nice to have the company.'

Esther Heinemann was a slim classy seventy-five year old lady with heavily powdered makeup and a mass of dyed jet-black hair in tiny curls. Her rouge laden, rosy cheeks, revealed a woman who still took pride in her appearance. Today, Esther was wearing her fashionable red velvet trouser suit. She always wore long sleeves as it covered up the marks from her diabetic insulin injections.

Lila Bozeman pulled up the spare chair. 'How is your friend?'

Esther explained with a puzzled expression. 'Well, just as you came in I'm sure she was trying to tell me something. She was muttering something about a necklace. Then she closed her eyes and fell asleep again. I expect the sedative they gave her was very strong.'

'You don't mind me asking, Esther, but I couldn't help noticing your Star of David pendant and your friend's *menorah brooch* pinned to her cardigan. You're both Jewish, aren't you?' she said with a smile.

'We are,' Esther replied. 'Golda and I originally came from strict Jewish families that lived in Slovakia. However we've lapsed a bit,' she said with a grin. 'Now we only go to the synagogue on Rosh Chodesh or other Jewish holidays.'

Lila Bozeman laughed. 'Just like me I'm afraid. My father would turn in his grave, God rest his soul if he knew. Him being a Rabbi, I had a strict Russian orthodox upbringing even for a girl.'

'You're Russian?'

'Yes, I still have a hint of a foreign accent, like yourself,' Lila joked, 'we stand out a mile us European Jews.'

Esther laughed. She liked Lila, even though they'd just met. Esther guessed, Lila had to be around the late sixties. She had a white complexion with a few liver spots, but the kind face revealed she had been very pretty once. With her greying hair pinned up, wearing a brown tweed jacket with matching skirt and shoes, Esther could see she was a person like herself who took pride in her appearance.

'So when did you come to England?' Esther enquired.

'It's a long story,' Lila Bozeman sighed. 'My family were persecuted in Russia for being Jews during the pogroms. My late father had been a Rabbi in the Ukraine but the Tsarist soldiers had destroyed our Synagogue. My mother's brother was a captain on a cargo ship, so we managed to escape with other immigrants to America. I grew up there in New York, and before the war I married Jacob Bozeman an American Jew.' Lila stopped and fumbled in her handbag. She took out a small bottle of Napoleon brandy. 'Do you have a couple of glasses? We mustn't let Matron know,' she winked.

Esther who liked the odd drink beamed back. The two plastic cups on Golda's bedside table were more than suitable as Lila poured a generous double for Esther.

Lila took a swig, which made her wince. 'That's better,' she said, and then continued. 'During the war, my husband was a pilot stationed in England flying B52 bombers over Berlin. Then when it finished, he stayed on and sent for me. We had no ties in America, as both our sets of parents were dead. So I've lived here ever since.' Lila took a sip of her brandy. 'We couldn't have kids so he was all I had.' She pulled out her handkerchief and sniffled. 'When he died from cancer seven years ago I was devastated.'

Esther leant across and squeezed Lila's hand.

'Oh, I'm being silly.' Lila dabbed her eyes. 'What about you, how long have you and Golda been over here?'

Esther's face darkened. 'During the war when the Nazis overran Slovakia, our families were interned because we were Jews. We were sent to Pullhausen Concentration Camp in cattle trucks.' Esther showed Lila the tattooed number on her arm.

'Oh my God!' Lila Bozeman put a hand to her mouth in shock.

'Golda and I were the only survivors. The rest of our families were killed.' Esther took a sip of her brandy to steady her nerves and then carried on. 'Mind you, it was Golda who suffered the most. Golda and her twin sister Rosa were sent to the medical block to suffer experiments at the hands of

Dr Joachim Eisele. Like the infamous Dr Mengele in Auschwitz, Eisele had an interest in twins. They were subjected to injections in the eyes with horrible stuff. That's why Golda has to wear dark glasses. Anyway, Rosa died but Golda managed to survive.'

Lila put a hand on Esther's shoulder. 'You poor things.'

All of a sudden, Esther's eyes widened. 'I wonder,' she said. 'Maybe Golda recognised someone from the camp.' Her mind was racing. 'Maybe the doctor? Perhaps she —'

The knock on the door stopped her in midsentence. Matron Olinski popped her head in and asked, 'How is she doing?'

Esther composed herself. 'She's still asleep, Matron, and muttering things.'

The matron leant over Golda. 'Yes, well she would be. The sedative would have taken care of that and she's probably a bit delirious still. As the doctor said, we'll see how she is in the morning.'

The matron turned to leave when Esther asked her diplomatically, 'Matron, do you think Golda recognised someone from the war?'

'From the war, what do you mean, my Dear?'

'Well...' Esther hesitated and then said, 'Golda and myself were prisoners in a Nazi Concentration Camp at Pullhausen. She kept shouting, "The Beast of Pullhausen!" I think maybe she recognised one of the guards or perhaps a doctor from the medical block.' Esther pushed up her sleeve and showed the numbered tattoo.

The matron gasped in horror. 'I've never met a camp survivor; it must have been too horrible for words?'

Esther tactfully asked, 'Although it's none of my business, Matron, I understand Doctor Eder is German. How well do you know him?'

'The Doctor?' she said astonished. 'I can vouch for Doctor Eder. His medical career is beyond reproach,' she said haughtily. The matron leant in closer and lowered her voice. 'I know first-hand when he was interviewed for the job at the home some years ago. I saw his record. I won't have anything said about him.'

The matron sat down on the side of the bed and glanced at Golda with a sympathetic expression. Then she turned to Esther. 'I'm telling you this information in the strictest confidence because I know you must be upset with your friend and looking for reasons why this happened. However, Doctor Eder is a good man. He practiced in Dresden. When the war came, he joined the Luftwaffe as a doctor in the medical unit but later served as a pilot. Then his plane was shot down and he was taken prisoner by the British in 1945. He was interned and sent to a camp in England as a POW. After the war, as all his family were killed in the bombings, he stayed on in this country and became a GP. He's been married and then divorced with no children.'

Matron Olinski paused, 'I know it must be hard for you to accept, Esther, after what you and Golda have been through, but he's not a war criminal believe me.'

Esther raised her hands in submission. 'I just had to ask the question, Matron. Probably I'm clutching at straws.'

The matron gave Esther a hug. 'I'd be doing the same if it was my friend lying there. With all that suffering you both endured, some like yourself handle it better than others. It all must have got too much for her. Probably *thought* she saw something that reminded her of the camp.'

The matron looked out of the window wistfully. 'We've all suffered from the war in our own way. I came from Poland but escaped the Nazis and fled to England with my mother in 1939. My father stayed on to fight with the resistance but was killed in the Warsaw uprising. Then my mother died of cancer in 1957. She was everything to me.'

Matron Olinski pondered then shook herself out of it. She briskly raised herself from the bed and said cheerily, 'Still, we have to carry on, there's no point in dwelling on the past as one could go mad, and I've got work to do.' At the door, she reminded them, 'Sometimes the memories can get too much if we let ourselves think about them. Who knows? Maybe that was Golda's problem.'

*

At around 2:30 a.m. early morning, Golda, still woozy from her sedative, opened her eyes to a fuzzy shape in a white coat leaning over her. Golda became restless and suddenly her face turned to an expression of recognition. 'No please. I won't tell, I promise. Please don't hurt me.'

'It's okay; I've come to give you your medication.' The figure paused. 'Who else have you told?'

Golda, with a shaky voice, blurted out, 'Nobody, honestly...'

The white coat leant over her with a mean face and said in a barbed tone, 'I said, who else have you told?'

'No one, please believe me...'

'Ah, that's good.' The figure moved to the half open door and listened out, then quietly closed it. Confident they were not going to be disturbed, the white coat picked up the spare pillow. The feet positioned themselves to get a firm balance. Then the pillow slammed into Golda's face.

It didn't take long, about three minutes in all. The neck muscles bulged, while both hands pushed down and shook with the pressure. Golda bucked and kicked until everything went limp.

Suddenly the grip on the pillow relaxed. The figure moved away, its heart still pounding, breathing in sharp snatches of air, trying not to be heard. Then it thumbed the lids of the staring eyes and checked the pulse, finally smiling with satisfaction.

Cautiously opening the door, making sure all was clear, the white coat quickly disappeared down the corridor.

The next morning at 7:30 a.m. care worker Gwen Maddocks entered Golda's room with a small breakfast. 'Good morning, My Darling. I've brought you a little toast and butter.'

Gwen spoke in a broad Welsh accent and liked to make a fuss of all the residents. She'd worked at the home for the last six-years and everybody liked her. Part of her routine was to come into the rooms every day to make the beds and do general cleaning. Aged 52 with a bubbly personality and a shock of red bobbed hair that framed a round face with a rosy-cheeked complexion; she was always in her green work coat, wearing over the top earrings and bold necklaces with large coloured beads. Gwen had been married and now had a grown up son and daughter living in London. She divorced four years ago but still maintained to everyone her relationship with her ex was good.

Gwen gently shook Golda. 'Come on, My Darling, it's time for—' She felt the hand, it was stone cold.

Gwen pulled the alarm cord. It signalled a flashing light on the panel in the corridor as well as in the doctor's and matron's office.

Matron Olinski appeared within seconds.

Gwen's expression said it all.

The Matron moved to the bed and felt for Golda's pulse. The coldness surprised her. 'She's been dead for hours, Gwen. I'll call Dr Eder.'

'What do you think it was, Mrs O? A heart attack? A stroke?'

'Could be either, Gwen. Better keep it quiet until the doctor's seen her. Cover her over and lock the door. I'll have to tell her friend Esther. God, I hope she doesn't freak out. That's all I need this morning.'

Gwen gave a sympathetic smile.

Later after examination, Dr Eder entered a heart seizure, caused from a panic attack and shock, on Golda's death certificate.

Esther, seeing Golda's room locked and then summoned to the matron's office, feared the worst. Lila who'd been hovering, offered to give Esther moral support and was by her side as she knocked on the matron's door.

On being told the news, Esther collapsed. Sitting in a chair, with the matron rubbing the back of her hand, she slowly recovered sipping a cup of sweet tea offered by Lila.

'I still can't believe it.' Esther dabbed her red eyes. 'She was fine at Ethel's party. I mean...she never complained of any heart problems.'

Dr Eder sat on the edge of the matron's desk and tried to explain. 'You see, it's not uncommon for someone like Golda who'd suffered a great deal of physical and mental anxiety over the years to have a cardiac arrest. Of course, the shock of what she saw or thought she saw at the party, probably compounded the stress which could have induced a heart attack even then and there, or later as in Golda's case.'

'Will there be an autopsy or post-mortem?' Esther inquired looking thoughtful.

The doctor smiled. 'Only if cause of death could not be ascertained or foul play was suspected. However, in Golda's case there was neither so I was confident in signing her death certificate.'

Esther, clutching the sides of her chair looking concerned, blurted out, 'I know she left a Will. She said she kept it in the matron's safe and that she wanted to be buried at Hoop Lane Cemetery Golders Green. She told me, she had a plot all sorted.'

'Don't worry, Esther. We'll make sure the arrangements are in accordance with her wishes.' The matron put an arm around her. 'Now you go and have a rest. Put your feet up. You've had a very trying morning.'

'I'll stay with her, Matron.' Lila Bozeman offered a hand. 'Come on, Esther, let's get you to the lounge and listen to the radio. Try and take your mind off it.'

'Thank you.' The matron acknowledged her help with a smile, while Esther, supported by Lila's arm, made her way out of the office.

Further down the corridor, Esther stopped just before the lounge door. 'Lila, there's something fishy about all this. It's all far too neat and tidy. Golda sees something. It terrifies her, she shouts out. Then next morning, she's dead. And we're told it was a heart attack waiting to happen. I reckon we're being fobbed off.'

'Esther, you have to see reason.' Lila tried to be sympathetic. 'You've had a doctor examine her. Why would he lie about the cause of death?'

'I don't know. Perhaps it's a cover-up. She mentioned the camp Pullhausen where she was a prisoner!' Esther's eyes widened. 'Maybe whoever she saw, killed her to make it look like a heart attack.' Esther pulled Lila closer. She looked both ways and said, 'Golda had always suspected the resident Doctor Karl Eder as being a former Nazi war criminal. Golda couldn't remember where she'd seen him. It may have been at a concentration camp or his photo on a wanted poster or even in a newspaper one time.'

'Esther, look it stands to reason that —'

'Esther interrupted, 'Golda never confided in anybody apart from me, in case she was wrong. She didn't want to look a fool.' Then her face lit up. 'The doctor had given Golda some new tablets to take recently. Perhaps the doctor realised she'd recognised him. Perhaps he'd increased the dosage of the tablets resulting in her having some sort of fit. Perhaps he was trying to make her have a heart attack?'

'Esther, don't be ridiculous.' Lila tried to reason with her. 'Just remember, all the well-known evil Nazis were probably rounded up and hanged or sent to prison. You're letting your imagination run away with you. Come on.' Lila opened the lounge door for her. 'Let's just relax, listen to a bit of radio.'

Breakfast left over smells of coffee and toast greeted them, including hints of lavender water and cheap cologne, from one or two residents dozing. With the wireless switched on low, they settled into their armchairs.

While Lila listened to the radio, Esther couldn't concentrate. She might just as well have been wearing earplugs. The more she thought about it, the more she had to find out. She'd have to do it alone. Lila, bless her, would think she was mad. Moreover, who could blame her? Doctors and staff had passed off what happened to Golda with a rational explanation. However, something clawed at Esther's brain.

*

Two days later, Esther saw her chance. Thursday afternoons as always, the doctor was away attending his other clinic in

Fulham. It was around two-fifteen after lunch and the lounge was full of residents either reading or sleeping. Lila's magazine had slipped from her hands into her lap as she snoozed. Esther watched her as she raised herself tentatively from the armchair.

She'd seen matron earlier from the window. Her hobby when she got the chance was watering and fussing with plants in the gardens. It was a sunny afternoon again, so hopefully matron would make the most of it out there.

With no one around, she approached the doctor's office. Esther tried the handle of his door and entered. The doctor left it unlocked on a Thursday for the cleaners. The smell of polish, disinfectant and empty paper bins indicated they'd been earlier.

The Venetian blinds were down, that was good; no one could look in. Esther tried the desk drawer. 'Shit!' she mumbled, it was locked. She instinctively lifted the blotter pad and, there it was looking up at her, the little metal key.

Her eyes glided over the drawer contents and then to the folders down below in the files section. Esther thumbed through some medical records until she found her own along with Golda's.

She studied Golda's record card. Esther saw no evidence of previous heart problems. However, old notes made by another doctor stated that Golda had different coloured eyes - Heterochromia iridum. It reported, on rare occasions heterochromia iridum can occur in one of a twin, male or female, also the patient had subsequent eye damage from concentration camp experiments.

She remembered Golda was a twin. The reason she and her sister were chosen for medical selection in the camp and, after what they did to her, why she always wore dark glasses.

She sorted through more folders, then her hand froze. She heard voices. Esther quickly tidied. Then someone tried the door handle; she was trapped. In a flash, she saw the louvered wardrobe. It was her only chance.

Through the slats, she could make out Dr Eder. It looked like he was changing his shirt. Esther held her breath as he opened the wardrobe door. She'd slid to the other side just in time as she watched his hand select a fresh one with a tie. Then she saw it. Esther put a hand to her mouth, the scar under his arm. She knew all SS were tattooed under their arms.

When her camp was liberated, the Americans by then had captured thousands of German prisoners, including SS posing as ordinary soldiers. Stripped to the waist they were forced to march past with their arms held high so an SS tattoo could be spotted. Some had been clever, tried to get rid of it by surgical means before they were captured. That way from a distance there was less chance of it being seen. However, close up like now, a resulting scar could mean a blood group tattoo had been erased.

Esther watched the doctor leave and then made her way back to the lounge. She nudged Lila with excitement. 'Lila - Lila, wake up! You'll never guess what I've just found out.'

Lila woke with a jolt and opened her eyes. 'Dear God, what's the matter?'

'Lila, I can't tell you here, let's go back to my room.'

Five minutes later, sitting together with a fresh cup of tea from Esther's small electric kettle and munching plain digestive biscuits, Esther gabbled out what she'd seen. 'I'm telling you as God is my maker; while I was hiding I saw a scar under his arm where a SS tattoo had been.'

Lila shook her head in bewilderment. 'You must be mad, what if you'd been caught? They could have sent for the police, had you for breaking in?'

Esther ignored her concern with a grin. 'But I wasn't caught. Also he had medical notes on Golda's eyes and the experiments she was subjected too.'

Lila sighed. 'Look Esther, you were hiding in a wardrobe. The light can play funny tricks. You perhaps think you saw something under his arm. More than likely it could have been a birth mark or a scar for something else.'

'Believe me, Lila, I know what I saw.'

'If that's what you want to believe, Esther. I know this Nazi revenge thing must run deep if you're a camp survivor. But you must face reality, it's highly unlikely he's a war criminal on the run.'

'Lila, it's not highly unlikely he's a war criminal on the run, he *is* a war criminal on the run. Probably in disguise, but not enough to fool Golda. She recognised him.'

Lila sighed again. 'I can only sympathise with you. I've only seen the horror pictures and films of the concentration camps as an outsider. To have actually been there like yourself is too horrible to contemplate.'

Esther buried her head in her hands. 'For many years I couldn't talk about it, tried to shut it out of my mind. But now with Golda and what's happened.'

'If you want to get it off your chest, Esther, I'm prepared to listen.' Lila drew up her chair. 'I've never met a camp survivor before; to understand what it was like first-hand.'

Esther composed herself, as if trying to find some inner strength. 'You had no idea, not knowing from one minute to the next if you were going to die. You could be hanged, shot or gassed, they didn't care. Sometimes it was for their amusement or official with your name on an extermination list.'

Lila put her hand on Esther's shoulder. 'Go on, I want to hear.'

Esther breathed in deeply. 'Even at the onset, the Germans had fooled our families into signing up for resettlement. When the Nazis overran Slovakia, we were ordered to report to the local railway station with luggage. They told us we were going to be rehoused near the Swiss border with beautiful views of the Alps. We would be working on collective farms with the opportunity to rent our own house. It was a trick of course. Over the station speakers a man called out, *Leave your luggage, don't worry it will follow.* Once inside the cattle trucks it was too late. None of us realised it was a one-way ticket to Pullhausen Concentration Camp.

'We travelled for two-days without water, and just an overflowing bucket for a toilet. Crammed in so tight you couldn't sit properly. Some of the very young and the old died on the journey.'

Esther took a sip of her tea.

'Let me top you up with that.' Lila took out from her handbag the small bottle of Napoleon brandy and poured two fingers worth into each cup.

Esther swigged, felt the warmth and then continued. 'When we arrived late at night, it was like hell on earth. As the doors opened we were blinded by floodlights. SS guards cursed us to get down, their Alsatians barking, straining at the leash. We were forced to jump a four-foot drop while soldiers shouted *Raus! Raus!* Hitting us with their riding whips and rifle butts. We had arrived at the camp.

'Then inmates called Kapos, dressed in their striped uniforms, worked like sheep dogs organising men and women into separate rows. Using sticks, they hit, pushed us and cursed until two selection queues were formed. Bodies that had already succumbed, were thrown out of the cattle trucks and carted away very quickly. Their grisly intrusion considered an insult before the commandant's eyes. When all was finished, the Kapos stood to attention and bowed to him with their caps removed.

'That's when I first saw him, the commandant of Pullhausen Concentration Camp, Doctor Karl Borch. He was in his immaculate grey uniform with an entourage of machine guns and guard dogs either side of him. The grand master of life and death, smiled and spoke while subordinates dutifully nodded. Now and again, his white gloved hands motioned, as if conducting an orchestra.

'The queue I was in with Golda and her sister moved slowly. Up ahead we could see the very young and elderly sent to the right; the healthy looking were sent to the left. We didn't give it a thought at first. Eventually when our turn came, we were directed to the left.

'In total there were nine-hundred of us, all women. We were marched in rows of five through a set of iron gates with the letters ARBEIT MACHT FREI welded at the top.

'I passed a female guard holding a riding whip. I wanted to shout out to her, why are we being treated like this? Then I saw her lash out repeatedly at a Jewish girl who had stumbled, and I thought better of it.

'As the SS shouted *Raus! Raus!* We were pushed and prodded into a large dilapidated building with a sign that read Delousing Centre. We were forced to strip. Most of us had never stood naked in front of strangers. Then, one by one, we were pushed into a chair to have our heads shaved. A rough hand manhandled my head, as the rattle of electric shears cut and scraped, tearing hair from my scalp. Then the shouting and pushing continued as we were herded into large baths of disinfectant. The green liquid stinging, as if it would eat the flesh off our bodies. Then more shouting and pushing until we lined up single file and had a striped woollen smock tossed at us as we passed.

'Because of no underwear, the coarseness of the wool on our bodies was unbearable. From there, we were funnelled through a door into another room with benches and long tables. There, Polish inmates, sat ten women down at a time for tattooing. The painful needle jabbed you repeatedly until blood ran with black ink. Finally, after being branded and numbered like cattle, we were moved and counted into groups of one-hundred and fifty, and made to stand outside our designated huts for roll call. This usually took over two hours while a block leader, supervised by an SS Warden, would walk up and down the rows counting and striking out with a stick to anyone that fidgeted. Eventually, after we were dismissed, women assigned as block leaders would dish out food. This consisted of a small piece of bread, some lard or margarine, and occasionally about 100 grams of salted pork.

Lila had gone pale as if she was about to faint. She took a swig of brandy and then blinked as it found its way. 'I've never heard anything so terrible.'

Esther looked at her concerned. 'Do you want me to carry on?'

Lila closed her eyes, then tentatively nodded as if summoning up the strength.

'During the day they played opera through the camp speakers. I never saw her, but Golda said the SS. Oberaufseherin, Greta Binz, liked to listen as she made her selections for the medical block - she supervised the women's medical block. I later learnt she liked Puccini; her favourite being *One Fine Day* from Madam Butterfly. I heard that played many times.

'She and the notorious camp physician, Dr Joachim Eisele, were an item. They would take it in turn to hand pick inmates with certain features or anomalies. Like twins and so on, that would suit their research, as they called it. To show his affection, he would make her presents. They say, amongst many was a lampshade made from the skin of inmates with tattoos, and a necklace with human eyeballs.'

Lila put a hand to her mouth in horror. 'Stop-stop, that's enough. I'm sorry, Esther. It's just too much for me.'

'It's okay, Lila, but you asked me to tell you.'

'I know - I know. It's just... too horrible to hear anymore.' She breathed in deep. 'I've got to get some fresh air, come on let's go for a stroll around the garden, we'll change the subject, talk about something else.' As Lila opened the door, she flinched back in shock. Gwen Maddocks was standing there.

Gwen looked flustered and embarrassed, as if she'd been caught red handed eaves-dropping. 'Oh – oh I'm sorry, My Darlings,' she said. 'Just come to let you know, Esther, about the funeral arrangements for Golda.'

*

The next afternoon, the local newspapers dropped through the letterbox. Spread out on the table before teatime, some of the residents were busy reading. A few had to lean in close holding their magnifying glass. Suddenly Edith, an elderly lady with blue rinse hair wearing a shawl, looked up. 'Hey, Ethel, you're famous.' She leant across and showed her. 'Got your name and picture in the paper for your hundredth birthday.'

Ethel beamed at herself sitting there posing in a couple of group photos. The paper went around the table for the others to see and then someone discarded it to the magazine rack.

Maureen Galbraith fidgeted nervously as she sorted out the tea things. As a natural blonde with sharp features, fair skin and a tall slim build, she could have passed for Swedish or Danish origin any day. Nevertheless, even wearing her blue work coat with her hair tied back, she looked younger than her fifty years.

Being divorced and living alone, she knew jobs were hard to come by as one became older. This was her fourth year at the home as a care worker. As far as she was concerned, this was the last chance saloon. She had been lucky to get the job, considering. With forged references, she'd got away with it. Now all she had to do was keep her head down and blend in. Always be obliging with a smile. Let them know, nothing was too much trouble, and most important of all, while out, keep the face covered. Even in summer, a light scarf worn high up around the mouth with a pulled down floppy hat would suffice.

During the hubbub of teatime, a pair of eyes watched carefully. Afterwards, as the trolley made its way across the carpet to the clatter of plates and cups being cleared, the television came on. *The Phil Silvers Show* had started. While most of them watched, fingers swiftly slipped the newspaper from the magazine rack and tucked it away.

Later while alone, the figure bent over the newspaper. The eyeglass hovered around the neck of the woman in the picture sitting with Ethel. It was hard to focus at first and then the blurring began to sharpen. A deep breath exhaled upon realisation. *Shit, the necklace, it's visible. That's what the Jewish bitch must have seen. Am I a silly cow or what?*

Must remember not to wear it next time. Hopefully no one else noticed, including the doctor. Thank Christ he still doesn't recognise me. Just lucky it never jogged his memory.

Dr Eder stood behind Ethel smiling at the camera. Now she clearly recognised him. She carefully tore out the newspaper picture and put in her pocket.

*

The following afternoon as it was warm and sunny, Esther decided to sit in the garden with her current Mills and Boone. Her favourite seat was just off the path by a dry stone wall. From here, she could take in the smells and the colours of the rose beds and sweet pea. While blue forget-me-nots framed the crazy paving slabs of the path either side, an abundance of marigolds in the distance, spread across her vision like a sea of yellow daisies.

Esther loved to watch the odd bee hop from one white hydrangea shrub to a blue one, then onto a pink, then back again. Butterflies fascinated her as well, her favourites being the large white and the common blue. She would rest her book if one of them hovered close, flapping and dancing, so dainty she thought, like a ballerina.

The music was soothing; *Dove Sono* from *The Marriage of Figaro* was coming from the speaker overhead. Matron Olinski had fitted speakers in the corridors and communal rooms as well as the garden. She was an opera lover and liked to listen to her favourites wherever she was working. She'd got the idea of background music from the local supermarket and had read somewhere the Japanese used it in offices and factories. She was sure it helped to calm down some of the boisterous residents especially after their medication.

Esther closed her eyes. The warm afternoon and the Countess's aria from Figaro were making her sleepy. As the book slipped from her fingers, her head drooped and then came a faint rhythmical snore in time with the rising and falling of her chest. Typical garden sounds surrounded her; the summer shrill of chaffinches, the throaty rasp of a magpie, crickets revving up in the grass. Esther continued to snooze until the SS guard's Alsatian dog bit her. She yelled and jolted upright. It had been another bad dream.

She had no idea how long she'd dozed. However, something was wrong. It was the music from the speakers. Fear and panic were taking control. Esther began to tremble. Slowly, the horrors of the camp came flooding back. The terrible shouts and screams inside her head. The blinding searchlights. Fearsome dogs barking, straining at the leash. Pleadings from the sick being forced into trucks. Guards striking out with their whips.

Esther looked up. The music overhead? Now she recognised it. Giacomo Puccini's, *Madam Butterfly*. It was the SS Oberaufseherin, Greta Binz's favourite.

Esther stood up. She held onto the back of the bench to steady herself. She closed her eyes and took deep breathes. Her head was clearing. There was no one around. Esther took a hesitant step. Then clutching her book she started walking towards the matron's office. As Esther's steps quickened, Maria Callas was singing *One Fine Day*. The music seemed to be getting louder and louder. Somebody was taunting her. Some cruel bastard's idea of a joke she thought. As she approached the doorway from the garden, the volume increased. Esther put her hands to her ears. She began to run in panic along the corridor. A couple of residents moved out of her way in astonishment. They stopped and looked back at her. The corridor was becoming narrower and longer.

Esther began to feel dizzy; she felt she was back in the camp, being herded along to the showers. The opera from the speakers mingled with cries and shouts inside her head. She couldn't take much more. Feverishly turning the handle, the music instantly stopped as she burst through the matron's door. There was no one in her office.

The Decca record player sat on the sideboard. All Esther heard was the repeating tick of the needle as it rode in the last outer groove of the LP. She lifted the arm to its rightful place. As the turntable slowed, she saw the RCA label along with, *Giacomo Puccini's Favourites*, in fancy gold lettering. Esther moved to the window overlooking the garden. She saw the matron still busy pottering with the plants. Esther clenched her fists. Was someone taunting her, teasing her? Hoping she'd go mad or have a heart attack?

Esther returned to her room. She lay on the bed thinking. After around twenty minutes, she'd thought it through.

*

Lila Bozeman woke with a start. Esther was shaking her. 'Lila - Lila! I've just realised something.' They were in the lounge, and Lila had dozed off with a magazine in her lap.

Lila looked startled. 'Dear, God, I thought you were going to tell me the place was on fire for a moment. What's up?'

'I've been thinking. It doesn't add up with the doctor.'

'Give it a rest, Esther; we're not back to him again are we?'

'No - no, what I mean is, I reckon he's what they say he is. Just an ordinary GP doing his job. Look, it makes sense. I remember Golda telling me there was only one camp doctor, who carried out the experiments and he was prosecuted and got ten years or something. The other doctors were killed trying to escape the Allies. But that evil bitch who ran the women's medical block, Greta Binz the SS. Oberaufseherin, she was the worst. Three of her guards were hanged for what they did. Golda said Binz was caught but then escaped. She'd read it in the news.'

'So, what are you saying?'

'Perhaps Golda recognised this Binz. It would make more sense.'

Lila nodded, 'You could be right.'

'And let's be honest, we're not just talking about one of the frail old residents here. It could be the Matron or Gwen, even Maureen?'

'Just hang on, Esther. Don't start jumping to conclusions straight away. You had the doctor in the frame only a few days ago.'

Esther wasn't listening. 'And another thing. That time Golda was trying to tell me something while I was leaning over her. Something about a necklace. She kept on muttering "necklace." That Gwen the staff carer. She always wears a necklace?'

'Now Esther, what have I said about jumping to conclusions?'

*

Every morning, lunchtime and evening, one of the qualified home carers walked around with her trolley to hand out medicines and tablets to the residents. She was supposed to lock the dispensary cupboard but sometimes she forgot.

The figure waited for her to leave and then rummaged the shelves and drawers for the insulin packs.

That afternoon just after lunch, a conversation was taking place in Esther's room.

'I brought your insulin. Dispensary collared me while I was coming to pay you a visit. See how you were.'

Esther's shaky hands took the box and fumbled with it.

The friendly voice said, 'Let me do that for you. Just relax, Esther, you've had a trying time.'

'Would you, you're so kind.'

The deft fingers pulled out the syringe and removed the small needle guard. Turning away, two phials snapped off. The syringe greedily sucked up the liquid. Turning back, 'Now, where do you usually have it?' the friendly voice asked.

When all was still, the insulin packaging was hidden beneath Esther's pillows to make out she'd stolen the phials.

*

Later that afternoon just before tea, Lila was surprised Esther hadn't come to the lounge. 'I'll just pop along and see where she is, Gwen. Save you the trouble while you're preparing the table.'

'Would you, My Darling.' Gwen replied. 'Tell her it's her favourite today. Cheese on toast and Eccles cakes.' She beamed a smile at Lila.

Not five minutes later, all hell broke loose. Lila had pulled the panic cord and met Gwen and the matron in the corridor rushing to Esther's room. Lila was just about to faint but was saved by Gwen and helped to the nearest chair.

'She's dead, she's dead, dear God.' Lila was wailing, *'She's dead, she's dead, Oh my God, she's dead.'*

Gwen and Maureen tried to pacify her, while Matron Olinsky entered Esther's room and found her slumped in a chair. Her hand was still clutching the syringe. On the table next to her was the suicide note:

Sorry to cause such a fuss, but I'm tired of living. I want to join my friend Golda, especially after all we've been through together. I couldn't leave her alone now...

The matron picked up the note. Her hand was shaking. She saw the two extra broken phials including Esther's dosage. She called for Gwen.

'Yes Mrs O.' Gwen came into the room and put a hand to her mouth in shock.

Matron showed her the note. 'Nothing's been reported missing from dispensary, has it, Gwen?'

'Not that I know of, Mrs O.'

'She must have saved up the insulin herself, purposely gone without so she could overdose.'

Gwen looked over the scene. 'It looks that way, Mrs O. Poor Lovey, she was such a nice lady.' Gwen pulled out a handkerchief and dabbed her eyes.

'You stay here, Gwen and keep an eye on things and I'll call the police. Maureen will have to see to their teas. I'll tell her.'

'Right you are, Mrs O.'

Later that afternoon, after the police had taken photographs, fingerprints and bagged up evidence, seemingly satisfied with the suicide note, that it had been self-inflicted after finding the hidden insulin. Esther's body was removed to the local police mortuary awaiting a post-mortem.

Lila was given a sedative and wheeled back to her room in a wheelchair. Dr Eder and the matron called in to see her while she was fast asleep.

Standing by her bed the matron sighed. 'She really has been through the wars, poor thing. Seeing her friend dead must have been such a shock.'

The doctor leaned over and felt Lila's pulse. Checking it against his watch he said, 'Yes you're right, Matron. Very unfortunate to have experienced that. Never mind. She seems to be stable now. Make sure whoever's on duty to pop in during the night to keep an eye on her.'

'Will do, doctor.'

CHAPTER NINETEEN

Dr Eder excused himself. He didn't want to be late. It was his evening class tonight at the local school. For the last two years, he'd taken up art.

On the way home he stopped off for fish and chips, ready to take indoors and eat out of the paper. It would save on washing up. As he turned the key to his flat, his front door swung inwards. With the briefcase in one hand and the fish and chips tucked under his arm, he stepped into the hallway and pushed it closed. Being June, it was still light so he didn't bother to turn on his florescent strips in the kitchen. Placing the fish and chips on the table, he was suddenly grabbed from behind.

The doctor cried out in alarm as the three of them forced him to the floor, gagging him. While two sat on his chest and legs, the other one tore open his jacket and shirt. Lifting his left arm, they saw the tattoo scar. Then they rolled him over binding his arms behind his back. With two holding guns, and the other with a knife at his throat, he wasn't going to fight back.

Dr Eder recognised their language as they shouted to each other in Hebrew. Then they hauled him up into a chair. Wearing balaclavas, they slapped his face a couple of times to show they meant business. The tallest one grabbed his shirt. He seemed to be the leader. The other two stood behind the doctor and nudged him with their guns.

'We know who you are so don't lie; your blood group scar confirms it. SS Doctor Karl Borch, former Commandant of Pullhausen Concentration Camp. With your chief physician Dr Joachim Eisele, you carried out experiments on the inmates. A court in Nuremberg sentenced you to death in your absence.'

One of them behind pressed a gun with a silencer against his head.

The tallest one in front, drew up a chair and sat facing him close up with the knife to his throat. 'Mossad have been following you for the last two months. However, our commander wants bigger fish to fry. We want Greta Binz the former SS Oberaufseherin of Pullhausen Concentration Camp. We have reason to believe you know her whereabouts?'

The doctor frantically shook his head.

'Take his gag off,' he said to the one behind. He pressed the knife. 'If you call out or make a sound I'll slit you from ear to ear.'

'Honest, I have no idea.' The doctor swallowed. His eyes were focused on the blade in front of him. 'Why would I know where she is?'

'You worked with her. You were her friend.' The Mossad agent pressed the knife firmly against the doctor's throat drawing a trickle of blood.

'I had nothing to do with that evil cow. Believe me, it was Eisele. He was the one she went around with.' The doctor lowered his eyes at the blade and then said quickly. 'I thought they hanged her, sentenced her to death?'

'The tribunal were sympathetic. She got life in an institution because of diminished responsibility. Of not sound mind to stand trial. Then the Bitch escaped. We reckon the Odessa boys must have helped her. You wouldn't know anything about that of course?' The agent twitched the blade drawing some more blood.

'No - no, please dear God. I'm telling the truth.' The doctor's eyes were filled with terror. 'I would tell you where she was otherwise. I hated the evil bitch.'

The agent pondered, then to the doctor's relief it seemed as if he might believe him. He withdrew the knife. 'Now listen to me carefully. The new head of Mossad wants Greta Binz. It's personal. Apparently, Binz killed his mother and sister in the camp. So we're here to do his bidding. The problem is, we have no resources to abduct her out of the country, so he wants her dead.'

The agent stood up and stretched his legs. He fiddled with the paper parcel until a pile of chips spilled out. He picked one up and chewed on it. 'They need more salt.' He grinned at the doctor and then turned serious. 'David Ben-Gurion our Israeli prime minister, doesn't want to kidnap her and jeopardise relations with Great Britain. She wasn't high enough to warrant a show trial like Eichmann. So he wants her exterminated,' he grinned again. 'As your crowd used to call it.'

The doctor blinked and tried to smile at the joke. Anything to keep him agreeable he thought.

The agent sat down again and pulled a couple of photographs from his jacket. 'SS Oberaufseherin, Greta Binz may have had plastic surgery according to some of our contacts and probably dyed her hair. Former inmates recognised the medallion she wore at selections.' He held up the photo. 'It was the Hünenkreuz Medal of Purity. Looks like a silver iron cross with diagonal swords. She wore it all the time.'

The doctor focused. The picture was obviously taken by a prisoner and smuggled out. It showed Greta Binz in front of a line of prisoners. In uniform, she was proudly wearing the medallion on the outside of her tunic with her riding whip tucked under her arm. In the background, a woman dressed in a striped smock hung from a gallows. Probably an example for the prisoners.

The agent continued, 'The medallion you see in the photo appeared to be her favourite piece of jewellery. She may still wear it. You haven't seen a woman wearing this at the Prince Regent Home for the Elderly?'

The doctor looked at the picture again and shook his head.

The agent showed him the other photo. 'From information gathered, we know she is in disguise posing as a care worker at the Prince Regent.' The agent gave a soft hidden smile through his balaclava. 'That I believe is where you are the resident physician.'

The doctor was speechless. The photo showed Gwen Maddocks. It looked like it was taken while she was being followed.

'Do you recognise her?'

The doctor nodded. 'Dear, God. It's Gwen, Gwen Maddocks.'

'You have to admit, it seems more than coincidence to have two war criminals working under one roof. For all I know you could be shielding or helping each other?'

'No, I swear I didn't recognise her as that evil bitch,' the doctor pleaded, 'it was so long ago, and like you said, with plastic—'

The agent interrupted. 'Now you have a choice. Kill her or be exposed yourself. We don't care how you do it. It can look like suicide; you can even run her over in a bloody car. As long as she is dead within five days. We will give you a number to phone when you've done it. We'll of course, double check ourselves.'

The agent took out more photos from his jacket. 'We know before the war ended, you deserted from Pullhausen camp and took on the identity of another doctor. A Doctor Karl Eder. Then you were captured and interned maintaining his identity. However, unfortunately for you, these photos clearly show you had worked at Pullhausen.'

The doctor's jaw dropped. There he was in black and white posing with his SS medical team with their glasses raised for a Christmas Day toast. Dr Joachim Eisele had his arm around his shoulder. Another one taken in a laboratory, wearing white coats this time. While he looked on, Dr Joachim Eisele was cutting into the emaciated body of a dead Jew lying on a slab.

'As the real SS commandant Doctor Karl Borch was never captured by the Allies, there are some outstanding charges pending that were raised in your absence during war crime tribunals. Helping Joachim Eisele being one. Nevertheless, if these photographs found their way to the police and the press, you would be arrested and any respectability you had achieved in this country would be worthless. Do I make myself clear?'

The doctor nodded.

'As I said, make it look like suicide. But if you get caught, Mossad and the prime minister of Israel would deny all knowledge of your actions. Untie his hands.'

One of them behind pulled a knife and slit the rope.

The doctor rubbed his wrists. He was thinking. He'd kill his own grandmother to get them off his back.

'One other thing. Don't try making a run for it. We're watching you twenty-four hours a day. If you do, with these photos found on you, Scotland Yard aren't going to rush around to find who killed an old SS Commandant.'

The doctor looked worried. 'If I carry out what you want, how do I know you won't still expose me? Or kill me?'

'You'll have to take our word for it.' The agent leaned in close menacingly. 'You and that bitch Binz or Maddocks as she calls herself, would be both dead if we had our way.

Fortunately, for you it's political. Has to be hush-hush. Mustn't come back to us. You understand?'

The doctor nodded.

'Oh, and one more thing.' The tall agent pulled out a key. 'Isser Harel, head of Mossad is a generous man. In five days' time at the left luggage locker on Charing Cross Station, you will find five-hundred pounds in an envelope for your services.' He handed the doctor the key. 'I for one think he's mad giving money to an old Nazi. But we have to follow orders.'

CHAPTER TWENTY

He watched Gwen through a crack in the door. The rota pinned to the kitchen wall was right. It was her turn to make the afternoon teas for the residents. As always, she got the big teapot ready then made herself a small one on the side. Listening out, making sure no one was around; she took out the small whisky bottle. A quick nip from the neck followed by a splash in her tea, and it was hidden again.

It shouldn't take long, he thought. 300 milligrams of morphine was more than enough. Hopefully, she wouldn't detect the bitter taste in the alcohol. It was fortunate she kept the whisky overnight in her locker. He'd also hidden some morphine phials there and a couple of needles. Make out she was a user. Directly she was unconscious, he would inject her to look like Gwen had overdosed by mistake.

Gwen leant against the table and slurped her tea.

Late afternoon it was the Matron who raised the alarm. She found Gwen unconscious on the floor. While waiting for the ambulance, the Matron with Maureen tried to revive her. However, it was too late. Gwen died on the way to emergency.

Later after the news broke, the police and the press had a field day. A heart attack they could swallow, but two more deaths in the same month was stretching the realms of coincidence.

The Chief Inspector on the case had the care home cordoned off, while officers combed through dispensary records and medicine logbooks. Staff lockers were searched, and fingerprints taken off cups, glasses, door handles and anything else that could determine if foul play had taken place. While a police room was set aside for interviewing staff, news reporters jostled at the entrance of the home for a photo or a comment from people coming and going that might offer snippets of information.

Although a post mortem confirmed Gwen Maddocks had died of a morphine overdose, her grown up son and daughter were devastated and didn't believe their mother was a junky. They were sure the post mortem findings were incorrect and lobbied the Coroner to hold an inquest.

With increasing pressure by the press, with headlines asking, how dangerous drugs held at the home had been made available in large quantities to a resident and staff member, without any pharmaceutical monitoring in place, resulting in them taking their lives, was totally irresponsible.

At the Coroner's inquest, Julian Mortimer-Soames highlighted, 'Drugs paraphernalia had been found in the staff locker of Gwen Maddocks. In addition, the post-mortem examination indicated a high amount of morphine in the blood stream, enough to be within the fatal range, and various puncture needle marks observed in her left arm and upper thigh.'

The Coroner concluded, 'Maddocks death had been a drug related overdose by mistake and there was no indication she intended to take her own life. Unfortunately, hard drug users sometimes forget their dosage and tolerance levels, resulting in fatal consequences.'

The summing up had resulted in an outburst from the gallery. Members of her family shouted, 'It's a cover up. Our mother wasn't a drug addict. It's all lies, totally lies.'

*

After Gwen's funeral, back at the home, the matron held a small reception with drinks and nibbles. She thought it would be a fitting gesture as Gwen had been popular with the residents.

With two other part time staff, Matron Olinski with Maureen, fussed around serving egg and tomato, cheese and ham and fish paste sandwiches. The mood was jovial, considering. Many smiles with a few flushed faces, bore witness to two empty sherry bottles, including a third well on the way.

With everyone catered for, the matron relaxed. She knew it had been a close call. The Coroner's inquest had been a nightmare. At one point, it looked like she was in the frame. It was *her* overall responsibility to ensure all drugs were locked away and dispensed correctly with someone present as a double check. The press for a couple of days had called for her resignation. Thankfully, Dr Karl Eder had backed her up. He vouched for her good character and the health and safety of the home. The Coroner seemed to agree; it would be difficult to control a morphine addicted care worker who had the trust of her supervisor and colleagues. Noting, not once had her addiction surfaced to make others aware, while she helped to deliver drugs and medicines to residents as part of her daily routine.

Maureen was grateful the heat was off. Thankfully, the press hadn't delved into staff backgrounds. Still, she had to be careful. While she stood to the side watching the residents, she fingered her necklace and thought of Gwen. Gwen had given it to her from amongst her garish collection. It was chunky and heavy and she knew Maureen had liked it. However, it was difficult to believe Gwen was dead; *and* a drug addict, even more so.

Maureen thought how easily she could have gone the same way. What she had done to those women all those years ago had left their scars. Only now and again did the feelings surface. Feelings to hurt them, hit them, slap them. She had full reign then. God, that power had been so beautiful. *Standing in front of the mirror in uniform, she'd been a somebody. She'd liked it when they backed away from her. The fear in their eyes said it all.* She'd been a firm believer in *euthanasia. Had helped a few of the useless ones along the way. Some of them deserved it, especially if they were late for roll call, as she called it, or too weak to get out of bed and make their presence seen. She'd make her selections unbeknown to them; then see them later. The sheer horror on their faces as she approached. 'I'm bathing you tonight,' she'd tell them. Some accepted their fate, they'd heard the stories, others would whine out a plea.*

Then the relations demanding answers, not happy being fobbed off. A reporter posing as a maintenance man with a hidden camera. Witness statements, all pointing a finger at her. Being well and truly fitted up. None of them knew the pressures of being a senior staff nurse in a mental hospital.

The electric shock treatment in the institution was the worst. Some of the staff believed she'd deserved it. Retribution for what she'd done. After that, prison with rehabilitation. Doing craft work, gardening and sowing mailbags. While, in front of the governor every six months for parole application, until finally, walking through the gates to the waiting taxi.

*

Lila Bozeman chatted in a small group. Although a temporary newcomer, she was popular during her brief stay. Easy to talk to and prepared to listen. Liked by the staff as well, especially as she could look after herself at meal times, toilet and bath nights. As Lila exchanged pleasantries with some residents over the excellent fruitcake, she fondled the Hünenkreuz Medal of Purity medallion inside her black cardigan.

CHAPTER TWENTY-ONE

The decorators had gone, leaving new wallpaper and carpet throughout, and the smell of paint and varnish lingered through some of the rooms. Greta Binz had returned to her care home in Golders Green. She hardly recognised the place. However, she'd recognised Dr Karl Borch alright, the Commandant of Pullhausen Concentration Camp, posing as Dr Karl Eder. Even though he now had a slight receding hairline, and put on a little weight since she last saw him fifteen years ago.

Greta Binz was glad the heat was off. The stress of impersonating Lila Bozeman with the grey hair wig and aging makeup to look in her sixties, was enough on its own. And the hassle of possibly being recognized by an old Nazi doctor or a couple of Jewish residents. It was a close call. However, she had more to worry about. The Aaron Rosenthal Jewish Home for the elderly in Golders Green had decided to increase its care prices. The board of governors in its wisdom, wanted payback for the decorating that had been carried out. Each resident and their direct relation received a letter stating the new increase.

Greta had worked out her sums. Her savings were dwindling fast. The other residents with their pensions and trusts funds were sitting pretty. The home was her cover. Without it she'd be lost. The thought of living out of hostels with drunks and deadbeats, as well as having to fill out social security and benefit forms spurred her into action.

Standing at the book check-out in Golders Green town hall library, Greta had specifically asked the librarian for books about Nazi concentration camps. The elderly female assistant in the tweed suit and greying hair pinned up in a bun, rummaged through some index cards and then looked over her glasses and pointed to a clutch of bookcases across the large room. She told Greta they had five books on the subject including information on the Nuremberg Trials.

With only one other person in the partitioned off reading room, Greta sat far apart with four of the books she had found. Flicking the few pages that contained newsreel photographs of camp atrocities and captured SS Nazi personnel known to be particular sadists, she breathed in deeply at a photograph of herself. Greta nervously looked up, however, the elderly gentleman across the table was concentrating on his reading.

Keeping an eye on him, she carefully slid the book under the table and tore out the page. Greta thumbed the last book and froze at the group photograph. There he was standing next to Joachim in his full SS- Commandant's uniform. It looked like they were in a relaxed mood sharing a joke while each smoking a cigarette. Under the picture the title read: Left to right SS- Doctor Karl Borch, Commandant of Pullhausen Concentration Camp and SS- Chief Physician Dr Joachim Eisele. Again, Greta looked up tentatively. She looked through the window of the partition, and then with her eyes fixed on the elderly gentleman, she slid the book out of sight and removed the page.

On the way to the local post office, Greta passed a waste bin and dumped the screwed up picture of herself. Then, when the queue had thinned down at the counter, she asked the male post office assistant for a copy each of the two Nazi doctors and the newspaper picture of Ethel's party.

Handing over ten pennies while muttering an excuse she was writing a novel about the war, the disinterested assistant loaded the Xerox coin operated Photostat machine. Two minutes later, Greta had two clear copies for her blackmail plan.

*

After nearly five weeks, Dr Karl Borch began to relax. He hadn't heard any more from the Mossad group. They must have been satisfied. He'd collected his five-hundred pounds from the left luggage locker. Small compensation for his troubles.

It was on Monday morning at breakfast before he left for work when the doctor turned as the letterbox snapped and his post thudded lightly onto the doormat. With his coffee in hand, he sauntered over and picked up the usual clutch of bills and drug company circulars.

The smart buff envelope stood out. Typed with the false name he was using, Dr Karl Eder, and his address just below the postage stamp, he hesitated. Although he hadn't heard from Mossad, that still didn't mean to say they didn't want to kill him. The first thing that came to mind was a letter bomb.

The doctor crouched and eyed the letter. He carefully picked it up by the corner and took it to the kitchen. Holding it up to the fluorescent ceiling strip light, he could see the shadow of an enclosure inside but no wires or anything that looked suspicious. He immediately tore it open.

His eyes swam over the Photostat copies of the pictures showing himself with his Chief Physician Dr Joachim Eisele posing at Pullhausen Concentration Camp and the other in the group at Ethel's party. The accompanying letter in printed Biro stated: *Be at Brentwood Station phone booths at 4pm sharp tomorrow and await telephone call, or I'll go to the police with the pictures.* He read it again to take it all in.

*

It was 3:58 p.m. and not quite rush hour yet. The doctor hovered; he pushed the two unoccupied phone booth doors open so he could listen out.

At the first ring, he lurched like a gazelle that had been spotted by a cheetah. He exploded into the booth clutching up the receiver panting hard.

'Yes-Yes, it's me Doctor Karl Eder,' he said.

'Listen to me carefully.'

He thought the voice sounded muffled. A bit high for a man. Maybe a woman. Probably talking with a handkerchief over the mouthpiece. 'What do you want?'

'Shut up and listen. I know you are SS Doctor Karl Borch, former Commandant of Pullhausen Concentration Camp. I will without hesitation report you to the police with the pictures, if you do not do as I say. It shouldn't be too hard for them to find you, considering I know your address and where you are working. Knowing who you are they may want to examine more closely the deaths that occurred at the Prince Regent Care Home. The victims may have recognised you. A good excuse to get rid of them.'

'I had nothing to do—'

'Shut up! Now this is how we play it. You've got three days to get one-thousand pounds.'

'Three days. Where am I going to get that sort of money in three days?'

'You are a Doctor. As far as I know doctors earn good money, and frankly I don't give a shit where you get it from. Now listen carefully. I suggest you write this down.'

The doctor fumbled in his pockets and found a pen with a café napkin.

'This Thursday evening, you will take one-thousand-pounds in used notes and place it in your Gladstone medical bag. You will then take the nine-forty-five evening train from Basildon Station to West Horndon Station. Get on the end trailing carriage and sit near a left-hand-carriage door, forward moving position. At a certain point during the journey, the train will stop. It won't be a station. Then push down the carriage door window and throw the bag out onto the track.'

'How do I know you won't try this again? Next month - next year?' the doctor shouted down the phone.

'You'll just have to trust me.'

'Okay, I'll get your money,' he said.

'I just knew, Doctor Karl Borch, former Commandant of Pullhausen Concentration Camp, you'd see sense.'

CHAPTER TWENTY-TWO

By nine-forty it wasn't busy. Basildon Central was winding down for the day. The diesel with its four carriages was in. The Doctor made his way past four seated people and sat as near as possible to the carriage door. He eyed them; two gentlemen and an elderly couple. The couple smiled at him as he took his seat. The compartment smelt of stale cigarettes and pipe smoke. Opening his newspaper he quickly buried his face pretending to read.

The Doctor clutched his bag. Thoughts swam through his mind. *Who the shit was it? Not Mossad. They wouldn't give money and then take it back. Must be someone at the home? Someone at Ethel's group picture. Has to be one of the staff. That helper Maureen? Or perhaps the matron? Yes the matron. She was from Poland. She may have been a camp prisoner but never said because she recognised me. Waited for a chance to pay me back, the Bitch. Yes it has to be her.*

He'd managed to scrape a thousand pounds together. Thank God, he hadn't spent the five-hundred pounds Mossad payment. For the other, he'd used five-hundred pounds of his own savings. It had cleaned him out.

The Doctor mulled over his situation as he rocked with the motion of the train. That Bitch matron had his arse nailed to the barn door, and knew it. She could have gone to the police with the information. But, oh no. Perhaps the reward wasn't big enough. She wanted more. Perhaps payback for some long nosed Jew relation that died in his camp. This Bitch would blackmail him again and again. Stood to reason. She'd want to see him squirm. However, now he knew it was the matron, he could get his own back. Get rid of her like he'd done with that Binz or Maddocks as she called herself.

The Doctor put his hand in his pocket. He felt the ball-peen hammer. It reassured him. He'd also brought along an old service revolver as a backup. Purchased some years ago along with a small tin box of ammunition, in case he may have been cornered somewhere because of his situation, he'd never had to fire it. However, the hammer was first choice as it made no noise. The gun was a last resort. In his other jacket pocket he checked the real money. That was also a last resort in case he was forced to hand it over.

The night before, he'd spent a couple of hours cutting up newspaper pages to the size of twenty-pound notes, and adding to the bundle three real notes top and bottom. Fixed with an elastic band he hoped it would fool them for a while in the dark.

At Laindon station, the last of the four passengers stepped off. The carriage was now empty. As it continued, the Doctor stood up and slightly swayed with the train as he moved to a seat nearer the door. He sat down, then shifted uncomfortably.

Suddenly there was a blast on the driver's horn and he lurched sideways as the train braked sharply and then slurred to a halt. The Doctor raised himself tentatively and moved to a window. He shielded his eyes and tried to look out, but the reflected light from the carriage made it difficult.

Before he parted with the bag, he had to make sure this was the spot. He pushed the carriage door window down and leant out. In the distance he could see West Horndon Station all lit up. A man with a torch, probably the driver, was playing the beam around, surveying something at the front of the train.

The Doctor turned as the interconnecting carriage door opened. The ticket collector, a large fat man wearing a cap and wreaking of stale tobacco, with a waist that could easily have burst his British Rail uniform trousers, looked around and then spoke loudly in a well-prepared, reassuring little speech. 'Just to let you know we have an obstruction on the line and the matter is being dealt with. Please do not make any attempt to get off the train and don't worry, we will be moving shortly.' With that, he closed the door and was gone.

The Doctor was convinced. This had to be the drop. He took the bag, leant out of the carriage window and looked into the darkness. It was a warm July evening. He swung the Gladstone medical bag, backwards and forwards in an exaggerated motion. He wanted to stand out, wanted the person to see where he was going to throw it. With a heave the Doctor let go and it bounced and then came to rest by the side of the track.

He stared down into the darkness and could make out the shape. The Doctor crouched and made his way to the opposite side of the carriage. He moved to the door, pushed the window down and then turned the outside handle. It swung open. There was a steep embankment directly in front. Not a lot of space, but enough.

'*Jesus!*' The Doctor cried out as he hit the steep grass and then rolled back under a large steel wheel. He frantically scrambled out from underneath the carriage, thinking it might start rolling again at any moment. Brushing himself down, he temporarily examined his left grazed knee and the torn trouser legging. He listened out; all quiet apart from the hissing of the diesel up front. Using the carriage as support, he carefully trod his way to the rear of the train.

Suddenly, crunching noises. Someone nearby was walking on the sleeper gravel.

The Doctor crouched; as he peered around the end carriage he could see the Gladstone bag and a figure approaching. Although it was clear with a full moon, he couldn't tell from the silhouette if it was a man or a woman. The figure was picking its way along the track, stopping, looking around, moving on and then stopping again.

The Doctor hesitated. Was it a railway worker doing its job? Last minute checks before moving off? If it was, where was the torch?

The Doctor looked behind; he had to be quick, he saw the lights of an oncoming train coming the other way. Then a horn sounded. He heard carriage doors closing. His own train was about to move off.

The figure stopped. At about thirty-feet away it spotted the bag. It began to move quickly, coming towards him. Then the horn of the approaching train sounded. The figure checked, looked at the oncoming lights and continued faster.

The Doctor felt in his pocket. He took out the hammer and held it down by his side.

Then the figure tripped and half stumbled to one knee. It mumbled, 'Shit! You mother–'

The Doctor was near enough to hear the cursing and could see it was a woman.

The figure got up, brushed itself down.

Up front, the horn sounded again and the Doctor's train started moving off. His cover was gone.

The figure crouched in the dark, but its eyes were only for the Gladstone bag containing all that money. On the opposite line, the chugging of the approaching diesel train was getting louder.

It was now at the bag. The figure stooped to pick it up and then tried to open it. It was having trouble with the clasp.

The Doctor had twenty-five feet to cover. He looked behind. The diesel was getting nearer - looming out of the dark like a giant angry serpent, all lit up screeching out its rage.

The figure opened the bag and grabbed the money; standing there totally oblivious, feverishly flicking the notes and then realising. *'Newspaper, you Cheating Bastard!'*

The Doctor moved in with a fixated and purposeful look. Like a lion that had crept behind a wildebeest on its knees at a water hole, he was upon her, swinging the hammer to the back of her head.

She half turned as the blow glanced off.

Then he tried to hit her again but she ducked.

She swore, *'You fucking Bastard!'* Then grabbed him, pulling the Doctor down. The hammer dropped from his hand. They wrestled and her wig fell off but she managed to get on top. She grabbed the hammer and tried to hit him, but he had her arm. Then with her left hand, she threw gravel into the Doctor's eyes. Wincing and blinking, he let her go, then screamed as she smashed the hammer onto his nose.

'Greta Binz!' The Doctor managed to cry out looking up at her with blood pouring down his chin.

Sitting astride him she prepared to strike again and then froze.

'Greta Binz, you're supposed to be dead. I killed you. What the hell—? Get off me, You Bitch!'

She hesitated for a second knowing she'd been recognised. In that instant he grabbed for the hammer and made her drop it.

The noise behind her was deafening. Greta could feel the approaching heat - smell the warm sickly oil. They were lit up in the oncoming train's headlights. The horn sounded again.

The Doctor reached inside his jacket and got tangled up trying to pull out the Smith and Wesson .38. Greta caught a glimpse of steel and instantly grabbed at it. It went off, then fired off again, missing her as her hand clutched the barrel - she yelled out as the metal burned.

Still astride him they wrestled, both her hands holding his with the gun. It went off again and the bullet slammed into her shoulder. She recoiled and nearly fell off him. Her hand felt for the burning pain while the other one feverishly clawed at the gravel until her fingers felt the wooden handle. She grabbed at the hammer and swung it down into his face again.

Blood from his broken nose sprayed her. The Doctor screamed with pain and it made him drop the gun. Again, she tried to get up, but he was pulling her down.

Even with his injuries, the Doctor wrestled with her, shouted at her, *'You Bitch! You lousy Bitch!'*

She rolled with him between the rails, dropping the hammer again, trying to kick him away, break free. Greta was feeling light headed. Losing blood. She could feel the vibration of the giant steel wheels as they bore down on them. The Doctor wasn't going to let go.

Out of the corner of her eye, she saw the gun, just beyond reach. Her fingers clutched at nothing. The train was less than fifty-yards away. The ground was shaking like an earthquake.

The Doctor began to cough, some blood clogging in his throat. He relaxed.

Greta strained and her fingers wrapped around the gun barrel. She looked behind; the steaming monster was nearly upon them. She wasn't going to make it. With one last exhausted lunge, Greta smashed the gun handle into his forehead. Blood spurted out of his nose and mouth as she pushed him away. She rolled and rolled in the gravel across the sleepers, crying out in pain as her head and knees hit the steel rail passing over it.

It was as if the devil had invited her in. Hell's door had opened; the heat, the wind, the roar with the burning stench of diesel thundered past, taking the Doctor with it.

Greta lay there on her back, not quite believing. Breathing in deep snatches, she looked at the stars. All of a sudden, she felt cold and started to shiver. Her shoulder was burning and felt wet. She touched it and held up her hand, mesmerized. It was covered in blood.

Greta pulled herself up. She swayed a bit, unsteady, taking in what had happened. She took a step, stopped, hesitated, then straightened herself and slowly walked over to the Gladstone bag. She reached down for it.

Proudly holding the bag, she walked slowly along the track; it was surreal in the moonlight, as if strolling down Bond Street on a Saturday afternoon.

She spotted the hammer. Close by was the gun. Picking up the items, she wiped them on her sleeve. She checked the chamber, there were three bullets remaining. Greta carefully wrapped the gun in some bits of bloodied newspaper she found by her feet, then she put it in the bag.

The first part of the Doctor she came across, was a left leg. Greta nudged it with her toe, as if it might still be alive;

perhaps start moving of its own accord. She carried on another fifteen yards and then, on the edge of the right-hand rail, she saw an arm cut off at the elbow.

She stepped over to look at it. The left hand little finger twitched nervously, as if beckoning her to come closer. Again, she carelessly poked it with her foot, then turned and slowly walked on.

Greta had gone another twenty-yards when she saw the shape. It was the moaning, as it dragged itself over the railway sleepers that had attracted her. Leaving a glistening trail of smeared blood in the moonlight, it moved like a gigantic slug.

Walking ahead of it, she blocked its way. The pitiful thing in front of her stopped. It stared carefully at her shoes, recognizing them and then lifted its head.

'Please help me?' The Doctor said weakly with pleading eyes. 'Look...look, take the money.' He rolled over onto the stump of his left arm and bellowed with pain. With the remaining hand, he opened his jacket giving Greta access. She knelt down and put her hand inside the pocket. The envelope felt warm and slick as she withdrew it. At that point, she turned and vomited at the side of the track. The heaving action made her shoulder explode with more pain and she saw coloured spots before her eyes.

Greta leant back and took deep breaths, she spat some phlegm a couple of times and then dabbed her mouth with a sleeve. Using the same sleeve, she wiped the envelope and tore it open. She checked the amount. Then she placed the bundle of twenty-pound notes into the bag.

The Doctor could hardly speak; he was losing blood fast. He managed to whisper, 'Don't leave me here, please help me?'

'Did you park a car?' She kicked his leg stump and the Doctor screamed, *'Ahhh!!!... Yes - Yes. Please God, don't, I beg you?'*

She kicked his stump again and he screamed with pain. 'Where are the car keys?' She didn't wait for a reply. Greta took a deep breath and fumbled again through his ripped jacket, wincing until her fingers felt the slippery key ring. She pulled them out and wiped the leather tag and the two identical keys.

'What's the car, and where is it? And don't lie; otherwise you'll know real pain.' She moved to kick his stump again.

He put up the arm he had left and pleaded. 'No, please. I'll tell you anything. It's a white P-5 Rover, WFS 143 reg.' The Doctor tried to raise himself. He had to pause to get his energy and then he said weakly, 'It's up ahead in the station car park.' He collapsed back exhausted, turning to cough up blood and spitting on the side of the track.

Greta sighed with relief; she clutched her shoulder, the pain was making her feel dizzy. She pushed her hair back leaving a bloody scuff on her forehead.

The Doctor in desperation bellowed out again as he rolled onto his stomach. His remaining hand clutched the bottom of Greta's coat. He looked up at her, whining, begging her to get help, get an ambulance.

However, she wasn't looking at him. Greta was focused on the approaching distant lights.

CHAPTER TWENTY-TWO

The Doctors eyes followed hers. He saw the oncoming train.

He shuffled and slithered towards her, slipping and slopping in his blood. 'Don't leave me here,' he begged, 'I'll give you anything…Pleeeese…'

Greta stooped and patted him on the head. 'Goodbye, Doctor Karl Borch, former Commandant of Pullhausen Concentration Camp. It's been nice doing business with you.' She moved off along the side of the track amidst his last desperate cries.

Greta, clutching her bloody shoulder while holding the bag, walked unsteadily by the rails towards the station. Shivering with cold and feeling dizzy, she knew she'd lost a lot of blood.

As she approached the level crossing just before the station, the flashing warning lights started up and the long gates swung open, as if allowing her a grand entrance - like some Cleopatra or Boudicca coming home after a great battle.

Greta suddenly turned to the sound of the Doctors last scream. It was drowned out as the ten-forty-five to Basildon swept over him. And then there was nothing. It was as if, Doctor Karl Borch had never existed.

Greta ducked down as she approached the station. With great effort and now spitting blood, she clambered up onto the platform. Thankfully at this time of night the place was deserted. She leant against the station wall to get her breath. She looked down and realized blood from her wound was puddling the concrete floor. Greta winced and moved off out of the station towards the car park. A trail of blood marked her way.

After a while, the white apparition of a Rover P-5 appeared out of the dark. It was the only remaining parked car. She checked the registration and then fumbled with the two keys as she eased herself into the posh leather driver's seat. The exertion made her cry out as she clutched her shoulder at the bursting pain and white spots flashed before her eyes.

With the Gladstone bag on her lap she took deep breaths to steady herself. Then she spotted a small bottle of Napoleon brandy tucked in the glove compartment. Greta unscrewed the cap and wiped the top. She took a swig and winced. 'Needed that,' she mumbled.

Greta relaxed and gazed through the windscreen, trance like, fondling her neck charm, the Hünenkreuz Medal of Purity. She looked down at it and smiled. Maybe it brought her luck? Greta winced at a new surge of pain. Then maybe it didn't. She took another small swig; the initial sting now becoming a warm glow. After a few more swigs the shoulder pain seemed to dull. Then her eyelids grew heavy; they flickered briefly and then closed. The brandy bottle slipped slowly from her fingers.

Greta said a few things incomprehensible; and then twitched as sleep took over.

CHAPTER TWENTY-THREE

'Come on, hurry up, Magda, the car's here,' Martin, her tall good-looking brother, shouted up the stairs. At 33 years old, he liked to think he still had a good head of dark hair, just thinning a bit at the temples. He fussed with his fingers at the slight widow's peak in Magda's hallway mirror while he waited for her.

'Give me five seconds and I'll be with you,' she called from the bedroom.

It was the usual panic. Earlier, Magda had received the urgent telephone call for her to give blood at the hospital, and then she phoned her brother.

That was the problem being AB Negative. Magda's blood group was one of the rarest. Only around 1 in 170 people had this type.

She'd started giving blood when she moved with her brother from Germany to London six years ago in 1954. They'd come over through a recruitment drive that was set up by the Royal Army Medical Corps stationed in Berlin. The lack of British military doctors and other medical specialists in the three services after the war, had prompted a lot of training opportunities. They'd both taken advantage of this. Martin was about to qualify as a doctor in the RAMC while Magda worked as an optician in the outpatients department at Moorfields Eye Hospital. Only having one eye herself, she wanted to give something back, help others.

With no ties to keep them, leaving Germany wasn't hard. Their mother was dead and the rest of the family had died in the bombing. As for their father, they hadn't heard from him in years. Although he was a wanted war criminal, they were sure he'd been captured by the Americans when they overran his camp at Pullhausen, and probably shot on the spot in some orgy of revenge.

The hospital had sent its emergency blood donor car to Magda's flat in Earls Court. As they climbed in, the driver switched on the flashing blue light and they sped off into the early July morning.

Because Magda lived on her own, Martin always went with her. From his training accommodation at the college, he'd come round to Magda's flat to lend moral support. She got very nervous having to lie down and give blood. Her experiences of forced blood tests at the time she was sterilised, had left their mark.

Now in her middle thirties and tall like her brother, Magda was still attractive with an almost white complexion, and she still retained her flaxen hair braids that were usually pinned up during her work day. Still single, she'd kept a slim figure. *'Painfully thin,'* her brother Martin would joke, and add, *'You need to eat more cream cakes and chocolate, Sis...'*

In all the time Magda had been a blood donor, she'd only fainted twice. Still, after a lie down and a cup of sweet tea with a biscuit, she was glad to see a friendly face.

Within ten-minutes, they'd swept into the Edgware Hospital entrance and pulled up at the emergency parking bays by reception. Magda quickly climbed out and walked through the swing doors to check-in. She was immediately confronted by the warm sickly smells of surgical spirit, while the white uniforms of hospital staff, stood out against the austere green décor of the walls and floor.

Martin had thanked the driver and ambled in behind her. He'd brought his book of exam medical notes as usual and was quite prepared to settle down and swot in the waiting room with a cup of coffee from the visitor's canteen.

At reception, Magda handed over her blood card. The duty nurse quickly phoned through, and another nurse immediately appeared and asked Magda to follow her. Walking briskly to the transfusion room which was the floor above, the nurse casually informed Magda it was for a gunshot victim who'd just arrived and was immediately going into surgery.

They were about to step into the lift when a team of doctors and nurses came running down the corridor wheeling a patient on a stretcher attached to a drip and some tubes. They called to them to hold the doors as it was an emergency. Magda and the young nurse let them enter first and then, with some room available, they stood against the doors.

As they began to ascend, Magda turned and saw the victim was a woman laid out covered in blood wearing an oxygen mask. She was moaning and trying to pull the mask off.

'My God, poor thing.' Magda put a hand to her mouth in shock.

'She's the one with your blood group,' the nurse replied. 'Looks like a gunshot wound but she didn't say how it happened. Still, the police will be here soon. They may get her statement if we're lucky.'

At that moment the patient became very agitated, she ripped her mask off and started waving one arm about and pointed, '*Borch... Borch... Magda Borch...*'

While two nurses restrained her, Magda leant over the woman. Her brain searched for recognition. She knew the face from somewhere. Was it an old optician patient of hers? Magda affectionately grabbed her hand. 'Yes that's me. How do you know my—'

Just then, the doors opened for the floor of the operating theatre. Magda and the nurse quickly stepped aside to let the others get out.

Suddenly the patient grabbed Magda's sleeve and tried to pull her along. She moaned out, '*Borch it's you, remember Westerberg Detention Centre?*'

Magda was walking quickly alongside the bed. '*Yes – yes, I was there but who are...*'

She coughed some blood and then whispered, 'It's me, Binz. Greta Binze.'

The sudden realisation hit her. 'Greta Binz... It... can't be...' Magda stopped and watched them run with the bed down the corridor.

The nurse put her arm around her shoulder, 'You okay? Is it someone you know?'

Magda stared into space. 'Yes...Yes, someone a long time ago.'

At that moment, a commotion started up at the theatre entrance. A doctor was doing chest compressions on the patient and breathing into the mouth. Another doctor administered an injection and checked the drip. As Magda and the nurse watched, the process continued.

After a few minutes they gradually began to give up. Finally the doctor shook his head and closed the patients staring eyes.

A nurse came down the corridor and spoke. 'I'm so sorry about your friend, but you won't be needed. She lost too much blood.'

'She wasn't really a —'

The nurse interrupted. 'Would you like to pay your last respects?'

'Well yes... I suppose... so.' Magda, still a little shocked, walked with the nurse to the bed, where the body was now in a cubicle surrounded by curtains.

The nurse swished them open and pulled the green sheet back and then discretely stayed outside.

Leaning close, Magda recognised her now. She whispered, 'For someone who looked so beautiful and yet could be so wicked, God bless.'

It was then she noticed the medallion, where the buttons of the bloodied blouse had been ripped away. 'Dear God!' Magda fondled the Hünenkreuz Medal of Purity. On the back was engraved Greta's rare blood group - AB Negative. Her thoughts went back to her school, to the presentation. It seemed a life time of events and disasters had occurred since then. She was about to slip off the medallion and stopped. Then she said to no one, 'On second thoughts, Greta, you keep it. It never brought me much luck either.'

Coming soon for thriller readers... `MAVIS BONE PRIVATE INVESTIGATOR AND THE PERFECT MURDERS` by B.P.Smythe.....

Free paperback and kindle copies to Amazon and Goodreads reviewers: Contact barrysmythe@hotmail.com

TO BE RELEASED IN 2019

PLEASE BE AWARE, READERS MUST NOT DISCLOSE THE ENDING OF THIS BOOK. THIS ALLOWS OTHERS TO ENJOY THE BOOK TO ITS ENTIRETY. AT THE TIME OF PURCHASE, CUSTOMERS MUST SIGN A PLEDGE TO UPHOLD THIS. PEEKING OR THUMBING THROUGH PAGES OF COPIES ON BOOK SHELVES IS STRICTLY FORBIDDEN.
Author B.P.Smythe

Lightning Source UK Ltd.
Milton Keynes UK
UKHW021459150519
342717UK00006B/370/P

9 781911 412885